"COME H[ERE]
BESIDE M[E]."

"Please," Abbie said softly. "I wish you'd stay."

"Why?" Dane asked huskily, his eyes searching hers.

"I want to be with you. You make me forget all the bad things."

Sweet sudden prickles of desire ricocheted through her body when he stretched out beside her and his hand came to rest on the flat of her stomach.

"This may not be such a wise thing to do," Dane said, his fingers tracing the satin edge of her robe.

"You don't want to be here?" she asked, looking up at him.

"Yes, but . . . I don't want you to regret what might happen."

"I take full responsibility for what's happening," Abbie said earnestly. "Let's not think of anything but what's between us now."

Taking her in his arms, Dane complied.

Dear Reader,

Superromance is proud to present The Rainbow Hills
Series, a very special trilogy conceived by a very
special author, Sally Garrett. A former Phoenix
corporate accountant who has relocated to a small
Montana ranching community, Sally understands
both urban and country life-styles. She's able to
write about three American farm women and their
families in a way that even the most confirmed city
dweller will find compelling.

Today, when most of us buy all our food at the local
market, it's easy to forget the women and men who
labor long and hard on farms to sustain the nation.
Sally's books make these people *unforgettable*.
Abigail, Eileen and Callie, the strong-willed
Kentucky women who vow as girlhood friends to
overcome all adversity together, exemplify all that is
best in the human spirit. It is our hope that as you
share the triumphs and sorrows of the Rainbow Hills
women, you will be uplifted by their courage and
their joyful discovery that love can indeed overcome
all obstacles.

Happy reading!

Marsha Zinberg

Marsha Zinberg,
Senior Editor,
Superromance.

Sally Garrett
RAINBOW HILLS SERIES

WEAVER OF DREAMS

Harlequin Books

TORONTO • NEW YORK • LONDON
AMSTERDAM • PARIS • SYDNEY • HAMBURG
STOCKHOLM • ATHENS • TOKYO • MILAN

To Arthur and Margaret Christensen,
whose willingness and patience
over the past three lambing seasons
helped turn this Arizona native
into a bona fide Montana lamber.

Published January 1987

First printing November 1986

ISBN 0-373-70243-4

ABOUT THE AUTHOR

Since her first Superromance, *Until Forever*, published in 1983, Sally Garrett has attracted a wide following of loyal readers. *Weaver of Dreams* is the first book in Sally's newest series, a trilogy about three cousins from rural Kentucky. Like the women she writes about, Sally loves living far from the city. With her biggest fan, husband Montie, Sally makes her home in beautiful Montana.

Books by Sally Garrett

HARLEQUIN SUPERROMANCE

90–UNTIL FOREVER
139–MOUNTAIN SKIES
173–NORTHERN FIRES
201–TWIN BRIDGES
225–UNTIL NOW

Don't miss any of our special offers. Write to us at the following address for information on our newest releases.

Harlequin Reader Service
901 Fuhrmann Blvd., P.O. Box 1397, Buffalo, NY 14240
Canadian address: P.O. Box 603,
Fort Erie, Ont. L2A 5X3

Acknowledgment:

Dane and Abbie and the Graften sheep ranch are from my imagination, but without the helpful assistance of the following people, this story could never have been completed: Margaret and Arthur Christensen, who ranch on the Sweetwater; Gladys and John Conover, who ranch up the Blacktail; Elsie Laden; Jim, Jerry and Chuck, who kept running into me wherever they sheared; and Kay Rice, a fan from *Until Forever* days, who shared her spinning and weaving skills with me.

If this story occasionally smells of sheep, it's because I've helped with deliveries and doctored newborn lambs, elastrated, painted and branded, worked on a docking crew, fed the bum lambs, cleaned more jugs than I can count, climbed the hills, checked the drop pens, eartagged, wrangled the sheep for shearing, weighed fleeces . . . and loved every minute of it.

ABBIE'S PROLOGUE

THE THREE GIRLS worked their way along the creek bank, the soles of their feet now callused by a summer of freedom from shoes.

Eleven-year-old Abigail Hardesty stopped to examine a fern growing at the water's edge. She brushed her curly red hair from her eyes as she squatted to get a closer look.

Her cousin, Eileen Hardesty, paused several steps ahead. About to have her thirteenth birthday, Eileen was the self-proclaimed leader of the three cousins. She'd assumed the role when Abbie had come to live with her natural father's cousin and his wife three years earlier.

"Come on, Abbie, you're such a poke-along," Eileen chided. "I have to get back by five to help Jordan and Les with the milking." Eileen jumped to a boulder in the stream, patting one of her long brown braids. She teetered on the rock, her arms waving in the air to catch her balance, but she had to take one quick step into the creek in order to save herself from falling on her behind. "Frankly, I don't see why Daddy won't buy a milking machine like your Uncle Harry did. Cripes, I shouldn't have to do milking at my age."

Abbie tore her gaze away from the beautiful fern and frowned at her cousin. "Uncle Harry says the machine will pay for itself in no time, now that all of my...cousins have left home."

Eileen put her fists on her slender waist, her budding breasts pushing against her cotton blouse as she danced from one boulder to another. "I thought you were going to start calling them your *brothers*, just to please Aunt Minnie."

Abbie's green eyes grew troubled. "I tried, but I . . . couldn't. They're not my brothers, and if my daddy hadn't been killed in that coal mine, and if my momma and my stepdaddy hadn't moved to Lexington, and if . . ."

"That's a lot of ifs," Callie Hardesty murmured.

Abbie and Eileen turned to the black-haired eight-year-old who often accompanied them on their explorations.

"And what do you know?" Abbie asked, determined to fight the tears that threatened to fill her eyes. Her mother's sudden decision to relinquish her only daughter still caused her anguish. "If my stepdaddy had had a job, they would have kept me with them. Aunt Minnie said so. You don't know nothing! You're just a spoiled and pampered little brat!"

"I am not!" Callie retorted, her brown eyes snapping. "Just 'cause I'm not as old as you and Eileen doesn't mean I'm a dummy. My momma says if I know what I want, I can get it. It's that simple."

"You're not so smart," Eileen said, hopping to the bank and walking back to join the other girls. "My momma says everyone should plan for something else besides what they want, just in case things don't work out. Momma says you should never put all your eggs in one basket."

Abbie whirled to face Eileen. "Aunt Minnie says if you work hard and don't lose sight of what you want, you can usually get it." She smiled. "Aunt Minnie says I'm just stubborn enough to get what I want. Each and every night, after I've said my prayers, I think about what I'll be when I grow up."

"Me, too," Eileen agreed. "My brother says I'll never make it, but I know he's wrong. I'm going to win a scholarship to college and someday I'll be an independent woman and the boss of a whole bunch of men. Wouldn't that be a barrel of fun? My brothers say they would never work for a girl!"

"I don't want to be anyone's boss," Abbie replied somberly. "But I don't want someone bossing me around, either. I want to be free. Aunt Minnie takes good care of me, and I love her for it, and she says she and Uncle Harry took me in because they love me and not because they had to do it, but still I'm certainly not spoiled like some girls I know." She cast a scornful side glance at the petite Callie.

"Well, I know what I want, too," Callie said, refusing to back away from Abbie's challenge.

"And what might that be?" Eileen asked.

Callie smiled, her cherub features lighting up. "I'm gonna marry Bobby Joe Huff."

"Bobby Joe?" Eileen bent double in laughter. "That skinny little boy with all those freckles?" She covered her mouth with her hand. "Does Bobby Joe know what you have in store for him?"

Callie traced a pattern in the mud with her big toe and smiled. "No, but I gave him a valentine last spring and he didn't tear it up."

"Are you going to give him a few years to grow up?" Abbie asked, suspecting that they were carrying their teasing too far.

"'Course," Callie replied. "But when he asks me, I'll say yes."

"I thought you were going to be a rich and famous singer, playing the dulcimer," Abbie said accusingly. "You're always saying your momma is just as good as Maybelle Carter and you're prettier than any of her girls. How are you going to be a singer and marry that ugly Bobby Joe Huff?"

Callie stuck out her tongue at Abbie. "I'll just do both. I'll only sing at the Grand Old Opry on Saturday nights. Bobby Joe and me are gonna get married and have three little girls and three little boys."

"Finish high school first," Eileen warned.

Abbie stared across the creek to a field of tobacco in the distance. "I don't ever want to pick tobacco worms again, and I don't want to marry a coal miner. They just get killed and leave you with a bunch of kids you can't feed."

Eileen nodded. "That's why I'm going to college."

"But college costs a lot of money," Abbie said.

"Sure, but if you make good grades you can get a scholarship that will pay your way," Eileen explained. "Mrs. Gray at the high school told me all about it. She says it's never too early to start working for your goals. I want to go to Western Kentucky University or maybe somewhere out of state. When I graduate, maybe I can have my own business."

"What kind of business?" Abbie asked, wondering why anyone would want to run a business.

"A department store, or a secretarial service like Miss Masters has in Central City, or maybe I'll own a coal company and boss all the men around."

Abbie grimaced. "That would be terrible. You'd be dirty all the time. Yuck. And what if you have a cave-in?"

"That's better than picking those awful tobacco worms every year. Anyway, I'd rather get away from here. I could own a store that sells cloth and yarn," Eileen countered. "Just imagine being able to buy a whole bolt of material at one time and not have to use all the scraps like my momma always does." She sighed.

Abbie smiled. "I'm going to be a weaver. Ever since Aunt Minnie showed me how to spin and weave I've known just what I want to be. I want to make tapestries so huge they'll have to put up buildings around them. Someday I'll be in the Guinness Book of World Records. Then you can all be jealous of me."

"Who'd be jealous of you with that ugly red hair and those freckles?" Callie sneered.

Abbie bristled. "My hair is better than yours. Who'd want plain black hair? It looks like you've been working in a coal mine all your life . . . and it's straight as a string. At least mine is curly. And I like my freckles."

Eileen stepped between the quarreling cousins. "Stop it, you two. You're both pretty and you both have pretty hair. Red goes with your green eyes, Abbie. And Callie's brown eyes are perfect with her black hair." She patted her own wispy locks. "Momma says God gave me brown hair to match my eyes, too. She says you gotta make the best of what He gives you. Isn't that what the preacher said in church last Sunday morning? Now shake hands and make up. We don't have time to fight today."

"Yeah," Abbie agreed. "School starts next Monday." She extended her hand to her younger cousin. "I'm sorry, Callie. Your hair is okay. I . . . I just don't like anyone making fun of my hair. Aunt Minnie says it won't always be so red." She glared at Callie. "Well, aren't you going to be a good sport and shake?"

"I guess so," Callie replied, reluctantly extending her small hand.

Abbie resisted the urge to squeeze Callie's hand hard. "Friends and sisters again?" Eileen asked, looking from one to the other.

"Sure." Callie cocked her head to one side, opened her mouth once, then closed it.

"Now what?" Abbie asked. "Say it or shut up."

"What's a tapestry?" Callie asked. "You said you were gonna make giant tapestries when you grow up."

"It's a picture made from weaving, silly," Abbie replied. "You decide what you want it to look like and then you just make it. Aunt Minnie is teaching me how."

"You're lucky to live with Aunt Minnie," Eileen said. "She treats you just like you were her own. I think that's neat."

Abbie smiled. "Aunt Minnie says when my momma called and told her about me, and said that she didn't have money to feed me and that they were moving away, Aunt Minnie wanted me right away. She told my momma that she had three boys and she wanted a girl. 'Course, my real daddy and momma used to come visit Aunt Minnie and Uncle Harry all the time, so it's not like we didn't know each other. Aunt Minnie had red hair when she was little and her eyes are green, too. People are always thinking I'm her real daughter."

"It's still not like having your *real* mother," Callie said.

Abbie frowned at Callie.

"But it's the next best thing," Eileen said, reaching for Callie's hand. "Now let's get moving before it's too late."

The trio scampered along the bank until they found their secret meeting place, a small glen hidden in the thick undergrowth in a wooded area not far from the creek.

The glen was less than four feet across, but at the rear was the small opening of a shallow cave where they had built up a cache of treats over the long warm summer.

As the three girls sat in a circle, munching on oatmeal cookies from Aunt Minnie's kitchen, Abbie enjoyed the silence. She didn't want to talk about herself and her past. Only the future held promise. With Aunt Minnie's encouragement she knew she would someday become a famous weaver of pictures, a weaver of dreams that would come true. *Yes,* she decided, *someday when I grow up, I'll be a weaver of dreams.*

Eileen's voice interrupted her daydreams.

"Did Aunt Minnie keep her promise?"

Abbie smiled and reached into the pocket of her shorts, withdrawing a brown paper sack. "Yes. But we can't look at them yet," she said. "First we must have our meeting, then we'll see what she made us."

Eileen nodded, her amber eyes serious as she reached for Abbie's hand as well as Callie's. "The last meeting, until next summer, of the Rainbow Hills Secret Society of Sisters and Friends will now come to order. Any old business?" she asked, scanning the other two faces. "Any new business?" Callie and Abbie sat quietly until Eileen elbowed Abbie. "New business!"

"Oh," Abbie exclaimed. "I was . . ."

"Daydreaming again?" The gentle smile on Eileen's pretty features eased the pain of discovery for Abbie.

Abbie raised her hand. "I have some new business. Aunt Minnie has been making us each something special. I have them here," she said, opening the sack. "Here's one for you," she said as she handed a small package wrapped in white tissue paper to Eileen. "And one for you, pipsqueak," she said, handing Callie an identical package. "And one for me."

Filled with anticipation, they unwrapped their presents.

"Oh, it's fabulous," Eileen murmured.

"It's . . . it's wonderful," Callie agreed.

Abbie gasped as she stared down at the gold locket in her cupped hand. "It's so beautiful." She leaned toward Callie. "Are they all alike?"

"Almost," Eileen said, after studying the other two lockets. "But each has our own initial on the front. See?" She pointed to the fancy script letter *E* on her locket.

"Do they open?" Callie asked, fiddling with the tiny clasp.

"They should," Abbie replied. Suddenly the gold cover sprang open revealing the inner compartments. On the left was a tiny counted cross-stitch image of a rainbow. On a hillside stood three strong trees. On the right were tiny clipped photos of the girls, one of the previous year's school photos. On the back of the gold case were inscribed the words, "Sisters and Friends."

Abbie whistled softly. "The three trees must represent us. Aunt Minnie must have worked for hours and hours on these." She glanced up at the other girls. "I never saw her working on them, not even once. She kept it a secret, truly a secret. Let's put them on."

Abbie and Eileen helped each other with the clasps at the ends of the delicate gold chains, then admired one another's lockets.

"Oh," Abbie exclaimed, turning to Callie, who was sitting forlornly and holding her locket and chain in her hand. "We didn't mean to forget you, pipsqueak. Here, let me help you." She fastened the chain around Callie's neck and lifted her black hair out of the way while Eileen adjusted the locket, which hung a few inches below Callie's throat.

Callie beamed. "Do I look as pretty as you do?" she asked, searching the faces of her older cousins for approval.

"You sure do," Eileen replied and Abbie nodded.

"Now let's make our promises," Abbie suggested. "We'll never never take these off...or if we do, we'll never lose them, and we'll always remember what we want to be when we grow up...and we'll stay in touch with each other, always."

"And we'll always be willing to help each other if we need help," Eileen added. "We'll never be too proud to ask for help. Now, that's important," she said, shaking her index finger at the two younger cousins.

"Yes," Abbie added. "The members of the Rainbow Hills Secret Society of Sisters and Friends will never forget each other, and we'll be best friends forever and ever, even when we're grown up and living far far away from here, and our matching lockets will prove it. Now let's promise, out loud." She reached for Callie's and Eileen's hands.

Gripping one another's hands tightly, they sat cross-legged in a circle and closed their eyes, repeating their sacred vows to be sisters and friends always.

CHAPTER ONE

"WHO'S IT FROM, BOSS?" Moses Parish asked as he took another sip of coffee from his chipped blue mug. "Your sister Maren, your brother Ejner or one of their attorneys?"

Dane Grasten squinted at the embossed crest of the University of Utah on the stationery he held before acknowledging Moses's question. "None of them, but it's only a matter of time before they stir up trouble again. With Petra prodding them, I'm surprised I haven't heard already." He smiled cynically. "Enough about my loving sisters and brothers. Thank goodness, Knud and Anna have been supportive through the years." He shook the letter. "It's from Emil Christensen in the agriculture department at the university. He wants me to take on another graduate student he thinks can become a ninety days' wonder in the sheep business, depending on the guy's plans for the rest of his summer break."

"What's the fellow's name?" Moses asked.

"A.B. Hardesty," Dane replied, running his hand through his blond hair. His jaw tightened, causing his features to appear sterner than usual. He returned his attention to the brief letter. "Emil says this one is older than most of his students but filled with potential. Hmm." He shook his head. "The doc keeps emphasizing the fellow's dedication and says he's sure that this one is just what I've always needed. I wonder what he means by that? Says he goes by his initials A.B. and that he has his own housing so only meals and salary have to be negotiated.''

"He must have a pickup and camper," Moses said, chuckling. "No need for a feller to live in a camper while he's here. You and me rattle around in this here house since your ma and pa moved away. Frankly, I like it when it's filled with people."

Dane nodded and took a bite of his scrambled eggs. "I agree, Mose. When I find myself talking too often to the ewes and lambs, I know it's time to seek out another person, even if it's an opinionated college student." He frowned. "Was I so filled with my own importance at that age?"

Moses laughed. "I can recall a few times you and your pa got into it when you came home at Christmas time during your first year at that university in Pocatello, Idaho. Want me to refresh your memory with the details?"

Dane held up his hand. "That's not necessary. Perhaps it's a good thing I dropped out after two years to work here full-time with Dad." He closed his eyes and for several seconds gave in to missing his parents' presence in his life.

Dane had grown up hearing his family history. He had been the unexpected but much loved sixth child, born when his mother was forty-five and his older brothers and sisters were all grown. In many ways he had felt like an only child. His aunts and uncles had spoiled him and, in their own way, so had his parents.

Dane's paternal grandfather had emigrated from Denmark and Axel Grasten, Dane's father, had always been very proud to be the first Grasten born on American soil. Traditions and values from the old country had fostered Dane's sense of commitment to his family. As a young man, he'd had no second thoughts when he took over the management of the Grasten sheep ranch to relieve his aging parents. They had stayed on the property for years afterward until moving out of state.

"It's hard to believe they're gone," Dane murmured.

"Your folks?" Moses asked. "Or..."

"Mom and Dad, of course."

"I thought you might still be pining for that pretty wife of yours," Moses replied.

"Lil?" Dane asked, surprised at his foreman's remark. "Hardly. You know how much she hated living here. She never helped, never tried to learn what was going on. Lil only complained about the endlessness of the work."

"Did you ever hear from her after that letter from Texas?" Moses asked.

"Once after the divorce was final," Dane said. "Some things are wrong from the start. I was young and we married for the wrong reasons." He shifted uncomfortably under the older man's intense gaze. "We all make mistakes."

"She was sure a pretty eyeful, but not the type of wife you need here. Now my Pauline, she was the right kind of woman for this life. Why, we were married for forty years and we always worked side by side until..." He stared at his cup for several seconds.

Dane nodded. "Cancer can strike at any time, Mose. Sometimes there's nothing anyone can do. I'm sure you still miss her."

"She's been gone for four lambings now," Moses said wistfully. "I'm old and set in my ways but you're a young man, boss, and you need a woman around here."

"I'm satisfied," Dane replied tersely. "I have several women who..."

"But you don't care a hill of beans about any one of them."

Dane glanced at his foreman. "Do you know so much about my personal life?"

Moses shook his head emphatically. "Damn right. I know that a man at thirty-eight still has reason to hope he'll find a good woman." He chuckled. "Remember those twin sisters who came here three years ago?"

Dane smiled. "Alma and Alta? Unforgettable. They arrived in the middle of lambing, uninvited but ready to work, and all they did was tag along after me and make a nuisance of themselves. I sent them packing after supper the second day." He glanced at Moses, whose gaze was distant and expression somber. *He's probably thinking about Pauline,* Dane reflected, allowing his sixty-four-year-old foreman a few moments of introspection.

Dane glanced at his watch, then at his lifelong friend's closed eyes. "Are you dozing?" he asked. "There's work to do at the lambing tents. We still have two without canvas tops. You can nap after dinner."

"I wasn't snoozing," Moses replied, straightening. "Just thinking about your folks. I'm glad they came to their senses and moved to a warmer climate. No blizzards in southern California. This cold gets to a person over the years."

"Are you thinking of leaving, too?" Dane asked.

"'Course not. Where would I go?" Moses reached across the oak table and tapped the letter. "What do you think? Gonna let that professor cousin of yours sucker you one more time?"

"I could use the help. Maybe the student can handle himself in the kitchen." He frowned at the overcooked scrambled eggs growing cold on his plate. "I sure get tired of kitchen duty."

"You say that every time it's your week to cook," Moses grumbled. "I feel the same way about doing the cleanup."

Dane smiled. "If Trudy Mayers is available during March and April again this year, I'll bribe her with a pay increase. Her cooking during lambing makes up for yours and mine the rest of the year." He picked up the letter and scanned it again. "I don't know if I want to take another chance." He shook his head. "After last year..."

"I understand," Moses said, laughing heartily. "After last spring and that young feller from Terraton, Ideho I didn't think you would ever let another intern set foot on the place."

Dane grinned, thinking back to the arrogant twenty-two-year-old student who had challenged everything Dane tried to teach him, usually prefacing his remarks with "Professor So-and-So says..." or worse yet, "That's not the way Dr. So-and-So told us it should be done."

The young man had lasted less than two weeks. The end had come when Dane lost his temper and laid down an ultimatum: listen or leave. The student had packed his belongings sometime during the night and slipped away from the rambling two-story white frame house, escaping in the shiny new Bronco his father had given him as a graduation present. The student had left a terse note of resignation and a promise to report "everything" to his advisor at the university.

"I did swear I'd never get taken again, didn't I?" Dane's blue eyes glinted when the light fixture over the long oak table cast its beam across his face. He rose from his chair. "Still I could use the help. Lambing can get out of control at times and I haven't heard if Oscar and Wilma are coming back this year."

"Lordy, I hope so," Moses said, perking up. "A spring without that pretty Wilma just wouldn't seem right."

"I think you've got a crush on that woman and won't admit it," Dane said. "She thinks a lot of you, too. I can tell by the way she feeds you."

Moses huffed as he carried his dishes to the sink.

"I'm sure she's as anxious to return as you are to have her," Dane said. "Blackie Swensen called and asked to be night lamber again this year. He has a friend he wants to bring."

"Girl or boy?" Moses asked, grinning.

Dane smiled. "An old sheepherder from the Dubois, Idaho area who wants to work the season. Blackie says he's good."

"So why ain't he herding in Ide-ho?" Moses asked as he ambled back to the table.

"The owners lost the place to the bank." Dane stuffed his letter back into its envelope and headed toward his office.

"So whatcha gonna do, boss?" Moses called after him.

"I'll give him a chance," Dane called back over his shoulder. "It's only fair."

ABIGAIL HARDESTY WAS ECSTATIC when the letter from the Montana sheep rancher finally arrived. She had returned from a three-day weaving seminar in Seattle and her adrenaline was high.

The workshop on tapestries had been her favorite, even though the demonstration she had given of spinning on an antique great wheel had brought her a good deal of personal recognition.

She touched the manila envelope, caressing the writing of her name: A. B. Hardesty.

Dr. Christensen had suggested that she apply for one of the openings in the agricultural internship program. Under the plan, regional ranchers gave students hands-on experience as they worked under the tutelage of experts in their field of interest. The professor had cautioned her that although he knew of her outstanding performance as a graduate student in animal husbandry, a potential employer might react differently when he learned that her undergraduate degree had been in fiber arts.

"But I've picked up the science credits I needed," she had reminded him.

"Yes, but a prospective employer might only notice the arts part of your undergraduate studies. I'll write a personal letter of recommendation. There's a special place in Montana I have in mind. The owner is my second cousin on my mother's side. The two of you would be perfect together. You have something special to offer, Abbie, and my cousin needs someone like you to shake him up a little. He's the best in the business but can get too settled in his ways at times. Once the ranch was a showcase operation, but lately he's reverted to some old-style techniques and I think you could help him update his operation."

Abbie and Dr. Christensen had become more than just teacher and student. He had invited her to his home, introduced her to his wife and two married children and encouraged her to ignore the chauvinism of some of the male students. "There are only three of you women in the program this year," he said, "and you're definitely the prettiest as well as the smartest."

"But my brain and ability are what counts," she had insisted. "Not my looks. If I was fortunate enough to inherit good looks from my ancestors, that's no cause to carry on like some of those younger men do. It's positively embarrassing. I wish they would grow up."

Dr. Christensen had understood when she explained her driving need to learn more about the sheep that produced the fine wool she enjoyed working with. Only fulfilling that need could satisfy her goal of someday understanding every facet of the fiber arts. From the sheep to wool and its cleaning, on to spinning and dyeing to the exact shades her design required, to weaving the fine yarn into beautiful tapestries that told stories of unusual detail—she wanted to know it all.

Her tapestries always included people, although one of her art instructors had cautioned her about the difficulty of depicting people in the design of the cartoons and translating them to the warp and weft of the fabric.

She tightened her grip on the letter. This man, who owned a small band of registered and purebred Lincoln sheep, was her newest goal. Not really the man, she amended, only his sheep. No, not his sheep, either. What she wanted now was the man's knowledge, the opportunity to draw on his vast experience. He also ran several bands of Rambouillet-Targhee crossbred sheep, and Dr. Christensen had spoken about his work with quarter Finn ewes. But her interest lay in the Lincolns, whose long-fiber fleeces with the beautiful crimp were very desirable in hand spinning and strong enough to be used in her larger wall hangings.

She smoothed her short, wavy auburn hair, wondering what the spring and summer would hold for her on the remote sheep ranch in the mountains of southwestern Montana. She hoped she would have six months of solid learning, a chance to do some dyeing and time to complete several small wall hangings on the tapestry

loom. She had already set up the loom on the dining table in the motor home that would be her residence on
wheels for the next half year.

She had purchased the motor home two summers ago
when she sold the small crafts shop she'd owned since
graduating from college. For the past two years she had
concentrated on the graduate program at the University
of Utah. A grant from a state arts foundation had eased
the burden of income loss, and her grades had brought
her a special scholarship the second year. Small commissions from patrons of the crafts shop had turned her
apartment into a weaver's studio, with a six-harness
treadle loom and an upright tapestry frame loom taking
up most of the living space. The comforts of an unclut-
tered home were luxuries she had set aside.

Such sacrifices were short term considering the prize
waiting at the end of the internship: her own studio, fully
equipped with assorted looms to produce works of vary-
ing widths, laundry facilities, a corner devoted to her
spinning, wall space for hanging skeins and whatever else
she chose and lots of storage for her cleaned fleeces. The
studio would have large windows and a huge skylight to
let in natural sunlight and save on utilities. She would
even have an outdoor fireplace for dyeing her yarns in
good weather.

She smiled, touching the envelope again. How many
times had she sketched her dream studio? The more experienced she became, the more she revised her design.
But why not? Dreams could come true if a person believed enough, and was willing to work hard to make
them a reality.

The studio would be located on a small piece of land,
with enough acres to rotate her own flock and prevent
damage to the natural grasses from overgrazing. She

didn't know where her land would be, but she was sure she would recognize the right place when she saw it. Abbie had set aside part of the money from the sale of her crafts shop and invested it. Her confidence in her plans grew each time an interest statement arrived.

She would have a flock of sheep to supply her with all the fleeces she would need and enough surplus to sell to augment her income. Perhaps some day she would even hire an assistant to help with some of the more labor-intensive tasks, but which ones? She loved to card the wool, to spin, to design the tapestries. Dyeing was perhaps her favorite job, other than the weaving itself.

She laughed aloud, her clear melodious voice startling her for a moment. Her Aunt Minnie had been right. She was a fanatic at times: obsessed when the muses worked overtime, single-minded when starting a new project and exhausted when the finished piece came off the loom.

Several weaving friends had warned her to leave the business of raising sheep to agricultural experts. But she had made her decision. And decisions could always be reconsidered.

Being free of emotional encumbrances was an advantage; Abbie had no man demanding that she stay home to have meals ready on his schedule without consideration to her own, no one to make fun of her weaving and the moods she often found herself in when sketching the cartoons. Recently she had switched from colored pencils to oil pastels in order to blend the shades more subtly. The paper designs had to be just right before she could begin weaving. She loved to move the yarn butterflies back and forth between the warp threads and watch the images grow before her eyes.

Suddenly she sobered and stopped her reverie. What if she hadn't been accepted?

She ripped open the envelope, her fingers trembling as she unfolded the letter. Her eyes scanned the page and she breathed a sigh of relief. She was to report to the ranch as soon as possible. Lambing had begun the first week in March. When the owner deemed her experienced enough, she would be expected to assume her share of the weekly shifts of night lambing. She would have one day off per week but should be prepared to work that day if emergencies arose. In several brief sentences her prospective boss described the worst possible weather conditions of spring in the northern Rockies. "The only time clock at the Grasten Sweetwater Livestock Company has a twenty-four-hour day on its face," he wrote.

"He's making a point of the long, hard hours," she murmured aloud. Was he warning her? What if the work proved to be more difficult than she'd anticipated? Would he fire her on the spot? Surely not.

D. A. Grasten would be her employer, instructor and mentor for the next six months.

Dr. Christensen had said the man had been in the business all his life, that his family had been on the same property for generations. Abigail wondered if he had a large family. She envisioned a Danish wife named Helga with blond braids, and several blue-eyed children. There were probably grandchildren as well, since he had been in the sheep business for many years.

Perhaps he would take her under his wing and treat her like a daughter. She would offer to help in the kitchen and get on the good side of his wife, clean the lambing pens better than anyone else, even stay awake during night lambing although she had always been one to go to sleep with the chickens and rise at the first sign of dawn.

One way or another, she would convince this Mr. Grasten that she was just the intern he had always hoped for. Dr. Christensen had spoken briefly about the problems with last year's student.

"Please, Abbie, never say 'Professor So-and-So says that's not the way to do it.' Dane Grasten is a staunch believer in practical experience. If you start out on the right footing, you'll find him the perfect teacher."

"What is he like?" she'd asked.

Dr. Christensen had only shrugged. "Taller than the average fellow. Good looking for his age. Blond and blue eyed like most Danes, but he might be getting gray by now. I haven't seen him in a few years. I last saw him at a family reunion about five years ago and although we've never socialized, we stay in touch. When I started this program twelve years ago, his was the first name on my list. He has character. When he shakes on something, it's as good as a written contract, better sometimes. I think you are just what Dane Grasten needs and I'm sure he'll agree once he gets to know you."

She laid the letter on the counter and put a frozen dinner in the microwave. In minutes she was seated at the table, eating her meal and thinking about the internship. While she ate, she reached for a piece of paper and began making a list of the items she would need.

Dr. Christensen had warned her that lambing could be messy, that newborn lambs were wet and slippery, but that the ewes were generally maternal and anxious to care for their young. He'd also cautioned her that the spring weather in the Montana mountains was characterized by sudden storms that could drop several feet of snow within hours, and that the temperature could plummet to below zero during the nights, freezing and killing a newborn lamb in minutes. She decided she'd need several pair of thermal underwear, waterproof overshoes, practical work gloves and two or three coveralls.

An hour later, as she undressed for bed, Abbie smiled. She had already jotted a brief note of acknowledgement to Mr. Grasten, committing herself to a March 20th arrival date. She had signed it A. B. Hardesty, the signature she had been using since leaving home in western Kentucky.

The bed sheets were cold as she slid beneath the covers. She had much work to do before she left. Abbie had a friend who wanted to sublet Abbie's apartment so her weaving equipment had to be taken down and crated and supplies packed, then moved to a storage unit she had rented a few miles from her apartment, along with a few pieces of furniture she owned.

She stretched, her feet pushing against the footboard of the maple bed. She was just a bit more than five feet eight and physically fit due to her daily jogging routine. She exercised chiefly to counteract the broadening effects of sitting at the loom. Except for her hips, which she considered too rounded, she was pleased with her appearance. Now, she could put her conditioned body to work in a very physical way and prove to Mr. Grasten that she could handle any work he assigned to her.

Her weaving books and magazines and a handful of paperback novels would take up her leisure time for the six months she would be away. A modern translation of the Bible, its pages dog-eared and several passages marked with yellow highlighting pen, would go into the glove compartment of the motor home. Perhaps she would begin attending church again. She had become lax since leaving home.

The Bible reminded Abbie of her youth. As a feisty eight-year-old, she had gone to live with her Aunt Minnie and Uncle Harry, making the trip from Paducah to Central City, Kentucky, alone on a Greyhound bus. Her mother and stepfather had been unemployed for months and had tried to explain to her that she would be happier living with her natural father's cousin and his wife on a tobacco farm than in Louisville, where they were moving. Uncle Harry and Aunt Minnie Hardesty had picked her up at the bus depot and taken her home, treating her to an ice cream cone on the way.

Two years later, Minnie and Harry Hardesty had legally adopted Abbie into their family of three teenage boys. She had lived with them until winning a scholarship to attend art school in Utah. She loved her aunt and uncle dearly, but she'd never been able to forget her mother, who occasionally wrote one-page letters in an often illegible scrawl. Aunt Minnie had tried to help her decipher the words, but usually the matter was settled with a hug and a kiss on Abbie's cheek, with assurance that she was loved by her new family.

Her adoptive parents had sold the farm to Uncle Harry's brother and moved to Lexington three years earlier. Abbie smiled, thinking of Aunt Minnie, whose red hair and green eyes matched her own. Aunt Minnie had taught Sunday School all her adult life and still occasionally chided Abbie during her monthly phone calls for her lack of regular church attendance. Now Abbie made herself a promise to try to become more faithful, for her aunt's sake.

Perhaps, she considered, independent living had made her selfish. She enjoyed living alone. There was no one to hurt, no sensitive egos to soothe, only herself to account for. She loved her freedom.

She grinned, pulled the quilted comforter up under her chin and curled into a comfortable position. Pushing the pillow a few times to fit her cheek, she burrowed deeper into the covers.

Her thirtieth birthday would be in mid-August. Most childhood friends and relatives her own age had long since married and had children. Some were already on their second marriages.

But Abbie's life had taken a direction away from marriage and family. At times, she felt a twinge of regret. As a child she had learned to cope, surviving living in poverty with her mother, and later, the loss of her parent and the move to Drakesboro. She couldn't remember her natural father, but from a large box of old photos Aunt Minnie had managed to find a handful of pictures of a handsome young man with Abbie's straight brows and steady gaze.

Life on the tobacco farm had been no more affluent than what she'd known, but her aunt and uncle's love had been given unconditionally. Her fondest memories were of being accepted by her cousins, Eileen and Callie, who lived on neighboring farms.

Aunt Minnie had distracted Abbie from brooding about her mother's abandoning her by showing her how to use natural fibers for crafts: they soaked vines and used them to make doll furniture and wall hangings, they boiled the natural dyes from the leaves and berries that grew in the surrounding hills to dye pieces of fleece still in the grease, they combed and carded the wool. Aunt Minnie also taught Abbie to operate an old spinning wheel that had once belonged to Aunt Minnie's grandmother. Her two cousins had soon lost interest in such lessons but not young Abbie.

She would be forever indebted to her aunt for opening the world of spinning and weaving to her.

Leaving the rural Kentucky life-style and going west to school had opened another world for Abbie, and her determination to become financially independent had grown stronger year by year. Her aunt had encouraged her to not look back, to turn her energies to the future, and gradually, as Abbie matured into womanhood, she had begun to understand her aunt's philosophy.

Next week at this very time, she thought, she would be nestled in her motor home bed with half a day's work under her belt. She could hardly wait. Someday she would find a way to repay Aunt Minnie for everything.

CHAPTER TWO

ABBIE TURNED OFF Interstate 15 and headed toward her cousin's potato farm near Shelley, Idaho. Although she was anxious to make up for lost time, she could never drive past her cousin Eileen's farm without saying hello.

After spending most of the day with two weaving friends, she was running behind schedule. As her digital wristwatch changed to 5:00 p.m., she promised herself she would stay at Eileen's for only an hour or two.

Eileen Hardesty Mills was the oldest of the three cousins who had become inseparable during their childhood. The bonds established then had carried over into their adult lives even as their girlish dreams had been replaced by reality.

Eileen was the oldest and a natural leader. Two years younger was Abbie herself, the red-haired, green-eyed, free spirit of the cousins. Three years younger than Abbie was pretty Callie Hardesty, the only female cousin to inherit the Hardesty family traits of black hair and brown eyes. Callie had tagged along with the older girls as soon as she was old enough to discover the fun they had during the summers.

Abbie stayed in touch with Callie but had grown closer to Eileen over the years since they both moved west. Abbie's frustration over Callie's refusal to pull herself up by her bootstraps from a life of poverty had caused an unpleasant exchange of words between her and Callie over the phone a few years earlier. Now, although Abbie tried to understand Callie's predicament, their relationship had deteriorated to obligatory cards at Christmastime.

She turned into the lane leading to Eileen's home. On either side of the dirt lane were plowed fields waiting to receive the seed potatoes that would begin the growing cycle again. The motor home rolled to a stop near the front door of the house.

The screen door slammed and two brown-haired girls raced down the front steps as Abbie stepped out of her camper. She was immediately hugged around her waist by both girls. She stood patiently until slowly they loosened their holds on her.

"Hello, Jodie. Hi, Jolene," she said, smiling down at their almost identical faces, then impulsively kissed each rosy cheek. The twins were second graders. "Where's your mom?"

"She's taking care of Daddy," Jolene said, her face changing dramatically. "She said to bring you inside." Jolene took one of Abbie's hands while Jodie grabbed the other, and they led her up the steps and into the house.

Eileen's husband, Duncan, had suffered a series of falls two years earlier, and the diagnosis was multiple sclerosis. They had been hoping for a period of remission, but instead, he had been fighting recurring bouts of pneumonia and his limbs had weakened considerably. *Struck down in his prime,* Abbie thought as the twins led her into the living room.

"Abbie!"

Abbie turned to see her cousin entering from the hallway and held out her arms. "Eileen!"

The cousins embraced. When they parted, both had to wipe away some tears.

"Come," Eileen said, taking Abbie's hand and guiding her into the large blue and white kitchen. "Let's have some tea. I baked bread today. It's still warm. How about a slice with butter and homemade blackberry preserves? The girls and Jordan helped me pick them last summer."

Abbie smiled, trying to overlook Eileen's drawn features. "How could I resist an offer like that? Girls, want to join us?"

"Yes!" Jodie and Jolene cried, wriggling into their seats.

"Where's Jordan?" Abbie asked.

"He's out sorting potatoes in the second spud cellar. I hired two new employees and Jordan is showing them what to do. Isn't it telling that Duncan and I must ask our ten-year-old son to act as a foreman?" She closed her eyes for a few seconds.

"I'm sure Jordan is proud to be able to help," Abbie replied. "He's always been mature for his age." She spread a generous spoonful of blackberry preserves onto the bread and took a bite. "Delicious."

Within minutes the twins finished their snacks and raced outside. Abbie and Eileen sipped their tea, content to enjoy the quiet together for a few minutes.

"I can only stay an hour or so," Abbie said. "I wrote you about my job on the sheep ranch. I hope to get there tonight."

"But it's getting dark already," Eileen said, pushing a few loose strands of hair from her forehead. "Why don't you stay here tonight? We have lots of room."

Abbie shook her head. "No, I want to keep moving. I can always pull into a rest area if I can't stay awake. After all, I have my bed with me."

Eileen smiled, but the paleness in her cheeks remained. "You're quite the independent woman, aren't you?"

The comment made Abbie feel uncomfortable. "I suppose so, but it's my choice. I like my life-style, so please don't hold it against me." She smiled. "I think you're lucky, too, Eileen. You have Duncan and the children. You're never alone."

"Sometimes I wish I..." Eileen paused, staring out the window. "It's just that sometimes the pressure gets to me and I just want to...want to...run away and hide." She glanced toward Abbie and Abbie's heart went out to her cousin. "Do you think I'm wrong to feel that way...just sometimes?"

Abbie reached for Eileen's hand and gave it a squeeze. "Of course not, Eileen. How is Duncan? Any better?"

"He's had a series of urinary infections and he's become very depressed. The physician is trying some new medication but I don't think anything is going to work. Our physician told us that no one dies from MS, only the complications. Isn't that a terrific consolation?" She took another sip of tea. "He's going to die, Abbie."

"Oh, no," Abbie cried, "you can't say that!"

"But it's true," Eileen said calmly. "I thought we would grow old together, but now, after only eleven years, I'm going to lose him. I know it."

"You mustn't talk like that," Abbie scolded gently. "Where is that faith you've always had? Have you forgotten the power of prayer you've always believed in? I'm surprised to hear you talk so fatalistically now."

"Perhaps that's why I feel this way," Eileen replied. "Recently I've felt less frantic...almost as though this is all about to change. I love Duncan very much, but I feel as if we're saying our goodbyes." She smiled. "But

we've had a few bright spots in our lives. Did I tell you
about the reporter who came and interviewed us?''

"You mentioned him briefly in a letter, but that was
months ago," Abbie said, glad to see her cousin perk up.
"Tell me more."

"Well, he was from a regional magazine called *Western Living*. He was . . . very nice . . . likable. It's strange,
but I felt very comfortable with him." Eileen straightened in her chair. "He was writing a series of articles on
women in unusual occupations. I was his only potato
farmer. I was afraid he'd be cold and unemotional and
make us feel as if he was prying into our affairs, but he
didn't. I think he genuinely enjoyed meeting us. Even
Duncan said he was glad I accepted the request to be interviewed."

Eileen left the room and returned a few minutes later
carrying a magazine. "The reporter's name is Daniel
Page. He's single, quite handsome, I thought, and he
came again to visit when the article was published, and
stayed for most of the day. He left several copies with us.
He visited with Jordan in the spud cellars, spent over an
hour with Duncan, and then he and I had coffee." She
studied her hands for several seconds.

"He's the first man I've enjoyed talking to in a long
time, other than Duncan, of course," Eileen said. "It
must be his profession, knowing how to put a person at
ease. He called me his Spud Lady. Here," she said,
handing a copy of *Western Living* to Abbie. "The article
is on page thirty-four. Take this copy. You can read it
later. Dan . . . Mr. Page took some photos and managed
to make Duncan look healthy and me a little fatter."

"Thanks," Abbie said, flipping to the article and
scanning it. "Good-looking couple," she agreed.
"You've lost more weight, haven't you? You probably

forget to eat. Don't let yourself get sick, too. Who would take care of you? Remember our promise when we were young to always ask for help? It still applies.''

Eileen nodded. ''I know, but it's easier to help another than to ask for help yourself. You, me and Callie are all guilty of trying to be totally self-sufficient, aren't we?''

''At times,'' Abbie admitted. The subject changed, and the cousins enjoyed the chance to bring each other up to date with their news. Soon an hour had passed.

''I'd like to say hi to Duncan before I leave,'' Abbie said.

''Sure,'' Eileen replied, and Abbie followed her into Duncan's room. He was asleep.

''Tell him I was here,'' Abbie whispered as they left the room. ''I'll come back as soon as I can. Maybe this slave-driving sheep man I'll be working for will let me off a day and I can get back here this summer.''

''I hope so,'' Eileen replied and they hugged again.

''Stay in touch,'' Eileen called from the porch as Abbie turned the key in the ignition.

Abbie waved goodbye and drove toward the highway, wishing she could do something for the family caught up in a slowly unfolding tragedy. Still feeling helpless, she merged her vehicle with the northbound interstate traffic.

She glanced at the gas gauge and switched to the reserve tank as the north exit sign to Idaho Falls appeared.

''This darn motor home passes everything but a gas pump,'' she mumbled, and flipped on her turn signal. She took the next exit, rolled to a stop and waited for the cross traffic of a business loop street to clear. She scanned the street for a self-service gas station and spotted one a block to the left.

After filling the two gas tanks, she shook her head. Motor homes were definitely not the most economical way to travel, she reflected. But the security of having a bed, bath and kitchen traveling with her more than compensated for the expense. "Darn it," she grumbled, glancing at her watch again. She had hoped to reach the ranch a day early, but she was still more than 170 miles from her destination. The activities of the long day had drained her of energy. She didn't care for driving the twenty-six-foot-long vehicle at night.

She paid her bill and ran to the motor home. As she waited impatiently for the traffic to break, she noticed a neon sign.

"Budget rates," the sign teased. She thought of a hot shower and shampoo, a television set. . . . It might be the very last time to enjoy television for six months.

The tiny message beneath the sign cinched her decision. "RV Dump and Free Water." She could empty the gray water and top off her water supply. She had been speculating on how to conserve her vehicle's water supply once she reached her destination.

After registering and receiving a room key, Abbie checked one of the closets to verify her supply of dyeing materials and skeins of natural yarn were still safely in their boxes. *I hope this Mr. Grasten has an open mind about building outdoor fires and bubbling, boiling pots,* she thought, deciding to be discreet. She wanted to do some dyeing on one of her first days off. If her boss didn't approve . . . she could always use the small kitchen area of her motor home.

She walked a block to a fast-food restaurant and ordered a box of chicken pieces to go, then hurried back to her motel room. After a shower and a few minutes with the blow dryer, she ate. Half way through a suspense movie and a second drumstick, her eyelids began to droop.

THE NEXT MORNING Abbie awoke as the sun broke above the horizon. For a few seconds she didn't know where she was, but images of the sheep ranch came to mind.

The time spent in the bathroom using a hot brush to tame her auburn curls helped her to rethink her schedule and give her self-confidence a boost. She was still on time. She would skip breakfast and another three hours, four at the most, would find her at her destination. She would begin her training, get under the skin of Mr. Grasten and make herself indispensable to him so he would never want to do without her...until her six-month stay was up.

As she worked on her hair, Abbie studied the pencil sketch of a map her employer had sent her. Instructions below the diagram cautioned her that the road was dirt, winding, steep and narrow at times.

"Take the Sweetwater Road and check your odometer when you leave Dillon," he had warned. "The entrance is exactly twenty-five miles from town. Turn to the right and drive across the creek. You'll see the main house on your right. Only a fool could miss it. The sign reads Grasten Sweetwater Livestock Company, Founded 1884."

"Sounds a little bossy and boastful, too," she murmured as she folded the note and map and slid it into her jeans pocket. *Well, Mr. Grasten, I'm not a fool. I can find your darn house even in the dark. And you're in for a disappointment if you think I'm impressed with the age of your sheep ranch.*

After spending a few more minutes with her hair, Abbie was satisfied. Soft curls, brushed away from her face, accented her cheekbones. The tapered cut at the back of her head exposed her ears, and the tiny gold loop earrings heightened the softness of her neck.

She frowned at her image in the mirror. Perhaps she looked overdressed. She chuckled aloud as she gave herself a final perusal. How could a kelly-green-and-yellow baseball jersey, jeans and suede oxfords be considered overdressed? She was just nervous about meeting the ranch personnel. And she always wore the gold earrings. They had become a part of her, a substitute security blanket, she supposed, the way the locket from her Aunt Minnie had been years earlier.

Once she had caught the gold chain of the locket on her spinning wheel. Fearing it might get broken, she had removed it. Now the locket was safely inside a small wooden jewelry box. Whenever she felt tense, a touch of the cool gold loop earring would reassure her that she could handle whatever trouble might come her way.

A touch of clear-red lipstick was the extent of her makeup. As a teenager, she had tried to give her straight brows a hint of an arch, but Aunt Minnie had said she was wasting her time, that the straight brows came from her stubborn Hardesty heritage and reflected her determination to succeed. Eileen and Callie had inherited the same trait.

Her skin was clear, healthy and natural. What people saw was what they got. There was no permanent to curl her hair, no padded bra to accent an already full bustline, no heels to boost her height—only a pair of reading glasses she found herself using more frequently when designing the cartoons for the loom or reading at night.

Within the hour, she was driving north on the interstate, humming along to the strains of a new Tommy Hunter tape on the dashboard cassette player.

DANE GRASTEN ROLLED over onto his back and pulled the pillow with him, shoving it against his ears to block out the persistent pounding.

"Boss," Moses Parish's booming voice called through the closed door of Dane's bedroom, "are you awake?"

"Go away," Dane growled.

"Boss, I need you," Moses pleaded, knocking again.

"Tend to it yourself, Mose," Dane shouted. "That's what I pay you for."

"You don't pay me enough to handle this problem," Moses called back. "That agricultural intern is here."

"Well, put him to work."

"But . . ."

"If he needs a bed, have him bunk with you until tomorrow," Dane called. "I need more sleep." He rolled back onto his stomach.

Moses pounded on the door again. "Boss, you've got to take care of this yourself. I ain't lying!"

The high pitch in Moses's voice caught Dane's full attention. Whatever the problem, it had shaken the unshakable Moses.

"Okay," Dane called. "Give me five minutes to wake up. I'll be out."

"Be sure and dress," Moses warned.

"What the hell?" Dane rubbed his face with his hands and tried to open his eyes but the bright light of late morning blinded him. "Okay, okay, I'll dress and come solve your problem. Now, get away from that door. I'll meet you outside."

He listened to Moses's audible mumbling and receding boot steps. His body protested as he swung his long legs over the side of the bed and sat up, still holding his head in his hands.

Dane's head continued to pound from his being suddenly awakened after too little sleep. If he had to suffer through a hangover, he should at least be able to have some pleasant memories of the night before. The only living beings with him last night had been 250 pregnant Rambouillet-Targhee crossbred ewes in the drop pen between the lambing tents.

He had been on duty the past two nights, filling in for one of his helpers who was ill with the flu, and he'd had only cat naps during the day. His new day man had called in sick yesterday. Someone had left a gate open and the rams had disappeared from their pasture. He had sent Moses after them, and Moses had spent the better part of the day tracking them down.

Dane wasn't sure how many more days like these past few he could endure. Finding good workers grew more difficult each year. Moses Parish was right. What he needed was a willing wife and several strapping sons ready to take on some of the physical labor, sons who would be trained to replace him, to give him time away from the place.

He rubbed his face again and stood. Who was he fooling? He was thirty-eight years old with no heirs at all. Maybe he should have sold out to the insurance company that had approached him the previous summer. It's representative had made an almost irresistible offer and had promised a certified check within the week if he would sell. Now, for a moment, he questioned his own sanity for refusing.

Dane dressed and hurried to his bathroom, vowing to keep this interruption short and sweet. He'd show the student through the lambing tents and drop pens before assigning him some simple chores to keep him busy.

Within the hour the student would be occupied and Dane would be back in the sack.

Two bloodshot blue eyes stared back at him from the mirror as he ran a comb through his hair. Dane scolded himself for not visiting the barber in town weeks ago. He looked like one of the town drunks, and he felt as bad as he looked.

He grabbed his worn beige western hat and clean coveralls from the closet on the service porch and reached for his overboots. He had left his gloves in the cab of the pickup.

The brilliant sun reflecting off the snow cover in the yard and hills blinded him for several seconds as he stepped outside.

His eyes were playing a delectable trick on him. The woman standing beside a long motor home and chatting with Moses couldn't be the intern, so who was she? She was tall and slender, yet the denim coveralls seemed to accent her shapely curves and sexuality.

Dane swallowed, his mind a blank. He frowned heavily as he approached her. "You're...?"

She extended her hand and in the split seconds before he found himself accepting it, his gaze fell on the well manicured, unpolished nails at the tips of her long fingers. Her grasp was surprisingly strong and firm.

"Yes, I'm A. B. Hardesty, your new agriculture intern from Dr. Christensen's program."

"You can't be," Dane replied. "Dr. Christensen never said anything...about..." He groped for the appropriate words to send her packing. "You can't stay."

"Why not?" she asked, cutting him short.

"Because you're..." His gaze swept down her coveralls. "It wouldn't work. We need a man."

She stiffened. "I have the same training as the male students," she retorted. "I'm healthy and strong. You can't deny me a chance just because of my sex. That's illegal!" Her pretty mouth pulled down at the corners. "I know I can do the work. I can't go back now. We signed a contract!" As she stood her ground, her fingers found the tiny gold loop in her left ear and stroked it.

The kitchen door slammed behind Dane and a woman's voice shouted, "Dinner's on! Eat it now or do without," before the door slammed again.

Dane glanced at his watch. He'd slept longer than he'd originally thought, and for a few seconds, he felt out of control.

Moses chuckled. "That Wilma is never one to mince words." He glanced from Abbie to Dane. Dane's gaze followed his foreman's to Abbie. She was surely easy on the eyes, the rancher thought, but she had to go.

Abbie stepped forward. "Mr. Grasten, you're not involved in this. I should be talking to your...father. Dr. Christensen said I had nothing to worry about."

"I'm the only Grasten living here," Dane replied, stifling a yawn. He grumbled something under his breath and turned back toward the house.

"But you can't...just..."

He turned to her again, looming over her. "I'm the boss and I can do whatever I choose to. Get that straight, Hardesty."

Moses stepped between them. "Why don't we go eat and talk it over some more? Surely Miss Hardesty is entitled to that much."

Dane closed his bleary eyes, shielding them from the bright sunlight. "I suppose so," he said grudgingly. "Come inside and have dinner with us, Hardesty. Then we'll talk."

He disappeared through the storm door and into the kitchen. Moses motioned to Abbie to follow, but she didn't move.

"Is he always that disagreeable?" she asked. "I came here to work and learn, not to be fired before I've been given a fair chance."

Moses grinned. "The boss had a bad night."

"He looks it," she agreed.

"He's not a bad-looking feller when he's in a better mood."

"His looks are immaterial," Abbie said. "I want to learn the practical side of sheep raising. That's all."

"He can sure handle that," Moses commented, smiling at her. "The boss is a walking book of knowledge when it comes to sheep."

Abbie turned toward the motor home door. "Give the cook...Wilma...my apologies, but I'd rather...I have things I can do while...Mr. Grasten eats."

"No," Moses said, taking her arm and turning her toward the kitchen door. "The boss is always in a better mood after a good meal."

"Feed the beast?" she asked, unable to suppress a smile.

Moses nodded. "You're figuring him out already. Now, you come on inside with me, Miss Hardesty, and we'll work this out. We need you here. Give the boss a second chance."

Abbie hesitated.

"Please?" Moses coaxed, grinning.

"Okay, and please call me Abbie, Mr. Parish," she said.

"Then none of this Mr. Parish business. I'm just plain Moses."

CHAPTER THREE

ABBIE WATCHED THE WIRY MAN disappear through the door. Uncertainty held her back. She liked Moses Parish, but this Mr. Grasten was a different matter. Was the man always so surly? And how old was he? What had happened to the fatherly mentor she had created in her imagination?

If Dr. Christensen had led Grasten to believe she was a man, perhaps he had deceived her as well. Surely he knew that Grasten was more her own age than he'd implied. And where were Grasten's wife and children? Inside eating lunch, or *dinner* as the cook had so briskly stated? Was everyone but the friendly Moses in a bad mood?

When she had first spotted Grasten coming down the porch steps, she had assumed he was the owner's son and thought he must be recovering from a night on the town. Perhaps he had a drinking problem. She certainly didn't want to get involved with all *that* could mean. Was Grasten always so unkempt? He looked as if he hadn't shaved in days.

Reluctantly, Abbie approached the kitchen door and stepped inside. The kitchen was a surprise. It was much larger than she had expected, and painted a very pale yellow. The curtains at the sunny windows were a yellow-and-white check with tiny red and blue daisies scattered across the material. The cheeriness of the room lifted her spirits.

Six men were seated at a large oak table. She recognized only Moses. The woman named Wilma stood behind the chair closest to the working area of the kitchen. Her hand on the chair back laid claim to her position of authority.

Two chairs were empty, one at the head of the table and one at the right of the head.

Wilma pointed to the latter. "You take that one."

Six pairs of eyes watched her, but only Moses smiled.

"You sit here in my place, Abbie," he said, sliding into the chair next to the unoccupied one at the head of the table. He moved his cup of coffee to his new spot and motioned her to sit down.

"Thanks," she murmured as she sat.

Moses motioned to the other men. "That old bald-headed feller with the missing tooth is Oscar Hansen. He's the best night lamber I've ever known. He's on his way to bed right after dinner. He don't like to miss one of Wilma's meals. She might not offer him another one."

The man across from Abbie grinned, apparently not offended in the least by Moses's description.

"This here ugly one is Buck Jensen," Moses continued. "He don't say much, but he's a downright genius when the equipment breaks down."

A good-looking redheaded man, who couldn't be older than his mid-twenties, nodded to her but didn't say a word, his ruddy cheeks darkened with a rush of color.

Abbie nodded.

"Them's Blackie Swensen and Windy Schmidt," Moses said, motioning to two men in their fifties. "They're old sheepherders from Ide-ho. Blackie is our second night lamber this week. They both take sheep wagons to the high country in the summer. And this is Andy Given. He does whatever needs doing, and when the boss says jump, he asks, 'How high?'"

Abbie scanned the six curious faces, wondering how many were sizing her up. She extended her hand to each of them.

"I'll probably have trouble remembering all your names," she said, "so be patient with me, but I'm glad to be here and I'm looking forward to working with you."

There was only one empty chair remaining. "Where are the wife and children?" she whispered to Moses.

He looked puzzled for several seconds before chuckling "Oh," he said, "the boss ain't married and if he has any offspring, he don't claim the young 'uns."

The others around the table broke into rowdy laughter until Dane Grasten appeared from nowhere and slid into the empty chair. Abbie resisted the temptation to look his way.

"What's so funny?" Dane asked, scanning the grinning faces staring back at him.

Moses sobered. "I was just introducing everyone. This beautiful lady is Wilma Hansen. She's subbing for our regular cook who can't get here until next Monday. Wilma is Oscar's sister."

Wilma slapped at Moses with her dish towel and caught him on his ear.

"Cut it out, woman," he warned, "or I'll tell Miss Abbie how mean you can be when you set your mind to it." But he was grinning when he glanced at Abbie.

Wilma grumbled as she lowered herself into her chair, smoothing her short, wavy, graying hair. She frowned at everyone before bowing her head and giving the fastest blessing Abbie had ever heard.

"Now eat," Wilma commanded. "I've got work to do this afternoon. I don't want to be cooped up in this kitchen all day."

"Wilma would rather be tending the new lambs or riding the range with the sheep than inside this here fancy house," Moses teased. "And considering what she forces us to eat, it's a good thing." He ducked again as she flicked the dish towel at him.

"Cut it out, old lady, or I won't take you to the movie in town on Saturday night," Moses threatened. "Then we won't be able to go sparking up...."

The dish towel found its target again. But when Abbie glanced down the table to where Wilma sat, she was surprised to find her grinning, her brown eyes sparkling.

Abbie joined the others in the meal. The roast beef was tender enough to cut with a fork, the mashed potatoes and gravy prepared without artificial flavors. Two bowls were heaped with broccoli and corn. A gelatin salad followed the bowls of vegetables around the table. When a platter of fresh-baked rolls emptied, Wilma immediately refilled it.

Abbie watched the others, amazed at the quantity of food they consumed. She took another bite of the yeast roll, enjoying the thick scoop of freezer-made strawberry preserves on top. She couldn't remember when she had eaten so much delicious food.

"This was a marvelous meal, Wilma," she said, turning to the woman who had intimidated her with her first appearance on the porch. "It's as good as Aunt Minnie's dinners and I always thought she was the best cook in Kentucky."

"Thank you, Miz Grasten...I mean Miss Hardesty," Wilma replied. She rose quickly from the table. "But the meal isn't over yet." She disappeared behind the refrigerator door, and reappeared carrying two bowls. "Strawberries and whipped cream. Moses, you lazy sheepherder, get me that pan of yellow cake," she said, setting the bowls on the table and closing the refrigerator door with her shoe.

Moses retrieved the cake from the counter and placed it in front of Wilma, bending his lean body to give her a peck on the cheek. "Kiss the cook is my motto," he announced to the grinning crowd around the table. "You don't never want to get on the bad side of the cook."

"Where did you find strawberries at this time of year?" Dane asked from the head of the table.

Abbie's attention swung to the man who held her future in his hands. The change in his physical appearance was dramatic.

A clean-shaven face displayed the square set of his jaw, but the hollows beneath his prominent cheekbones lent his features a hard, lean look. The blue of his eyes was several shades darker than the sky overhead and reminded her of the indigo dye she had experimented with once early in her weaving career. They were no longer bloodshot.

His hair was lighter than she had first thought, with gentle waves lying against his forehead and the nape of his neck. He needed a haircut. Abbie found herself attracted to him without understanding why.

Nordic-looking men had never appealed to her. The few she had met during a skiing holiday at Sun Valley, Idaho a few years earlier had been handsome but arrogant and vain, flaunting the tans and well-developed physiques they had acquired in health spas. They had left no doubt about their goal of bedding every woman who responded to their overtures. Their arrogance and vanity had been a turnoff to her, but this man was different.

The difference didn't matter. Abbie knew it was fruitless to speculate about her new boss. She needed him for his expertise. She would be polite and cooperative. It was imperative for her own goals that she convince him that he needed her as much as she needed him.

She concentrated on her dessert plate of strawberries and cake, sure she would gain several pounds in no time if Wilma continued to serve such delicious meals. The thought of staying for six months brought her thoughts back to Dane Grasten, and she glanced his way.

He caught her gaze. "If the rest of you have nothing to do this afternoon, I know some drop pens that need to be checked, and two pens of twins that should have been docked yesterday, and a cow whose calf is having trouble suckling. The fence up by Dagmar Springs was damaged by elk last week. We still have two new gates to hang. If that's not enough..." He paused, waiting for the workers' reactions.

The men finished their dessert and rose as one, grumbling among themselves that they already had more work than they could handle.

Abbie remained in her chair.

"What about you, boss?" Moses asked. "Going back to bed?"

Dane rose from the table and studied the auburn curls of the woman still sitting two chairs away. "Miss Hardesty and I have things to discuss. Take over the lambing tents, Mose."

"But Windy and me were going to start the docking," Moses complained.

"You can do that later," Dane said. "Get someone started on branding the lambs. There's a list of numbers near the irons. And make sure the numbers are neat and legible. There's no need to waste time painting if the numbers are so smudged you can't read them. I'll be there in an hour or less to relieve you.''

Abbie's attention raced from worker to worker and back to Dane, wondering if anyone but Moses would challenge him.

He met her gaze, his voice still low and steady. ''Now, if you're through eating, Hardesty, let's get this over with.''

She rose to her full height. Dane sensed this woman wouldn't back down easily. Convincing her would certainly be a challenge, but he would make her see that the best course for both of them would be for her to agree to void their agreement and tactfully head back home. He couldn't recall where that was. Emil Christensen had mentioned something about her not being a Utah native. Her voice had a soft drawl that suggested a Southern heritage.

Damn Christensen. He would have to have a talk with the professor, relative or not. This deliberate deception, after last year's disaster, was more than Dane intended to tolerate.

''Hardesty, follow me,'' he said, trying to resist being affected by her troubled expression. ''We have to talk.''

Abbie followed him down the hallway. She watched the sway of his broad shoulders beneath the blue material of his shirt. Her eyes dropped to the worn leather belt holding up his jeans. She had expected to find his name stamped into the leather, but instead she'd read the initials, D. A. G. His stride loosened and her gaze dropped to his hips. They were broad enough to be in perfect proportion with the rest of his athletic body, yet trim and lean.

Giving in to admiring his form, she neglected to notice his change in stride and almost stumbled over his boot heel as he turned sharply into a side room. Steadying herself with one hand against the jamb, she paused by the door.

"Have a seat," he said, taking his place behind a scarred antique desk cluttered with papers and an open ledger.

She sat down, her bottom clinging precariously to the edge of the chair as she folded her hands tightly in her lap.

"Did you have any trouble finding the place?" he asked, leaning back in his swivel chair and studying her.

"I was watching the creek and didn't notice the house in the trees," she admitted. Recalling the terse comment about fools in his letter, she added, "But I realized right away I'd driven by it. I had to back up just a little bit." She smiled. "It's so large, I don't know how I could have missed it."

"It's harder to find when the trees are leafed out," he said, noting her tense posture.

"It must be very beautiful here in the summer," she said.

"My mother and sisters always thought so," he replied.

"Do you have a large family?" she asked.

"Three sisters and two brothers."

"That's wonderful," she said, smiling warmly. "I have three adopted brothers. They always teased me unmercifully. Well, actually they aren't adopted. I am. But we're related, we're cousins. I was the youngest and they could really make my life miserable when they set their minds to it."

His mouth softened. "I was born twenty years after all the others so some would say I was a little spoiled." He stared at her coveralls for a moment. "Why are you wearing coveralls already? Take them off and . . ."

She shot from her perch on the edge of the chair. Her hand had moved the zipper to her waist before they both realized she had taken him quite literally. The tail of a yellow knit shirt fell out.

"Not now!" he shouted, his mouth tightening. She was as high-strung as a cornered cat. "I just meant . . . you must be warm . . . in the house. I assume you're wearing jeans or whatever underneath." His gazed locked on her hand, which was still clutching the zipper tab. "Why don't you . . . slip out of them? You can do it here or in the bathroom. It's just down the hall on the right. I'll get us some fresh coffee."

He hurried from the room, leaving her standing alone and feeling like a fool. Taking his advice, she found the bathroom and wriggled out of the coveralls. She suspected he was about to ask her to leave. She wouldn't.

When she returned to the office, he sat at his desk again, stirring sugar into a steaming mug of coffee. She returned to the uncomfortable chair and waited for him to speak.

Dane studied her over the rim of his cup. The green in her sports jersey accented her eyes. He wondered what she would look like in a dress, something soft and clinging. Black, he decided, she would look terrific in black. His gaze wandered over the portion of her body showing above the desk. She was well-built, he thought. No, that sounded as if he was checking out a new tractor or a prospective ram. And the femininity of A. B. Hardesty was obvious to any man with half a brain.

"What does A. B. stand for?" he asked.

"Abigail Bernice, but people usually call me Abbie," she explained. "I've always used my initials in business.

And what about your name? Is it really just plain Dane?''

He set his cup down. ''My older brother Knud was nicknamed Swede by his schoolmates, and he fought many a battle because of it. When I came along, my mother decided to make it clear that the Grastens were Danish, so she named me Dane. At least I had it easy in the first grade. I was the first kid who could print his name.''

''No middle name?'' Abbie asked.

''Axel after my father,'' he explained. ''Enough about genealogy. Why didn't you use Abigail in your letter? Why the deception?''

She stiffened. ''It wasn't deception. Dr. Christensen said using my initials, as I usually do for business, would be fine. He was the first to suggest it.'' She dropped her gaze to Dane's hands. They were large and strong. She forced her attention back to his stern face. ''I didn't mean to deceive you, and I do need this internship. Dr. Christensen must have had his reasons.''

He took a deep breath and exhaled slowly. ''I'm sorry, Hardesty, but this just can't work. We're not set up for...a single woman...here.''

''What about Wilma, the cook?'' she demanded. ''Who is she married to?''

''No one.''

''Then my marital status is immaterial, isn't it? I plan to live in the motor home. I won't get in your way. Good grief, surely you'll at least give me a chance. I'm qualified! I'm just inexperienced! I need this time, Mr. Grasten. I could tell from the conversation at lunch...I mean dinner, that you're shorthanded. Try me! You might like...my work.''

Her outburst brought his attention from his coffee cup to her face. The heightened color in her cheeks brought out the auburn of her hair. Nice hairdo, he thought, pretty but practical. He wondered for a second if the curl was natural. *Damn it, what difference does it make to me if she perms her hair or not?* Dane thought.

"Your pipes will freeze."

"What?" she cried.

He grinned. "In the motor home...the pipes won't be able to take the cold."

"They're insulated. The man at the RV shop swore that..."

"He probably exaggerated," Dane replied, leaning back in his chair and rocking a few times. She certainly was persistent, almost bullheaded.

"Then I'll just...conserve what water I have...in buckets," Abbie insisted. Her slender brows furrowed. "It's my business anyway, but I know how to make do with what I have."

"But I'm responsible for my help...."

"Then I can stay?" She straightened in the chair, her hands gripping the edge of the desk.

She had lovely hands. Dane's gaze moved from her hands, up her arms to her heaving breasts, and he saw the faint edge of a lacy bra beneath the yellow jersey. His eyes traced the shadowy outline of her collarbone beneath the knit fabric where it disappeared into the kelly-green of one sleeve, and followed the sleeve to the bare skin of her forearm. A practical digital sports watch circled her left wrist.

He closed his eyes to block her from his field of vision as he considered the decision he thought he'd already made. He straightened in his chair.

"Three days," he said, and she inhaled sharply. "I'll give you three days. But don't be too proud to admit the work might be more than you can handle."

She beamed. "Oh, I won't . . . but I won't . . . I mean I will be able to handle the work. I know I will. Oh, Mr. Grasten, thank you. You won't regret this. Thank you." She rose from her chair and extended her hand.

"Please don't call me Mr. Grasten," he said, rising to his full six-foot-two-inch height. "It's just plain Dane." His features softened as he accepted her hand.

She smiled and reached for the coveralls on the back of her chair. "Now can I go to work?"

He gave her a genuine smile. "Do you have a pair of waterproof boots?"

"Of course," she replied. "They're in the Winnebago."

He nodded. "Meet me by the blue pickup in ten minutes. We'll drive to the lambing tents and I'll show you around. There's some hiking to do and lots of jugs to clean. You'll be sore tomorrow."

She nodded. "I can handle a few sore muscles."

Abbie sidled around him but he grabbed her sleeve. "Wait a minute."

Her eyes widened. "Yes?" she asked, her back pressed against the hall wall.

He released her sleeve. "I'll have Andy connect you to the house electricity."

She looked at him quizzically.

He smiled. "I mean your motor home. Do you have extra electrical cord?"

Her stiff posture relaxed. "Yes, I have a hundred feet of insulated, heavy-duty cord with three prongs and . . ." She dropped her gaze from his. "Yes, I have cord."

"Good, we'll get you all fixed up."

"It needs to be leveled, too," she said. "If I leave the keys, could he do that also?" She pulled a key ring from her jeans pocket and handed it to him.

His hand touched her shoulder. "You can have a room upstairs if you want. We have plenty of bedrooms."

"No."

"Okay, but if you change your mind . . ."

"I won't," she assured him. He motioned for her to precede him, and she returned to the kitchen. When she turned to ask him another question, he was gone.

"Better hustle," Wilma warned. "The boss don't take to dilly-dallying around."

"Of course," Abbie agreed, running out the kitchen door to the motor home. Within minutes she had pulled on the black overshoes, tucked the pant legs of her protective denim coveralls inside them and buckled them to her calves. The sky was spitting snow so she grabbed a cap she had knitted from her own spun yarn, her jacket and a pair of mittens. She scanned the interior of the vehicle wondering what else she might need. Slapping her jeans pocket, she confirmed that she had a pocketknife. She was ready.

Dane Grasten shook her confidence. He had an aura of competence and expertise that unnerved her. But weren't his abilities exactly the reason she'd come here?

"Of course," she murmured. "I've come to learn from the best, and Mr. Grasten sure looks like the best." She grinned, thinking about the change in his appearance since their first encounter.

She shook her head, chiding herself for stalling. Smoothing the front of her jacket, she reached for the doorknob. "Well, Dane Grasten, here I come, whether you're ready for me or not."

He was waiting impatiently in the truck cab. The minute she opened the door, he turned the key in the ignition and the engine came to life.

A quarter of a mile from the two-story house and a few hundred feet past a tiny log cabin, they approached a large wooden structure, long and low and painted barnred. Abbie's excitement grew. Behind the building were rows of pens running at right angles to a small creek and then up the hillside behind. The pens were empty.

"Where are the sheep? Isn't that your lambing shed?" she asked, pointing to the structure.

"No," he replied, barely glancing at the building.

"But it must be, it's..." Suddenly she saw the other end of the building. Part of the roof was missing and the remaining timbers of almost a quarter of the building were charred.

"It's burned," she gasped, turning to him. "How?"

"We had a fire," he said. "We use the old lambing tents now. It's not as convenient, but they've lasted all these years, so I'm glad we saved them."

"Oh, how sad. It looks like such a fine building. Why haven't you rebuilt it? How did the fire start?"

When Dane didn't answer, Abbie turned to look at him. His jaw was clenched, his eyes concentrating on the twisting dirt road. She must have hit a sensitive nerve, she decided, dropping the subject as the truck rolled to a stop near a compound of log buildings, each with a canvas roof. Sheep pens were everywhere, most of them filled with ewes and their lambs. He laid his hat on the seat between them and retrieved a blue and white corduroy cap with the ranch's name and emblem on the front.

"Do you have a cap?" he asked.

"This one," she said, showing him the knitted hat she'd brought along.

He reached behind the seat again. "Wear this," he said, offering her a cap identical to his. "It has ear flaps if the weather gets bad. You can use it while you're part of the crew."

He watched as she settled it on her head, her eyes hidden beneath the bill. He could see her grin but the rest of her face was in the shadow of the brim. "Let me adjust it," he said, removing the cap again. He tightened the straps and put the hat back on her head, straightening it as she glanced up at him. Their gazes locked for several seconds, until finally she tore hers away.

"It might wreck your hairdo," he warned.

"That's okay," she replied.

"Don't you care about your hair?" he asked. "Most women spend so much time... primping."

"Not me," she said, grinning. "My fingers will do if I can't find a comb. Thanks for the cap. Now, what should I do first?"

"Have you worked with sheep before?" he asked.

"No, but Dr. Christensen told me what to expect."

"Where did you grow up?"

"On my Uncle Harry's tobacco farm in western Kentucky." She grinned. "I know all about picking tobacco worms and pulling suckers. We had pigs and chickens and a worn-out Guernsey cow and, for a few years, several goats. I used to ride my cousin Callie's horse and we would pretend he was a thoroughbred on his way to Churchill Downs, but actually he was my uncle's plow horse and..." She stopped abruptly. "I'm sorry, I was rambling. I left there years ago. No, I've never worked with sheep but I'm willing to learn. I'll do anything you need done. Just try me."

"You may regret your promise by the end of the day."
He climbed down from the truck and she had to run to
catch up with him.

She tagged after him as he went through three of the
lambing tents, asking Moses questions about the ewes.
Each tent had a dozen small pens, and each pen held a
ewe and a new lamb.

"Are these the jugs?" she asked, laying her hand on
the wooden slat of the front panel of one pen.

Dane turned, and for a few seconds Abbie suspected
he had forgotten she was with him.

"That's right," he said. "These lambs were born during the night and this morning. Moses says they're all
doing fine."

"How long do you keep them inside?" she asked.

"They'll be branded and moved out tomorrow," he
replied, moving to the Dutch door and outside. She
quickened her pace.

"Don't you ever have twins?" she asked.

"Yes, and we try to keep them together in the next two
tents," he said. "These breeds usually have singles." His
eyes sparkled as he turned to her. "But wait until mid-
April. I've been experimenting with quarter Finn crosses
and they're famous for their multiple births. Triplets are
the norm. They're usually smaller but cute as can be."

"You sound very proud of them," Abbie said. "Why
do they lamb a month later?"

"I want time to give them special attention," he explained. "I've been trying to keep records on them from
year to year. You'll see...if you make it past the three-day
trial." He put his hand on her shoulder. "Come this way
and you can start your first job."

Circling around two more lambing tents, they arrived
at an open pen filled with eleven lambs ranging in age

from a day to more than a week. The minute the lambs spotted Dane, they began to bleat.

He laughed, leaning over the fence and holding his hand out to some of them. "These are the bums," he explained. "I haven't rigged up the automatic feeder yet, so we're still giving them bottles. You can be the nursemaid to these babies. The bottles and the milk replacer are in the hotbox in the hospital tent over there," he said, pointing to the next building. "Moses put the formula to warming when he came back. Give each lamb several ounces. They'll know to stop when their bellies are full."

He turned to Buck, who had a question. She frowned. Was that all the instruction he intended to give her? She headed toward the hospital tent and breathed a sigh of relief when she found Moses inside.

She explained her plight and together they filled four bottles with the formula.

"Come back when these are empty and I'll help you again," Moses promised. Sighing, Abbie headed back to the pens.

CHAPTER FOUR

CRADLING THE WARM BOTTLE in the crook of her arm, Abbie stepped through the gate. Suddenly, she was surrounded by bleating lambs. She tried to take a step and tripped over one overly aggressive baby. Feeling herself falling, she flung out her arm but missed the post holding up a nearby canvas-covered shelter. She shrieked as the bottles flew into the air and she landed in the straw and droppings of the pen, her face inches from the ground.

She tried to get up, but several curious lambs surrounded her. One frisky lamb climbed onto her back and nuzzled her hair. Afraid she might hurt it, she lay still, resting her forehead on her arms. She felt another lamb join the first on her back, but this one chose her rounded buttocks for its perch.

She wriggled her hips but the lamb didn't budge.

"This wasn't what I had in mind," Dane said.

She raised her head to find three of the other men leaning over the fence, grinning from ear to ear, while Dane moved through the gate.

"Get them off, please?" she asked. Mortified by her own clumsiness, Abbie felt her eyelids burn with tears. She vowed she wouldn't cry, not in front of these tough men. She tried to rid herself of the lambs on her back by wriggling her hips again.

"Nice move," Moses said. "Do that again."

She stopped immediately. A third lamb joined the others, and her head fell to her arms again. "Get them off," she pleaded. The first lamb walked light-footed toward her shoulders, paused, then put two tiny hoofs on her head. "Ouch!" she cried.

"That's enough fun, boys," Dane said, and the men returned to their duties. He shooed the lambs off her back and shoulders. His hands slipped beneath her armpits and he pulled her to her feet. "Are you hurt?" he asked, brushing the straw from her arms.

"A lot you care," she mumbled. "I could have stayed there all afternoon." She plucked at the straw in her hair.

"All you needed to do was roll over," he said. "They would have jumped off. They're playful and very surefooted." He tried to restrain his laughter.

She felt the hot moisture of a single tear slide down her cheek. "Don't you start laughing." She brushed the tear away and rubbed the back of her head where the lamb had stepped.

"Let me check you out," Dane said, turning her around and examining her. "I wouldn't want you to file a workman's injury claim against me in the first five minutes."

He buried his fingers in her hair, searching for an injury, and she leaned into his touch.

A bleating lamb brought them apart. Dane brushed the straw from the front of her coveralls and retrieved the bottles.

"Sorry, Hardesty," he said. "I shouldn't have laughed. I'm truly sorry." His pursed lips failed to hide his grin.

She tried to retain an indignant frown but couldn't. "It's okay," Abbie said, smiling gamely. "I should have watched where I was going." She took one of the bottles. "Now is there a technique to this?" she asked, looking at the hungry lambs.

Dane set one bottle on a nearby fence post and scooped up a lamb, then perched him on the two bales of straw beneath the canvas lean-to that acted as a weather break.

She watched him, awed by the sight of this rugged man displaying such tenderness toward a young orphaned lamb.

"Sit here beside me," he said, and she joined him on the straw bales. Soon she had fed two of the lambs. "I think you're getting the hang of it," he said, unfolding his long limbs. "I'll get some refills."

When Dane returned, he had three more filled bottles with black nipples attached. She glanced up as he latched the gate.

"Yes?" she murmured, returning her attention to the nursing lamb.

"You act as though you enjoy this," he said, reaching for another of the bums.

"What's not to like?" she said, her head bent over the tiny creature perched on her lap. When she looked up, he was staring at her. "Is something wrong?" she asked, the lamb's face nestled against her breast as it eagerly sucked on the bottle.

"No," he said and his frown gradually faded. He finished feeding the lamb and put it gently on the ground, "You're doing fine. I have some ewes and lambs to move to larger pens, so when you've finished here come find me and I'll give you your next assignment." He squinted at her. "I think you'll make a good straw engineer."

He was gone before she could ask what he meant.

She replenished the bottles and soon all the lambs were fed and settled for a nap.

She hurried to the hospital tent, cleaned the bottles and set them in a rack to dry, then went in search of Dane.

"Moses," she called, spotting him several pens away. He waved to her and she went to him.

"Can I help you, Abbie?" he asked, raking soiled straw into a pile before scooping it into a wheelbarrow.

She smiled as she approached him, touching the gold earring in her ear as she tried to remember the name of the job Dane had promised to teach her.

"I was looking for...Mr. Grasten," she said. "I've fed the bums and he said he'd show me how to be a straw...engineer?"

Moses grinned. "He did, did he? That rascal! Did he tell you what that involved?"

"No, and I can't find him anywhere," Abbie replied, turning around to see if he'd reappeared.

Moses grasped the handles of the wheelbarrow and began to push it toward the gate.

"I'll get it," she said, running ahead of him and holding the gate wide, then refastening it.

He dumped his load on a growing pile near a tractor with a front loader. "The boss went back to bed."

"At this hour?" she exclaimed. "It's only 3:00 p.m.."

"Mustn't criticize the boss," Moses warned.

"Oh, I didn't mean to do that, but..."

"He was up all night," Moses explained.

"I'd think he would know better than to party during a time as busy as this," Abbie said.

"He wasn't partying. The boss seldom lets his hair down for a party," Moses said. "Sometimes I wish he would. He's been on night lambing duty the past two nights because one of the men has been sick with the flu. Then yesterday we had some problems and he was up most of the day. He don't usually look like he did this morning, ma'am. Usually the boss is neat and tidy, but this morning he was bushed. You'll have to forgive him—not that he would care one way or the other.'' Moses removed his cap and scratched his thinning brown hair. "Come to think about it, he did shave after meeting you. Maybe he does care.''

Abbie felt the heat of a blush moving up her cheeks. "He needn't shave for me,'' she said.

"The boss does as he pleases,'' Moses said, grinning again. "He's a loner and he's independent, but that's just his way. Now about that straw engineering job. That means to clean the jugs. Come with me and I'll find you a pitchfork and a rake. The boss likes clean jugs for the ewes and their lambs. Cleaning jugs looks easy, but most new workers wake up the next morning and they can't move their arms.''

She followed him to a lambing tent filled with ewes, each with two lambs. He handed her the necessary tools.

"How do I clean the pens when the sheep are still in them?''

"Well, we do it like this,'' he said as he removed one of the gates. "These are all branded.'' For the first time she noticed the red numbers painted on the ewes' and lambs' backs. "So we'll move them outside to a larger pen where they can get used to the elements. I set the gates up earlier. If you'll shoo this momma and her young 'uns out, I'll work on the others.''

Soon they had the ewes and their lambs outside and moving down the lane to their new pen. Chaos reigned for several minutes as the ewes searched out their twins and rejected other frantic lambs. Moses and Abbie lingered at the gate, watching them.

"How do you like working with the sheep?'' Moses asked.

"Oh, I really enjoy it," she replied. "Of course I don't know much about it yet, but there's something about them that's . . . different. Maybe it's their size. They're manageable. And I love the bums. All the lambs."

"Don't get too attached to them," Moses warned. "All the wethers and some of the ewe lambs will go to market this fall."

"I know. I suppose you have to not think about that part of it when they're being born, but they're sure cute now." Abbie extended her hand to a curious lamb. "They're pretty and lovable." She sighed deeply. "It's so peaceful here." She turned around and leaned against the slats of the fence, scanning the valley before turning back to Moses.

Her gaze fell on the lambs for an instant before it rose to linger on the snow-covered hills behind the lambing area. "It's beautiful . . . isolated . . . but I don't feel isolated. Someone warned me that I might feel closed in by the mountains, but instead I feel as though I'm on top of the world. I really like it."

"You might change your opinion after a few months," Moses cautioned.

She shook her head. "Maybe, but . . . well, I've only been here for one afternoon. I'll withhold judgment for a few weeks." She smiled at him. "But I don't think I'll change my mind."

"You'll miss the city life," he warned.

"Not a chance," she said, laughing lightly. "Too many people pressing in around me and I yearn for the country. I'm used to being alone and doing things by myself. I plan to spend my spare time weaving. I have a frame loom in the motor home. I want to finish several commissions, then start on something new to depict my stay here. Who knows. Perhaps I'll put you in my next tapestry. It will have to be small because of the size of the loom, but I always put at least one person in my work. I guess it's become my trademark.''

"I've never seen anyone weaving before,'' Moses said.

"Come visit me sometime and I'll show you how it's done,'' Abbie said. "Now, can you show me what a straw engineer does? I wouldn't want the boss to find me just standing around talking.''

"You're right about that,'' Moses agreed. "The boss don't take kindly to yakking or smoking when there's work to be done.'' He squinted at her. "Do you smoke?''

She shook her head.

"Good. The boss's wife smoked.''

"Wife? So he has been married!'' The words slipped out before she could stop them. "What happened? Did she . . . is he widowed?''

"Divorced.'' Moses lowered his voice. "Her name was Lil, Lillian actually, and she never took to this kind of living. She liked to party, especially during the spring.''

"But that would be during lambing,'' Abbie said. "Surely she knew he couldn't leave.''

He grinned. "You've been here half a day and already you're showing more common sense than she ever did.''

"How long were they married?'' she asked.

"Two and a half years.''

"How recently?'' she asked, knowing she was prying.

"Almost ten years ago,'' Moses continued. "Did you see that big lambing shed on the way up here?''

She nodded. "It looked great...except for the burned-out portion. How did it happen? I asked, but he didn't answer.''

"The boss still don't like to talk about it much, but Lil set fire to it one night when she wanted to go to town and he wouldn't go with her.'' He paused, recalling the event.

"It was right in the middle of lambing. They had a big shouting match. A person couldn't help but know what was happening, but no one expected her to do a crazy thing like that. The shed was filled with more than a hundred ewes and their lambs. I'll never forget that night as long as I live. The panic of the animals. The barking of the dogs."

Moses frowned at Abbie. "The boss has this thing about fires and carelessness. He says they go together. Well," he said, "I've talked too much. Someday he'll rebuild it . . . when the time is right."

They walked together toward the empty lambing tent.

"Now you get to work and keep the boss happy," Moses said, leaving her alone.

By the time Abbie heard the dinner bell ring, the pens were cleaned and her arms were aching. She had finished four of the lambing tents. As she hung up her tools, she knew she'd discovered arm and back muscles she'd never used in her weaving.

She jogged to the motor home and washed up, then hurried to the kitchen. As the others gathered around the table for supper, Dane's chair remained empty. *He must still be asleep,* she thought, disturbed by an unusual feeling of loss each time she glanced at his empty chair.

The conversation centered around lambing until someone mentioned a dance band.

"The Music Tenders are playing at the Outfitters' Den," Buck Jensen announced. These were the first words Abbie had heard the young man speak since her arrival.

"Where's the Outfitters' Den?" she asked.

"Up the Ruby River at the bend about fifteen miles the other side of the dam, not too far from Alder," Moses said.

The landmarks meant nothing to Abbie. "Is there something special about them? Who are the Music Tenders?"

"They play western dance music," Buck said.

"The lead guitarist used to work here," Moses explained. "We try to catch him when they're in the area. Want to come along?"

"When? Maybe I'll have to work," she said.

"Sunday afternoon about three," Moses replied. "We usually try to cut the crew to the bare bones when the Tenders are around. Plan on it." He accepted a large platter of sliced ham and the conversation stopped.

She finished her meal, declining dessert. "Well," she said, rising from her chair. "I need a shower and then it's early to bed for me."

"Arms ache?" Moses asked.

"A little."

Several of the men chuckled.

"You'll get used to it," Wilma said, as Abbie gathered her plate and utensils and carried them to the sink.

"Can I help with cleanup?" Abbie asked, her shoulders sagging as she paused by the kitchen door.

"No, honey," Wilma said. "You look beat. We have an automatic dishwasher and Moses is about to offer to help with KP." Wilma glared at the surprised Moses as he opened his mouth to protest. "But the boss has a message for you," she informed Abbie. "Before he left for town he said to tell you to save your water and use our bathroom."

"But I . . ."

"He insisted. No excuses," Wilma said, as she turned back to her dessert.

"Don't challenge the boss," Moses added, "just like I don't challenge the cook."

Wilma's dish towel shot toward Moses and flicked the back of his neck.

"Ouch!" he cried, confirming Wilma's accuracy. "How the heck can you throw a curve with that rag?" he grumbled. As he gathered up his dirty dishes and moved toward the sink, he winked at Abbie. He stumbled as he passed Wilma's chair.

"Oh," Wilma gasped, swinging out of her chair to catch him. "Don't fall. Did you hurt yourself?" she asked, grabbing his arm.

Moses leaned against Wilma, resting his hand on her shoulder as he steadied himself. "Thanks, sweetie," he said, giving her a peck on the cheek. "You saved these old bones from breaking. If I'd fallen and broke my leg, you'd have to have tended to me in my sick bed. How would you have liked that?"

Wilma pulled away slightly, shaking her finger at him. "They shoot horses and old goats when they break their legs," she warned. "And you're no different. Puts them out of their misery right away. Now, if those spindly legs of yours will hold that bag of bones up long enough to help me, let's get to work."

Abbie was still smiling as she hurried to the motor home and gathered up a change of clothing and the toiletries needed for the shower. Moses and Wilma's love-hate relationship intrigued her, making her wonder how long their taunting and teasing had been going on. Had they ever considered getting married? Had either been married before?

She recalled what Wilma had said about their boss. *Dane Grasten went into town.* Why hadn't he said something?

He didn't have to answer to her, Abbie reminded herself. Hadn't he already said that he did as he pleased? Yet his image stayed with her while she took advantage of the offer of the bathroom.

The man was an enigma. He ruled the sheep ranch with an iron fist, yet he allowed his men time off to see a former employee and his band. He refused to rebuild the burned-out lambing shed with all its improvements. He insisted that she use the house bathroom and conserve her own water supply. He needed sleep yet he could recover suddenly when a trip to town was justified.

Perhaps he had a woman in town. *A woman.* How involved was he with her? The thought of a woman, an obviously significant woman in his life, troubled Abbie as she recalled the tidbits of information Moses had shared about Dane's former wife, Lil.

She stopped thinking about Dane Grasten's personal life as she dressed and gathered her soiled clothing. She would have to check into laundry facilities soon.

In the motor home, she had expected to drop off to sleep immediately, but her mind raced. After an hour of tossing and turning, she got up and went to the dining table. The loom was calling to her. Reaching for a sheet of graph paper, she began to sketch a design, her reading glasses perched on the bridge of her nose. The overall features of the new tapestry were selected; the sloping hills, behind which were rugged snowcapped peaks. Of course ewes and lambs had to be scattered throughout the design. A blue pickup truck was added.

Her hand moved the pencil quickly over the squares, almost as though it had a mind of its own. Beside the cab of the pickup a tall man stood, one hand on the door handle, the other on his hip. Two sheepdogs frolicked nearby.

She paused. Did the ranch use dogs for working the sheep? She'd seen none. Surely she would have if they'd been there. Yet she recalled noticing a row of doghouses not far from the back of the house.

The house. It was a grand house, a two-story clapboard structure well maintained with fresh white paint and gray trim. The interior was tastefully decorated with furniture from another era. Probably at one time it had been the pride and joy of some Grasten woman. Dane's mother, she assumed. Studying the sketch, she nodded. The design was coming together, the feel and flow of her ideas jelling quickly.

When Abbie finally glanced at the clock, she couldn't believe her eyes. It was eleven o'clock. Where had the time gone? The sound of a truck driving into the yard caught her ear. *Probably the lord of the manor coming home from his hot date,* she decided.

She tightened the belt of her long robe. The temperature outside was well below freezing but the interior of the motor home was warm and cozy from the propane furnace near the sleeping area. The storm that had been threatening had passed overhead and darkness had fallen on a clear sky.

Knowing she should turn out the light and try to sleep, she rose from the bench. Perhaps a cup of tea would help. She turned on the propane burner beneath the copper teapot.

There was a knock on the door, the sound reverberating in the quiet interior.

"Who is it?" she asked, touching the doorknob.

"Grasten...Dane Grasten," the voice outside replied. "If you're...presentable, could I come in?"

CHAPTER FIVE

"IT'S VERY LATE," Abbie replied, her hand still on the doorknob.

"I know. I saw your light and wondered if you were okay."

"I'm fine."

"I brought someone from town I think you might enjoy meeting."

Surely he wouldn't bring his woman friend to the ranch and take her to meet his newest employee. Who could it be? she wondered, knowing there was only one way to find out.

"Of course," Abbie said, holding open the door.

The motor home shrank in size when Dane's presence filled the interior. As she looked up at him, his features softened and almost evolved into a smile, highlighting his handsomeness. She realized she was still wearing her glasses and quickly removed them, tossing them onto the graph paper.

She laughed nervously. "You know how it is when you reach my age, the eyes are the first to go."

"It happens to us all," he agreed. "I had to get a pair a few years ago when I had trouble reading my own writing in the ranch ledgers."

"I'd expected you to be at least seventy years old, with a dozen grandchildren."

"Dr. Christensen has been playing games," Dane said. "He led me to believe you were a young man of about twenty-five."

"Maybe we should contact him and complain," she said, her gaze roaming over his torso.

"We'll wait three days," he replied. She avoided his eyes. Was he waiting for her to fail? Or anxious for her to go?

His sheepskin coat hung open and she noticed the well-tailored shirt he was wearing. "Wilma said you had dinner in town."

"Yes, with friends."

"Do you want to take your coat off?" she asked. "It's warm in here. I haven't turned the furnace down for the night. I've never stayed in the motor home for an extended period in such cold weather."

"I meant what I said about moving into the house," he said. "The others stay there."

She shook her head. "I'm sure I'll be fine here. I wouldn't want to impose or get in anyone's way."

"No problem," he said. "The house was built for a large family. There are bedrooms in the basement as well as on the second floor. My folks thought someday the place would be filled with their children and their grandchildren, but I'm the only one who stayed on the place. Moses and I rattle around in it except during lambing. Did Wilma give you my message?"

She nodded. "Thank you. It will save me a great deal of water. Working with sheep does tend to leave an odor."

"There's no sheep smell in here," he said, lifting his head and pretending to sniff the air.

She smiled. He accepted her suggestion, shrugging out of his heavy coat and carefully placing it over the back of the passenger seat in the front of the vehicle. When he turned to her, she suppressed an urge to go to him. Her heart thudded unexpectedly. Never had a man's proximity made her feel so womanly.

He wore a pale blue dress shirt made of the finest broadcloth and denim jeans. She turned again to the coat and saw the broad end of a tie, tiny red sheep scattered across a field of navy, dangling from one bulging pocket.

"A tie and dress shirt without a suit?" she teased.

"I had a photograph taken at the request of the local chapter of the Wool Growers. The photographer promised to focus on me from the chest up."

Nice focus, she thought, smiling as she turned her attention from his coat to his face. "I like your tie," she said. "It's unusual."

"It was a gag gift the year I was president of the Montana Wool Growers," he said. "I don't know where the secretary of the MWG found it. I suspect his wife had something to do with it. I don't wear it often."

"All this time to have your picture taken?" she inquired.

He shook his head. "I had an appointment with an attorney."

"Nothing serious, I hope," she said.

"A problem with the ranch," he explained. "Some of my brothers and sisters want to sell out their shares. It could get complicated. I needed to know where I stand if they begin to put pressure on the rest of the family."

"I hope it gets resolved," she said.

"So do I. If they can force us to sell, it could mean the end of all this," he said, waving his hand through the air. "Later I had dinner with some friends"

"We had leftover stew," Abbie said. "Don't tell Wilma, but I've had better."

"We had prime rib at the Eagle's Nest, a restaurant in town."

"Were many in your party?" she asked, wondering why she was prying into his affairs.

"Seven of us," he replied. "I was the odd man. A cattleman and his wife from south of town, a retired physician and his wife, the vet and his wife and me." He scanned the interior of the motor home. "Am I keeping you up?"

She shook her head. "No, I was working on a weaving design, then I decided to have a cup of tea before trying to get to sleep." Unable to understand the strong desire to be near him, Abbie searched for something to talk about that would keep him from leaving. "You look nice dressed up," she said.

"You don't think bib overalls are sexy?"

"Not terribly. Neither are coveralls."

"Depends on who's wearing them," he replied.

Abbie heard a sound like a whining animal. "What was that?" she asked, looking around.

"He's the guest I wanted to introduce," Dane said.

"He?" she asked as she heard another whine. "It sounds like a . . . dog."

She followed him to his coat. He stuck his head into the bulging patch pocket and withdrew a squirming young puppy.

She stepped closer. The animal in the cupped palm of Dane's hand was a fluffy ball of black, tan and an unusual mottled gray.

"Why it is a puppy," she exclaimed, "and so young."

The puppy raised his head, his sleepy doe eyes slowly opening. When he spotted Abbie, his tail began to wag furiously.

"He's darling." Reaching out, she touched one of his ears. "May I hold him?"

"Of course." Dane relinquished the puppy.

She cuddled the puppy against her cheek. Dane's somber expression relaxed into a grin.

"In a few months, his eyes will probably change," he said. "One will be blue while the other will stay brown."

"How unusual," she said. "I saw a dog like that once. He was beautiful." She lowered the puppy to her breast. "Would you like some tea? I made enough for two."

"Sure." He took a step toward the stove. "Where are the cups? I'll pour, since you're busy."

"Top cupboard to the left," Abbie replied, sliding into the bench again. With one hand, she pushed the loom to the back of the table, slid the sketch beneath the pad of graph paper and then pushed the pad and her glasses underneath the loom.

The puppy stretched his head and licked her chin a few times before settling down again in her arms.

Dane sat down across from her and slid one of the cups of tea toward her. "I'll take the puppy if you're tired of holding him."

"No, that's fine," she said, glancing down at the dozing animal. "Maybe I could put him on the bed. Will he stay asleep?"

"I'm sure," he said as she rose. He was still wondering why he had given in to the impulsive idea of using the pup he had brought from town as an excuse to see her again. He grew vividly aware of her movements, of her dark forest-green velour robe brushing against his shoulder and arm as she walked to the rear of the motor home. He rose and followed her, trying not to think about what she might—or might not be wearing beneath the attractive robe.

From a compartment she pulled out a woven afghan, its subtle earth and sky tones matching the animal's own fur. She fluffed it into a pillowy nest before depositing the sleeping puppy in its center. He stretched once, then curled up again, tucking his tiny nose beneath one paw. Abbie pulled the edges of the afghan up near the front of the nest she had made.

"Now he's safe and he won't fall out," she murmured, smiling down at the puppy.

"He's only a few weeks old," Dane said.

She whirled around, unaware that he had followed her.

"He might mess on it," he warned.

"It's washable."

"Are you sure?"

She nodded. "I made it. I even spun and dyed the yarn." Her voice was as soft as the fiber in the afghan.

Her face was inches from his. It was a lovely face, he thought. Her green eyes seemed to be searching his for a meaning he didn't understand himself. Her hair smelled of English lavender. He inhaled deeply, wanting to take her in his arms but knowing the only sensible action would be to step away.

His hand reached out, touching a curl caught in the gold loop of her earring. *Why the hell don't I just walk out?* Dane asked himself. She had been at the ranch for a matter of hours, yet he felt as if he had known her forever.

The silence hung heavily in the warm interior. She said something, but her voice was so soft he had to lean closer to hear her. "What did you say?"

She didn't repeat her words and his attention was drawn to her mouth. *I'm close enough to touch her lips,* he thought, *close enough to kiss them. They would be soft, warm.*

Abbie tentatively touched his shirtfront. Temptation was inches away. The reaction of his own body to her closeness was getting out of hand.

"No," she whispered, leaning closer, her body swaying against his.

"You're right," he murmured, taking her hands from his body and clasping them in his. He noticed her breathing was erratic. "I'm sorry," he said. "I didn't mean to...upset you. I...I just thought you'd enjoy seeing the pup."

She eased her hands from his. "I didn't mean anything...I don't know why I touched you. Our tea is getting cold," she said, her voice still husky. She cleared her throat as she sidled past him and hurried to the table and the tepid cups of tea. "I'll make some fresh."

He slid back onto the cushioned bench and watched her, enjoying each fluid movement she made.

"I'm sorry, Abbie," he said, studying her slender torso as she busied herself at the counter. "I usually don't put the make on my employees." The creases around his mouth softened as she turned to him with the teapot. "But then I've never had an employee quite like you. I'm sorry."

"Apology accepted," she said, smiling back at him. "I've never had an employer like you either. In fact, I've never had an employer at all. I've always worked for myself, as a weaver and running my crafts shop."

"You had your own business?" he asked.

"Yes, I carried needlecraft and weaving supplies. I converted one corner of the shop into a small gallery, where I took consignments as well as showed my own work. I sold the business when I decided to return to school," she said, stirring a few drops of honey into her tea. "Didn't Dr. Christensen tell you about me?"

He shook his head. "He said you were older and that you were unusually gifted. I assumed he meant in agriculture. He never mentioned your weaving talents. I didn't know you were already established in a career."

She took a sip of tea. "I never thought about it much. I've always been self-employed. It might take some getting used to, having a boss to answer to, but I'll try to manage."

"I've seen weaving demonstrations at the Wool Growers conferences," he said, admiring the graceful movements of her hands. "Some of those looms are rather large. Are yours?"

"I have a six-harness treadle loom, but I had to disassemble it when I moved here," she explained. "I have several other smaller models but I brought only this one with me." She touched the frame. "Weavers come with a lot of stuff. You should see my bags of rovings and a gray fleece I haven't had time to clean. When I dye the skeins of yarn, I really spread out. I can really make a mess sometimes." Her expression grew solemn. "Is it okay if I do some dyeing on my time off?"

He shrugged. "I don't see why not," he said, more interested in admiring her face than listening to what she said.

"Thanks." She smiled. "Now tell me about the puppy. Where did you get him?"

"He's part of a litter my Australian shepherd bitch had a few weeks ago."

"But I didn't see any dogs this afternoon," she said.

"They've been at the animal hospital in town," he explained. "The veterinarian, Dr. Bart Hanley, is a good friend and we discussed the animals and their problems. He agreed they would be better off here now, so I brought most of them home after dinner."

"Why were they at the vet's?" she asked.

"Someone poisoned them last week."

"Oh, no! That's terrible," she cried.

"Yes," he agreed quietly, and his hands encircled his warm cup.

He has such nice hands, she thought, *large and capable, yet gentle and sensitive.* "What happened?" she asked.

"The dogs have the run of the place," he explained. "We're close to the road and there's very little traffic, but Bart says he's positive someone tossed out some poisoned meat. It's happened at three other ranches on the Sweetwater. Two of the dogs died. The father of this litter is still at the vet's but he's going to make it. I brought the bitch and her surviving pups home this evening. Her milk passed the poison on to the pups and we lost three of them. This little guy is the strongest of the litter. He's fine, and two others are going to survive. You'd think we'd be immune to such problems way out here, but it can happen." His broad shoulders rose and fell as he exhaled slowly.

She glanced at Dane's face when he didn't continue. His personality was a mixture of strength and vulnerability, sophistication and expertise in his profession. His handsome features reflected genuine concern for the animals and people in his care. Under his strong facade, she sensed his emotions were carefully protected against possible injury, just as he sheltered those around him.

"I'm sorry to hear about the dogs," she said. "Can the puppies nurse from their mother now?"

He nodded, his eyes darkening as he talked. "Yes. We'll need them more than ever when they get older. These pups are destined to be working sheepdogs, but they won't be ready for training until next year. We'll have to buy two replacement dogs for the summer. We use them during the summer for grazing up in the mountains. A herder and two dogs can take care of a band of sheep with no problem. They're as necessary as the men.''

''How many sheep are there in a band?'' she asked.

''Ours have about a thousand,'' he said. ''We should have four bands this summer. We'll sell off most of the wether lambs this fall, keep some ewe lambs for replacements and weed out the older ewes that come up dry or have bad bags or are blind. There are lots of factors to consider. I hope the price for market lambs holds up.''

He scanned her features. ''So much for the lesson in sheep raising for one evening. How did your day go? Did you get all the jugs cleaned out?''

Abbie smiled. ''I'm now an experienced straw engineer, ready for the second day of my three-day trial,'' she assured him. ''I'm not prepared to quit yet.'' She rose from the bench and put her cup on the counter. ''But if I don't get some sleep I won't make it through tomorrow.''

''You could always try some night lambing,'' he said, joining her near the sink. His finger touched the lapel of her robe. ''That's where I'm going for an hour or two before I call it a day. Want to come with me?''

''Just the two of us?'' she asked, her hand coming to his before dropping to her side.

''No, Oscar and Blackie are working tonight. I want to make sure everything is okay. Would you like to get dressed and come with me?''

''I don't think that would be wise.'' She watched varied emotions play over his features.

''You're probably right,'' he said, retrieving his coat and moving to the door. ''Good night,'' he called, and he went outside.

She stood leaning against the closet door, her hand on her breast as she waited for her pulse to steady. She had wanted to go with him more than anything in the world, but something held her back. Her attraction to him was more than she could handle in her present state of exhaustion. She'd never longed for a man's touch as she did his, and yet they were practically strangers.

As Abbie turned out the lights, she realized Dane had left the puppy on the bed. She scooped him up, cuddling the animal safely in her arms, and ran out the door into the darkness.

"Dane, wait for me," she called.

In the distance, she saw a dark form stop and turn. She hurried to him. "You forgot the puppy," she said breathlessly. "He will want his mother before long."

In the darkness she could discern his features, the hard planes of his cheek and jaw.

"Thanks for bringing him to me," she whispered, steadying herself by grasping Dane's upper arm through his heavy coat. She pushed up on her toes and brushed his cheek with her lips. A gust of frigid air blew past them, sending a flurry of snowflakes swirling around her ankles.

The front of his leather coat hung open and suddenly she found herself and the puppy safely inside the fleece lining. Her arm slid around his waist as she gave in to the desire to be close to him. The warmth of his body surrounding her, bringing her to a sense of euphoria that sent her blood pulsing in her temples. His open lips touched her forehead and she tilted her face up to him.

"Yes?" she whispered.

"Yes," he agreed, his arms pulling her snugly against him. His warm breath caressed her cheek. She was hesitant to initiate a kiss but fearful it might not materialize if she didn't.

Dane touched her face and she leaned her cheek against his rough palm. She shifted, enabling him to touch her mouth with his fingers. A low moan escaped from her throat as his mouth covered hers. His lips were warm. Abbie clutched the back of his shirt, twisting as the kiss deepened. They clung to each other in the frigid night.

When the kiss was over, they were both breathless.

"Oh, God," Dane murmured.

She buried her face against his shoulder as a sudden burst of joy brought tears to her eyes.

Another gust of icy wind sprinkled her bare ankles with snow, reminding her of her attire. She tried to pull away.

"What's wrong?" he asked, his voice low and husky.

"My feet," she whispered. "They're . . . c-cold."

He leaned over her shoulder and caught sight of her thin satin slippers. "My God, woman, you're going to have frostbite if you don't get back inside." He chuckled. "It's just as well. This is crazy, us standing like this in the freezing darkness."

"Someone might see us," she murmured. "What would they think?"

"It's my place," he replied. "I can do what I want here, with whoever I want."

"But I can't," she said. "I want to work here for the next six months. I don't want anything to spoil that. I've only been here since noon. You've probably already gotten the wrong idea. I've never done such an irresponsible thing before in my life." Abbie tried to pull free from his embrace.

"You're not irresponsible, just impulsive," he replied, shaking her slightly, "and I promise to not hold it against you." He pulled her close inside the coat again and held her for several seconds. "But you're right. I'll try to have more control next time."

"There won't be a next time," Abbie insisted. "I came here to work, to learn about sheep raising. That's all."

He nodded slowly in the darkness. "I understand, Miss Hardesty . . . but it felt so right . . . didn't it?"

She stared at him, but didn't speak.

"Didn't it?" he asked again.

"Yes," she admitted, "but it's wrong. The other employees . . . you've got to treat us all alike."

"I can't do that."

"Why not?"

"I've never wanted to kiss Oscar or Moses . . . not even Wilma."

She pulled away, angry at his reply. "You're making fun of me! I should have known. I fell for one of the oldest tricks in the book, didn't I? You set me up! You were testing me. Now you'll start looking for ways you can take advantage of me. Well, I misread your intent, Mr. Grasten, but you can bet it won't happen again.

"Take the dog," she said, handing the puppy to him in the cupped palms of her hands. "I'm going to bed."

"Abbie, don't . . ." Dane protested, but before he could say more, she turned and ran to the motor home.

CHAPTER SIX

THE NEXT MORNING, Dane Grasten glanced at the clock above the stove when he heard footsteps on the back porch.

The other workers had all gathered for breakfast at seven, but the seat next to his remained empty. No one had commented on Abbie's absence. Now, as they finished, she had apparently decided to make an appearance.

The door opened and she hesitated, her hand resting on the knob as she surveyed the seating arrangement around the table.

Dane's gaze swept down her figure, then slowly worked its way up past the jeans, which weren't nearly as tight as some he'd seen, to the loose pink sweatshirt with the collar of a sage-green oxford-cloth shirt showing at the neckline. Her hair had been tamed since last night. She had pushed up the sleeves of the sweatshirt to reveal the buttoned cuffs at her slender wrists.

Her cheeks were rosy, her eyes shining with stubborn determination. She avoided his gaze, but her shoulders stiffened and he knew she was aware of his stare.

"This ain't no restaurant," Wilma declared. "You eat when the cook is ready."

"Yes, ma'am," Abbie replied. "I'm sorry."

Wilma's features relaxed into a warm grin. "But there's some flapjacks left. I reckon they'd taste pretty good with some of that jam you liked yesterday."

Abbie nodded silently and approached the table. Dane frowned, waiting to see if she would take the only empty chair. No one had been told to leave it, but some unspoken code had declared it hers.

He suppressed a yawn, and took another long drink of coffee. He hoped she'd had a miserable night's sleep, too. After putting the pup back into the box with the rest of the litter, he had considered going back to the motor home and apologizing, but when he had stopped several feet from the door, a dim light somewhere in the interior had gone out and he had cursed under his breath. Why did he owe her an apology when she had been the one to misunderstand?

Instead, he had pushed his exhausted body to its limit, climbed again into the blue truck and driven to the lambing tents a half mile away to check on Blackie and Oscar. In one of the tents, he had found a ewe having difficulty giving birth to her first lamb. She had been in labor for two hours, Blackie had said.

Dane had rolled up his dress-shirt sleeves past his elbows, liberally dowsed his hands and arms with liquid disinfectant and knelt by the distressed ewe. When he had examined her, he had found a breech lamb and when he had pulled it, it was dead. Within minutes he had selected a lamb from the bum pen, rubbed it in the birth fluids and convinced the new mother that it was her own. The ewe didn't seem to question her new baby's vigor and size. By the time he had called it a night, the lamb was suckling contentedly.

Dane had returned to the house just after two in the morning, glancing toward the motor home and wondering if Abbie was awake. As angry as she had been, probably not, he guessed. He had showered and stretched out on the bed but sleep had evaded him. After an hour he'd gone to the kitchen and turned on a light to find the makings of a roast-beef sandwich. Within minutes he'd had the sandwich and a glass of milk in his room. The sandwich had satisfied his stomach's emptiness, but another hunger had begun to grow and he didn't see any way to satisfy it. Abbie had made it clear she had regretted the brief encounter in the yard, but that only made the insatiable hunger worse.

Damn the woman, Dane had thought as a vivid image of her auburn hair and green eyes haunted him. *Damn Emil Christensen for tricking me into accepting her. Damn me for agreeing to let her stay. Two more days and she'll be gone,* he vowed as he rolled onto his stomach and tried not to think of her. He didn't need the troublesome distraction of Abigail Hardesty. The other women in his life were enough. They didn't ask for commitments. They were free and wanted to stay that way. And they didn't make him feel restless and hungry.

When the alarm clock sounded a few hours later, a cold shower had torn the cobwebs from his brain but the hunger lingered.

Now, as Moses motioned her to sit, Dane knew he would have trouble holding himself to the three-day trial.

Abbie slid into her chair. "Good morning," she murmured.

"You're late," Dane said, loudly enough for all to hear.

"I... overslept."

"She probably had trouble getting to sleep," Moses chimed in. "Sore muscles and all that hard work, Abbie?"

"Yes," she admitted, "but I'll work out the soreness today."

"Good," Dane said, and her gaze reluctantly shifted to his face. Her eyes were filled with doubt and regret.

"Do I feed my bums and clean jugs again today?" she asked, a touch of color brightening her cheeks.

Moses chuckled and both Dane and Abbie turned to him. "Here for a half a day and already she's claimed the bum lambs as hers. Possessive, ain't she?"

Dane came to her rescue, ignoring Moses's remark. "Later," he said, and her attention swung back to him. Damn those eyes, he thought, hating the burden they put on him, as though he held her future in his hands. He wanted to hold more than that, he acknowledged, but shook the disturbing thought away. "Windy," he said, glancing to the wizened older sheepherder from Idaho sitting several chairs away, "you and Buck can work on that new section of fencing this morning. I'll have Hardesty work with me. We'll take care of the feeding."

She groaned aloud. "Will that take very long?"

"A few hours," he replied. "We'll feed hay to the ewes that have lambed, the bucks in the upper pasture, the cows that have calved and the horses that are several miles to the south. So there's lots of territory to cover. Now eat something. We don't have all morning."

"I'm not hungry," she said, reaching for the coffeepot and pouring herself a cup.

"It's a long time till noon," he warned. "You need something in your stomach so your stamina holds up. It's steady work until dinner."

She stiffened. "I know what my body needs...." She dropped her gaze and concentrated on the steaming cup of coffee. "This will be enough."

"Stubborn," he growled.

Her mouth tightened but she didn't say a word. Her coffee was half finished when he stood.

"Okay then, Hardesty, let's go. The stock is waiting."

"Yes, sir." She rose and tugged the ribbing of her sweatshirt down around her shapely hips, opened her mouth to say something but apparently thought better of it. Instead she stood at attention and saluted him.

Moses sputtered his coffee and Wilma covered her mouth with her napkin. The others around the table stared at Dane and Abbie, speechless.

Dane suppressed the desire to smile and saluted back. Her face paled, then reddened.

"I'll get my sweater and coveralls," she said, brushing past him and out the kitchen door.

On the back porch, she pulled on a clean pair of insulated coveralls and sat on the top step to put on her overshoes. He sat down beside her and did the same, wondering what thoughts were going through her mind.

"About last night," she said, rising and hurrying down the steps, "it won't happen again, I promise you. Now, who else will be working with us?"

"No one."

"You mean I have to...spend the entire morning...?"

"Alone with me," he said. "Can you endure that on an empty stomach?"

She huffed. "You betcha!"

"Where are your gloves?" he asked.

She pulled her mittens from her coverall pocket.

"Good Lord, Hardesty, those aren't working gloves," he said. "They're for making snowballs. Is that all you have?"

She nodded. "I thought they might protect my... blisters," she said, turning her hands over to show him her palms. She had three open blisters.

Grimacing, Dane went to a storage cupboard and selected a new pair of leather gloves and another pair of cloth gloves. Returning to the porch, he tossed them to her, along with a can of bandages. "Fix your hands before they get infected. You'll be useless to me injured."

He watched while she fumbled with the tin and its contents. She carefully covered each red area. There were more tender spots on her hands than he had thought. Finally she closed the tin and tossed it back to him, hard enough to let him know he was pushing.

"Use the cloth gloves when you're working with the new lambs," he suggested, "but the leather ones will keep you from getting more blisters when you're pitching hay. Now, let's get moving."

She hurried to the blue truck but when she reached it, she was surprised to find him headed in another direction. He climbed into a battered white one-ton truck with red wooden panels extending the length of its bed, making side walls a few feet higher than the cab. He sounded the horn and she jumped.

In the seconds it took her to run to the different vehicle, she prayed for patience and endurance to make it through the morning. Her stomach growled, disturbing her request for divine intervention. She climbed into the cab and ignored him.

He drove past the lambing tents and stopped at a closed gate. "We always leave the gates the way we find them."

"Okay," she replied, glancing at the gate.

"The rider is always in charge of the gates," he said.

She climbed out, opened the gate and waited impatiently for him to drive through, closed the gate, then hopped into the back instead of rejoining him in the cab.

They drove to the hay corral and he backed the truck until it bumped a stack of baled hay.

"Load them up," he called, staying in the cab.

Abbie stared at the giant stack of bales. She had helped her uncle on the family farm in Kentucky. She knew how to sling bales of hay. With a tight-lipped smile, she began to stack the bales two by two on the bed of the truck.

"How many?" she shouted after she had loaded a dozen bales. Breathing heavily, she paused and leaned against the side panel of the truck. She wished she hadn't put on the sweater beneath the insulated coveralls. She was sweltering in the heat of her own body.

She unzipped the coveralls and wriggled out of the top portion. It fell to her hips and clung. She removed her sweater, then twisted the sweatshirt up and over her head. The tails of her oxford shirt pulled out of her jeans and for a few seconds she was afraid it might come off with the sweatshirt. The corduroy cap caught in the sweatshirt. She searched for it and finally found it, trying to smooth her rebellious curls with her fingers before replacing the cap.

As she tipped her head back, willing the muscles in her upper back to relax, she savored the chilling effect of the air on her body. She pulled the sticky fabric of her blouse from her stomach and flapped it several times in the air. She knew she was subjecting herself to pneumonia, but the air felt marvelous. She tested the skin just above her navel with the palm of her hand and found it dry.

I'd better cover up before he finds me, she thought, *but not yet.* Slowly Abbie rotated her shoulders, closing her eyes to block out the bright sunlight reflecting from the ground cover of snow.

What she needed was a good twelve hours of undisturbed sleep. Dreamless, deep sleep without a certain man's intrusive presence. Sleep that would replenish her energy supply to its usual high level. Wasn't Dane Grasten ever going to tell her how many more bales she had to load?

"So how many bales do you want?" she shouted as she enjoyed a last minute, leaning against the side of the panel. Abbie knew he couldn't see her with the stacked bales blocking the window of the cab.

The tail of the truck sank under his weight and her eyes shot open.

"Another six should do it," he said nonchalantly, leaning against the opposite panel.

"How long have you been standing there?" she asked, angry at finding herself under his perusal.

"Long enough," he said. "Too tired to finish?"

"Not on your life," she said. "I was just taking a break. Is that allowed?"

"After we feed the stock." He reached for a bale and tossed it onto the stack as if it was weightless.

She shoved her arms back into the coveralls and jerked the zipper up to her chest, then joined him in the work until the back of the truck was filled.

She wiped perspiration from her forehead and jumped down from the tailgate. "How can it be so warm when the air is below freezing?" she asked, uncomfortable under his intent gaze. "Stop staring at me."

He ignored her. "Don't wear the insulated coveralls unless you're going to be outside and not too active," he suggested. "The ones you wore yesterday would have been better. Want to go change?"

"No," she replied stubbornly. "I'll manage."

"Fine," he said. "Then let's go." He walked to the cab and paused. "Cut the baler twine and when I say ready, toss the flakes off the pitchfork as I drive along. Don't put the hay out too close or the stock will just trample it. Bet you don't have a knife," Dane said, reaching into his pocket.

She shoved her hand into the pocket of her coveralls and produced her pocketknife, waving it proudly in the air. "I win," she declared. "My uncle trained me to always carry a knife. Said it might help me out in an emergency sometime."

He laughed. "Chalk this one up for your side. Now let's get to work. Want to ride inside or back there?"

"How far before we begin feeding?" she asked.

"Five miles to the horses," he said. "We'll do them first and work our way back to the house."

"Inside," she replied, willing to swallow her pride for the sake of the comfort and warmth of the cab.

The next few hours were spent with Abbie balanced on the back of the truck while it bounced over the rough pastures. By the time the truck was empty of the bales, they had traveled dozens of miles, with Abbie jumping down to open and close so many gates she had lost count. She was positive no two gates had the same kind of closing device.

Gritting her teeth, she closed the final gate and climbed into the cab. The dinner bell rang in the distance.

"Good timing," Dane said, "I don't know about you, but I'm hungry."

She was tempted to ask why, since she had done most of the manual labor. Her stomach growled and she hoped he couldn't hear it. A second ringing of the bell sounded as he braked to a stop near the back porch.

"I'm going to change coveralls," she said, avoiding his I-told-you-so-smile. "I'll be there in a little bit."

When she entered the motor home, her gaze lingered on the bed in the rear. If only she had time for a nap, just a short one. She drew a glass of water and swallowed two aspirin, holding little hope that the pills would revive her for the afternoon.

A catnap would enable her to get through dinner seated next to Dane. Abbie was sure he had driven her harder than necessary. As she thought back over the morning, she almost burst into tears. He had been just plain mean and inconsiderate, she decided, as she crawled onto the king-size bed that filled the entire rear section of the motor home.

She pulled a pillow from the pile in one corner and tucked it beneath her cheek. *Just a catnap,* she vowed, but she was asleep within seconds after shutting her eyes.

"WHERE'S ABBIE?" MOSES ASKED, as the serving dishes began their progression around the table.

"Changing her clothes," Dane said, concentrating on the full gravy bowl as it began to wobble in Moses's hands.

Gravy slopped onto the plastic tablecloth as Moses reached past Abbie's empty place and offered it to Dane.

Moses frowned at Wilma. "Don't you know, woman, that you can't heap the gravy?"

"Be thankful you got some," Wilma retorted. "This cooking is not my dish. When the heck is Trudy going to get here, boss?"

"She called before breakfast this morning," Dane said, feeling as though that had been days ago. "She said she's been helping her daughter with a new baby, but now she's free. She'll be here day after tomorrow. Then it's to the lambing tents for you, Wilma.''

''Great!'' she replied. ''That's where I belong anyway, not cooped up in this kitchen.''

''What's wrong with the kitchen?'' Dane asked, spooning gravy over his mashed potatoes.

''Oh, it's a nice enough kitchen,'' Wilma replied, her brown eyes evaluating the room. ''It's the kind of kitchen that a missus would really love, cooking and feeding her man and their little ones, but not me.''

Moses cast an affectionate glance toward her. ''Ain't I worth cooking for, sweet thing?''

''You aren't my man and this isn't your kitchen,'' she retorted, ''so stay out of this.'' She returned her attention to Dane seated at the opposite end of the long table. ''This kitchen needs children and a wife who doesn't mind this kind of living.'' She took a slice of corn bread. ''It's none of my business, but this house needs a family again.''

''You're right, it's no one's business but mine.'' Dane's gaze swept the workers. ''You all are like a family, especially during lambing time. Most of you have been coming back for years, and the rest of the year, well...Moses and I get by.''

''It's not the same,'' Wilma mumbled under her breath.

After dessert, the men returned to their respective jobs, leaving Dane alone in the room with Wilma.

She busied herself with loading the dishwasher while Dane lingered a few minutes over a second cup of coffee.

''Your sister Anna called this morning,'' Wilma said.

Dane flinched and sat his cup down. ''Did she say what she wanted?''

Wilma shook her head. "Just told me I could give you the message that she's on your side...and Knud also. Are the others making trouble again, boss?"

Dane glanced out the window. "Just the usual. Moving to the city changes a person, I guess, makes them forget what it's like working on the land. Did Anna want me to call her back?"

"Didn't say," Wilma replied, then turned her attention to finding space for one final bowl in the dishwasher. Suddenly she straightened and frowned at him. "She's different, you know."

Startled at her outburst, Dane looked up. "Who? Anna?"

She jerked her head toward the backyard. "Abbie. Don't you do anything to hurt her, boss."

Dane sobered. "Why would I do that? Do you think I'm a mean taskmaster, Wilma?"

"You can overdo the bossing around sometimes, that's for sure," she said, putting her hands on her hips. "Just you be careful with her. She's different, and you'd be sorry if you did something to drive her away from here."

"I'd never drive her away," he replied. "If she leaves, it will be because she chooses to leave. She has a career already established. This is just a stop along the way for her. So don't get too fond of her. She'll be gone before any of us get to know her. First impressions aren't always valid."

"I heard you giving her three days," Wilma said. "I wasn't eavesdropping yesterday, but I was still in here cleaning up and I heard you two bickering about that agreement. Three days isn't long enough to test a person. It's not fair if she doesn't perform to your high-and-mighty standards and you drive her away. Sometimes you expect too much of another person."

Dane rose from his chair. "Wilma, that's enough. You make me sound like an insensitive ogre who gobbles up his employees and spits them out regularly. Am I that bad?"

Wilma's stiff stance softened a little. "Sorry, boss, I didn't mean to put it that way. I'm butting in where I don't belong, but I think I could get really fond of that young woman if she stays around a while."

So could I, Dane thought as he took his plate and silverware to the sink and reached for his cap. "If she quits, it won't be because I forced her to. You can depend on that. Now I have work to do and so do you. I'm going to find the missing Miss Hardesty and give her a lift to the lambing sheds. She must have decided to eat in her private little home on wheels. See you later," he said as he ambled from the room.

There was no response when he rapped lightly on the motor home door. He turned the knob. It was unlocked. He stepped inside, his eyes slowly adjusting to the shadowy interior.

"Abbie, are you here?" he called.

Movement in the rear caught his eye and he ventured closer.

She was asleep on the bed, her cheek pressed into the top edge of a pillow. She had pulled it close to her breast and now part of it lay beneath her.

"Abbie, are you okay?" he called softly. The window shades were still drawn from the night. He leaned closer, admiring her profile in the shadows of the room.

She turned onto her side and curled her legs, hugging the pillow tightly.

"Abbie, it's time to return to work," he called, his low-pitched voice sounding unnecessarily loud in the quiet vehicle. A wave of protectiveness swept over him as he continued to watch her. "Did you eat?" he asked, softening his tone.

She mumbled in her sleep.

"Abbie," he murmured, the name bordering on a caress. He resisted the urge to reach out and touch her. The green blouse had become twisted, exposing the creamy skin of her stomach, flat and firm as it disappeared beneath the band of her jeans.

"You're excused for the afternoon, Hardesty." He reached for the afghan she had used the night before for the puppy and draped the woven piece over her sleeping form, smiling a little as she burrowed into its warmth.

A tiny grin curled her lips and he wondered what she was dreaming about. Quietly, he left the motor home, locking the door behind him.

WHEN ABBIE AWOKE, the darkness surrounded her like a shroud. She cried out and tried to sit up but every muscle in her body rebelled. The pounding of her heart subsided as images of the long work morning came to mind. Gradually she gathered her wits and reached for the light. The digital clock told her it was several minutes past four in the morning.

"Oh, no," she moaned. "I've slept around the clock. How could I? Why didn't someone wake me?" Slowly she sat up, each movement of her arms and legs pure agony. Pushing herself out of bed, she staggered to the bathroom, then inched her way to the window in the door.

Looking toward the house, she saw two illuminated windows, one on the main floor and one upstairs.

This was the last day of her trial period. "If I can't work, he'll insist I go for sure," she said aloud. Perhaps one of the lights came from Dane's room. She would dress and go to the kitchen door. If it was unlocked, she would have a quick breakfast and volunteer to do whatever Dane wanted done.

Abbie wriggled into her jeans, groaning aloud as her bruised biceps protested. When she slipped into a red shirt, her fingers rebelled at working the buttons through the openings. Irritated, she wriggled out of the blouse and pulled a navy blue sweatshirt over her head, then ran a brush through her hair.

How could she possibly have slept for sixteen hours and not have awakened once? She pulled on a pair of warm woolen socks and grimaced. Even her toes and arches were stiff, and her fingers were ruined forever, she thought, wondering how she could ever spin or weave again.

She tied her shoes, trying to maneuver the laces without touching the blisters on two of her fingertips.

She reached for the coveralls that had been her excuse for returning to the motor home in the first place. Perhaps the walk to the house would help work out some of the kinks.

"I'll make it," she repeated over and over to herself as she crossed the frosty yard. She worked her way up the steps, one at a time. When she reached the door, she glanced at her watch. It was quarter to five. Surely no one would be up at this ungodly hour, she reasoned. But sounds came from the kitchen as she opened the door and stepped inside.

Dane Grasten stood by the stove, dressed in jeans and a yellow-and-navy-plaid flannel shirt but still in his stocking feet, pouring himself a cup of coffee.

As she closed the door, he turned to her, his blue eyes piercing. "Good morning," he said. "Catch up on your rest?"

CHAPTER SEVEN

ABBIE COULDN'T SUPPRESS a blush or a smile as she slid out of her jacket. "Yes," she said, eager to accept the steaming cup of coffee he held out.

He pulled it back a few inches. "How are the hands?"

She showed him her red and swollen palms. "I've never had so many blisters at one time," she admitted, reaching for the cup again. "I'm hungry enough to eat a horse this morning. Got one cooking on the stove? Until it's ready to serve, how about two aspirin for some aches and pains?"

Dane retrieved a large bottle of the pills and shook out two, offering them to her. She tried to get them without touching him, but failed. Images of that same hand touching her cheek two nights earlier brought a wave of longing. She gulped the aspirin down with a glass of water he had drawn.

"Now, about that horse . . ." she said.

"No horses available. We need them this summer," he said, laughing, "but we could whip up something else. Shall we toss a coin to see who cooks? Wilma refuses to start working in the kitchen before six." He reached for the coffeepot and gave her cup a partial refill. "You missed a few meals yesterday."

She took a sip and set the cup down on the counter, then flexed her hands a few times. "Why don't we work together?" she suggested. "Do you have potatoes?"

He nodded.

"And onions?"

He opened a pantry door and retrieved two potatoes and an onion.

"Eggs and bacon?"

He nodded, opening the refrigerator. "And juice. We have orange or cranberry. Wilma is a nut about vitamin C in the mornings."

"I'll do cottage fries," she said, "but they must have lots of onions in them. That's the way we fixed them in Kentucky when I was growing up."

"Perhaps Southerners settled the Pacific Northwest," he remarked. "That's the way my mother fixed them, too."

She grinned. "I doubt if your ancestors ever set foot in the South. Didn't they come in Viking boats across the Atlantic?"

He laughed. "Almost. My grandfather came from Denmark in 1880, but he landed in New York, made his way to St. Louis, took a steamer up the Missouri to Fort Benton, then hitched a ride on a freight wagon on its way to Bannack and got off and walked to Dillon, where a sheep rancher picked him up and took him home. He homesteaded a few years later right here. Did you notice that little log cabin this side of the burned-out lambing shed?"

She nodded. "It's very tiny."

"My grandparents lived there and had three children before they built a larger house beyond the lambing tents," he said. "My parents built this house in the twenties, when sheep raising was at a peak. I always considered my ancestors' route rather direct, but if you trace it on a map, I reckon it's a bit round about."

She smiled. "I'd expect lots of Norwegians and Swedes in this area with all these mountains, but the Danish? Isn't Denmark rather flat?"

"Rolling hills," he replied, grinning back at her. "Most of the country is at sea level and my grandfather told me once that the highest peak, and I use that term loosely, is about three hundred feet. We're standing at close to six thousand here."

"What brought your ancestors here?"

"Employment . . . and space," he said. "Denmark is a crowded country. Two of my great-uncles came first and sent word to my grandfather that if he could learn to work with sheep, he could become a rich man. He did, over the years, but the work was never easy. The country and its climate is quite different from his homeland. My parents have just left on their first trip to Denmark. They'll be gone for a month and hope to find some of their long-lost cousins. I'm glad for them." He took another sip of coffee. "And yours? I suppose they came over on the *Mayflower*."

"Not quite," she replied. "They arrived in 1634 at Jamestown on a ship from England," she said. "They were Scotch-Irish and they settled in Virginia for 150 years or so before moving on to Kentucky. Somewhere back then, one of my ancestors was a close friend and hunting companion of good ol' Daniel Boone himself."

She laughed. "I moved in with Aunt Minnie and Uncle Harry when I was eight years old. I loved to hear the stories of the men who risked their lives trying to explore Kentucky. Frankly, I don't know which stories were based on fact and which ones were purely fiction, but they were great to hear on warm summer nights when we sat outside and counted the stars. My cousin Callie and her momma would play the dulcimer and we'd sing those old-time hill songs, and my uncles would try to top each other with stories of the men and women who had preceded them. You wouldn't believe how difficult it was for the early settlers to get through the Cumberland Gap.''

"And what of your real parents?" he asked. "Do you know who they are?"

"Sure, but if I go back a generation, I'm right with the rest of the Hardesty clan," she said. "My dad and Uncle Harry were first cousins."

"What happened to your father?"

"He was killed in a cave-in at one of the Rainbow River mines," she said. "I was about six. We moved to Paducah a few months later."

"We?" he asked. "You mean your mother?"

"Yes, but I don't know much about her," she admitted. "She's still alive and writes every once in a while, but no one can ever read her writing. The last letter my Aunt Minnie received was from Newark, New Jersey. Can you imagine how frustrating it was, as a little girl, to get these letters and only be able to read every fourth or fifth word? She always sent me a five-dollar bill on my birthday, but she never called. Her maiden name was Smith, Bernice Smith. Can you imagine trying to track her down among all the Smiths in the east, and to make it worse, my stepfather's last name was Johnson. I decided long ago to consider the Hardesty side as my real family. It was much less stressful that way as/I grew up." She paused. "Good grief, I'll get carried away if I don't watch myself."

His somber blue eyes followed her movements as she took another sip of coffee. "Your Southern accent gets stronger when you talk about your family. Do you miss them?"

"At times, but I don't get back to visit very often," she said. "Most of them still live back there in the Rainbow Hills area near Drakesboro. Talking about them makes me a little homesick. Funny, after all these years."

"Fate must have dictated our paths would cross right here in this kitchen in southwestern Montana," he said.

"Probably because we're both hungry," she replied.

"Yes," Dane agreed. He sat his coffee cup down. "Now what about those potatoes and onions? The combination is one of my favorites."

"Great," she murmured, glancing around him toward the stove. "We've finally found something to agree on."

He was lounging against the corner of the stove, and she reached out to nudge him out of the way, touching his side without thinking. She jerked her hand away, but still he didn't move.

His hands fell to her shoulder. Her complexion paled as she looked up at him. His expression was serious and she wished he would smile or joke instead.

"I won't hurt you, Abbie," he promised softly, his lips barely moving. "And I'm sorry I worked you so hard yesterday. Today will be different."

"Promise?"

He nodded, his features changing into a warm smile, sending her heart thudding. She took his hands in hers and gently removed them from her shoulders, holding them for an instant longer than was necessary.

"We'd better start the potatoes," she said, turning to the sink. Abbie turned on the water to rinse the potatoes. When the warm tap water hit the damaged tissue of her palms, she shrieked from the pain shooting through every nerve ending. A burst of tears streamed down her cheeks. Unable to stop crying, she stood at the sink, holding her hands out to the air, willing the burning to recede.

"Crazy woman," Dane muttered, as he turned the water off and reached for a towel. Carefully he patted her hands dry. "You don't strike me as a woman who cries very easily," he murmured, his head still bowed over her wounded hands.

Abbie looked up at him again, her eyes sparkling with moisture. "I'm not," she insisted. "I'm really very tough," as if to negate her words, a burst of emotion brought new tears flowing down her cheeks. She tried to brush them away, but her hands were useless.

"Maybe too tough. Loners tend to get that way. Let me," he said, drying her cheeks.

"I'm okay, really!"

"No, you're not." He wiped the corner of one eye again. "You're beautiful." He kissed her on the spot he had just wiped, then lightly at the corner of her mouth.

"Thank you," she murmured, her hands finding their way to his waist again. "You're not bad looking yourself, when you don't frown so sternly. You'd look great with a mustache."

He laughed. "A mustache? Me? A mustache should be dark."

She shook her head. "No, a blond mustache would be . . . sexy."

"But it might tickle," he replied, and they laughed together.

She smiled up at him, enjoying the close contact. "Shouldn't we start this breakfast before the others get up?"

He nodded, letting his hands slide down her arms to her hands. "But first you must patch up these. You'll find all sizes of bandages in the bathroom. Help yourself."

Before Abbie could budge Wilma appeared in the entryway, dressed, but with her hair in rollers. "Who's making all the noise in my kitchen?" she demanded. Her mouth fell open when she spied Dane and Abbie, holding hands and standing inches apart. The awkward moment continued until she recovered her usual briskness. "If you're going to cook, you've got to do it for the whole damned bunch."

"We were discussing Abbie's hands," Dane said, turning Abbie's palms for Wilma's curious inspection.

"Good Lord," Wilma exclaimed. "You can't cook with those hands. You probably can't even work outside."

"Yes, I can," Abbie insisted, taking advantage of the moment to free herself from Dane's grasp. "Give me a few minutes to fix my hands and I'll be as able as anyone on the place." She laughed. "At least I've gotten enough rest for a while. I'll be back and help you with breakfast, Wilma. Isn't this a nice morning?"

After she had disappeared, Wilma turned to Dane. "And I was afraid you were going to be mean. You devil." Playfully, she punched him in his midsection. "But you still be careful and don't hurt her."

AFTER BREAKFAST ABBIE hitched a ride on the back of the hay truck to the lambing tents and spent the day learning the operation. The morning passed quickly as she became engrossed in the techniques of caring for the lambs: checking the drop pasture for newborns or ewes about to deliver, keeping the feeders filled, feeding the bum lambs. There were always a few jugs to clean. As she worked, she listened to Moses tell stories of past lambing seasons.

Dinner at noon consisted of ham and scalloped potatoes with all the trimmings. Abbie filled her plate, knowing she would burn off the calories in the afternoon.

And she did. The leather gloves protected her hands and she was able to clean the jugs as soon as Moses moved the day-old lambs and their mothers to larger outside pens. Gradually her muscles recovered as she worked out the soreness.

Darkness had descended when they gathered for supper. As the meal ended, Dane rose from his chair. "Well, folks, I've put off the paperwork stacked up in the office long enough. See you all in the morning. Blackie," he said, turning to one of the night lambers, "come get me if you have problems you can't handle during the night." He excused himself without a backward glance.

Abbie watched him go, hiding her disappointment. Perhaps she had read too much into the friendly exchange so early that morning. *Maybe I should leave well enough alone,* she thought, as the others left the table. Then she remembered that it was the third day of her trial period. She had a very legitimate reason to seek him out, after all.

Abbie helped Wilma with the kitchen chores. An hour later, she made her way to Dane's office. His blond head was bent over the ledger, a pair of glasses with silver frames beneath his furrowed brows. While one hand operated the keys of an electronic calculator, the index finger of his other hand followed a column of numbers down the page.

She rapped lightly on the doorjamb, disappointed at the irritated expression on his face at the interruption.

"Yes?" he asked, removing the glasses and dropping them onto the ledger. "Can I help you?"

The cool detachment in his tone threatened her confidence. "Have you decided...if I can stay? We agreed on a three-day trial. Do you remember?"

He tossed down the pencil he had been using and tipped his chair back on its springy base, peering at her under a thoughtful frown. "I haven't decided."

"But you promised," she exclaimed. "You said three days!"

"I'll decide when three days are up."

She stepped into the office. "What do you mean? I arrived on Monday and this is Wednesday. Isn't that three days?" She inhaled and put her fists on her hips.

Dane motioned for her to take a seat, but she declined the offer. *I could gaze at her forever,* he realized. Each time he had driven past the lambing area he had searched her out, usually spotting her auburn curls below the blue and white cap he had given her. Taller than two of the men, she had been easy to find when working outside in the pens. Twice she had waved. After the third drive-by of the morning, he had to admit he had been looking for excuses to find business nearby.

Now as he savored a few more seconds of merely admiring her, Dane searched for an excuse to keep her around. He jumped at the first idea that entered his mind. "I haven't gotten three days' work out of you," he said, maintaining his somber expression.

Her temper flared. "You're crazy. Monday, Tuesday, Wednesday; three days in any normal person's book."

"Does that mean you want to leave?" he asked.

"No," she said, glaring directly at him. "I like it here. I enjoy the work. The people are..." Her gaze dropped. "I like the people, too. I signed an agreement, but you're trying to weasel out of it. Now either make a decision or I'm going to call Dr. Christensen and complain. You're not being fair, leaving me dangling like this. I've made plans for the next several months and now you're threatening to ruin them all.'' Her cheeks flushed with color as she stood her ground. "Do you treat all your agricultural interns this way?"

"No," he admitted, "I don't. And I'm keeping my word on the three day work agreement. You arrived on Monday and worked half a day. Yesterday you worked the morning, so that finishes your first full day. Today you worked a full day. That makes two days. You're a day short." He tipped the chair back again and waited for her reaction.

"You make me feel as though I've received a stay of execution," she said, her shoulders relaxing beneath the navy sweatshirt.

He had never considered sweatshirts sexy before, but as he continued watching her, he felt himself responding in a very physical way. He dropped the chair back to an upright position. "Sit down," he said. "Please."

She sat, tucking one foot beneath her.

"Comfortable?" he asked.

"No," she said. "This is the most uncomfortable chair I've ever sat in."

He suppressed a smile. "I'll make a note of it. Anything else?"

"Yes."

He waited, watching her eyes dart from his face to the bookcases lining two of the walls, then across the desk to linger on his hands, before returning to his face. He wondered what she thought of him. He had never cared what a woman thought of his physical appearance. He recalled her comment about blond mustaches and ran his finger across his clean-shaven upper lip.

She smiled.

He sensed they were on the same wavelength. "What else can I do for you?"

"When is my day off?" she asked. "You said in your letter I would get one day off a week."

"Friday."

She frowned. "Why Friday?"

"Is there something wrong with Friday as a day off?"

"Well, no, but . . ." She shrugged.

"Others who have been here longer get Saturday or Sunday," he explained. "I try to spread the employees' days off to cover the week. No one else has Friday off. Do you have plans?"

She nodded. "I want to do some weaving."

"If you need to make a trip into town, check with Moses," he said. "He goes for the mail every few days and you can ride in with him. Or if he's not going, feel free to use one of the ranch vehicles, but tell someone you're taking it."

She studied her hands. "Sometime this summer . . . if I stay this summer . . . I would like go to Shelley, Idaho to visit my cousin."

"I assumed your relatives were all in Kentucky. Do you have cousins scattered all over the country?" he asked.

"No. This relative is special. We grew up together and are still best friends. Her husband is very ill and . . . she needs a distraction once in a while. She's too proud to ask for help."

"Sounds like pride runs in the family," he said, rubbing his chin with his fingers.

"Perhaps, and what's wrong with pride?"

"Sometimes it can get in the way of good judgment."

"I can think of worse traits," she challenged.

"Such as?"

"Stubbornness. Thinking you have to do it all your-self." She grinned. "And being a slave driver."

He laughed. "You may be right about the last. How are the sore muscles and blisters tonight?"

She straightened in the chair and put her foot back on the floor. "This morning when I first got out of bed, I was sure I had died and rigor mortis had set in." Abbie laughed. "I feel much better now. The day's work helped and my hands feel much better. Wilma gave me some salve to put on them. Stinks to high heaven, but she swore by it."

"Bag Balm?"

"How did you know?"

"That's Wilma's cure-all for what ails a person on the outside," he said, grinning at her. His blue eyes held her captive until finally he looked away.

She rose from her chair. "I'll leave you now, so you can get back to work. Thanks for the day off." She glanced over her shoulder at him as she lingered in the doorway. "I hope I'm still here to claim it."

ABBIE WAS MOVING some ewes and lambs to a larger pen the next afternoon when she heard someone call her name. When she looked up, Dane was standing beside the blue pickup, motioning to her.

She shooed the last few lambs through the gate and fastened it, then made her way down the lane to him. He didn't look very happy, she thought. Had he decided against her staying? If so, why had he decided to let her go? She had accepted each and every job assigned her, doing them carefully and thoroughly.

"Hardesty, it's time to talk," he said, when she stopped a few feet from him.

She shoved her fists into her coverall pockets. "Yes?"

He paused and she shifted her weight from one foot to the other.

"I've made my decision," he said.

She waited, but he didn't continue. "Well?" she said, hoping he wouldn't be offended by her prompting.

"You can stay."

Her eyes widened. "I can...stay?" Gradually her face broke into a smile and her eyes sparkled. "Do you mean it?"

"Of course," he said. "You're a natural with the ewes and lambs. We'd miss you if you left now. You seem to have won over all the other workers. They have insinuated that they would be very unhappy if I canned you. Moses and Wilma have each threatened to go on strike if I send you packing. So, we're stuck with each other for six months minus three days. Is it a deal?"

"It sure is!" Abbie reached for his hands and squeezed them tightly for several seconds. "Thanks," she murmured, "you won't regret this."

She dropped her grasp and whirled away, waving to Moses several pens away. He gave her a victory sign and waved back.

Dane watched her hurry back to her work. "I hope neither of us has regrets," he muttered beneath his breath.

HER DAY OFF was spent in total seclusion in the motor home, with only a few minutes taken for a mug of soup. The project on the loom was completed, and in the late afternoon Abbie removed the piece and tied the ends into short borders of fringe. She had begun to measure out the new warp threads for the loom when the dinner bell rang from the ranch house, announcing supper.

She made herself a promise to complete this exacting part of the weaving process and then begin spacing the warp threads on the loom during the evenings of the coming week. Hopefully, the next project would be well underway a week from now.

During supper, the talk around the table was about the Music Tenders band, due in the area on Sunday. Sadly, she told the others she would be working.

Sunday afternoon, she was heading back to the lambing area when the first truck, with Buck driving and Andy and two strangers squeezing into the cab, drove away from the yard. She waved, envying them their afternoon off.

Shortly before two, Moses arrived at the lambing tents in another ranch truck and honked the horn. Wilma was sitting beside him, wearing a dress.

"Let's go, Abbie," Moses called. "The boss has given you time off. Hop in and we'll drive you to the motor home and you can get all gussied up."

She hesitated. "I can't leave here. I'm alone and . . ."

Moses shook his head. "Windy is on his way down. He says he's too old and feeble to dance and the battery in his hearing aid is too shot to hear the music. He offered to take your place. Come on now, before the boss changes his mind."

"Okay," she agreed, climbing in beside Wilma. "Who all is going?" she asked, wondering if Dane would be staying at the ranch.

"Windy and Blackie are covering the place," Moses said, as he rolled to a stop near her motor home door.

"The boss is coming later with Oscar and Trudy." He grinned. "Now change into something real pretty like Wilma here, and let's go dancing!"

CHAPTER EIGHT

As ABBIE RUSHED through the motor home door, she wished she had time to shampoo and shower, but Moses and Wilma were anxious to leave. A quick wash would have to do.

She pushed the hangers back and forth in the closet, searching for something dressier than jeans, sweatshirt and baseball shirts.

"Ah," she said, sighing, as her eyes fell on the perfect choice. She yanked the prairie-style patchwork skirt from its hanger and held it up to her waist, the ruffle around its hemline falling just past her calf.

She changed her undergarments, chose a lacy slip and stepped into the skirt. A slate-blue chambray blouse complemented the blues and tans of the skirt. When she pulled on knee-high brown leather boots with two-inch heels and stood up, she was satisfied with her mirrored reflection.

Quickly, she folded a woven shawl into a triangle and draped it around her shoulders, tying its ends into a loose knot across her bosom. Its soft angora and mohair wool in chocolate, slate-blue and ivory shades would keep the chill away in case the bar was drafty. Once again, she wondered if she would meet Dane.

She hadn't seen much of him, other than at meal-times, since he had given his decision. Perhaps he had been avoiding her. Angry sparks had flown more than once, yet when he had kissed her that first night, flames of a different kind had begun to smolder.

It was much too easy for a woman to read more into a man's interest than was actually there. She had been guilty of the same mistake herself. *Women are emotional,* she thought, *while men are physical. Isn't that usually the way it works out?*

Abbie had no time or inclination to have a casual short-term affair with a man whose chosen profession kept him tied to the land. She laughed aloud as she brushed her hair and picked out a few pieces of straw and green alfalfa leaves.

"No time, no time, for daydreaming," she sang, as she pulled up her skirt and made a final adjustment to the tails of her blouse, tugging it firmly over her full breasts. The skirt always accented her slender waist, and tonight, just for tonight, she'd enjoy looking every inch a woman.

Dane Grasten could admire her from afar as she danced the evening away in the arms of the other cowboys and sheepherders. Let him find out for himself she was a female beneath the baggy sweatshirts and bulky coveralls.

No one would ever know how often he had intruded into her thoughts and how comfortable his presence had become there. This afternoon and evening was for fun and dancing, enjoying the company of these men and women who she knew only as sheep tenders and cooks. *The Boss*, as everyone on the place called him, would probably not show his face at such a frivolous occasion. But then again, he was unpredictable. If he did join them, would he find her attractive enough to ask her to dance?

The horn sounded outside and her meandering thoughts came to an abrupt halt. Grabbing a coat, she sailed out the door.

"Dillydallying women," Moses huffed as she got into the truck.

"Sorry," Abbie murmured.

"But from the looks of you, the time was well spent," Moses replied, winking at her as he turned the key in the ignition. "You're prettier than a newborn lamb."

"Coming from an old sheepherder like him," Wilma added, "that's quite a compliment, Abbie. I know someone who's in for a surprise."

"Thanks," Abbie murmured, hoping they were referring to Dane.

As Moses drove, the road twisted around the foothills and mountains, following the creek through the valleys until it joined a larger river, then along the southeast shore of a mountain reservoir.

"You been this way before?" Moses asked.

Abbie shook her head.

"This is the Ruby Reservoir," he explained. "It's the lifeblood of the ranchers in these parts. They own shares of it, entitling them to draw water for their fields. There'd be little hay without it."

"Does Dane get water from it?" she asked.

"Nah, he's got a few wells and the Sweetwater Creek and other sources, and unless it's a real dry summer he manages."

She concentrated on the countryside, but her thoughts were on Dane. "Do you think he'll come?"

Moses grinned. "He said he would try." He glanced her way. "Does it matter?"

She met his gaze. "It might."

She thought she heard a mumbled "Good" from both Moses and Wilma. "He doesn't take much time off, does he?" she asked.

"Ranching is full time," Wilma said. "That's the trouble with some women. They expect their men to work from nine to five, then have energy left to fool around all night."

"The stock needs looking after, day and night, rain, snow or sunshine, sick or well," Moses added. "The days start before sunup and don't end till the job is done."

"I know," Abbie replied. "Fortunately, I've always been an early riser." She smiled. "I grew up on a farm. In Salt Lake, I used to go jogging in the dark before my classes, then start weaving as soon as classes were over. Sometimes I wouldn't stop until midnight, but usually I wilt when the sun goes down. I prefer quiet evenings, talking to someone I enjoy being with, listening to music, working on my cartoons...."

Moses glanced her way. "You draw cartoons?"

She laughed. "Not the kind you're probably thinking of. My cartoons are the designs I use for a pattern when I weave."

"Like the patterns in counted cross-stitch?" Wilma asked.

Abbie nodded. "A little. I usually do a cartoon on graph paper, then enlarge it to fit beneath the warp threads on my loom. It tells me when to change the color or texture of my yarn and keeps me on track so the finished tapestry tells the story I'd originally planned."

"Sounds more complicated than a person would think," Wilma said, as they left the reservoir and continued on the dirt road.

"Ain't that the way with most things," Moses remarked. "Life tends to get complicated if you don't keep your guard up."

Abbie smile at them both. "All my tapestries tell a story, but sometimes I keep it a secret and let the viewer discover it for herself."

"Do only women view your work?" Wilma asked.

"No," Abbie said, "but men usually don't take time to study them. I've been working in the evenings on a new design. As soon as I finish my current project, I'll be starting on one that will tell of my stay here." She sighed deeply. "Time has a way of passing without a person noticing the days. One of these mornings I'll wake up and realize that six months have passed and the day has arrived to move on."

"Maybe the boss will ask you to stay," Moses said.

"I doubt it," Abbie replied. "He has his life pretty well established. I want a place of my own. He's been married before and . . . and I don't think he's forgotten her. That burned-out lambing shed is proof of that."

"Hell, I didn't mean get hitched," Moses said, grinning past Wilma to her. "I just meant to keep working with us. You have a way with the ewes and lambs."

Mortified at her response, Abbie shrank into her corner, vowing to keep her thoughts to herself from now on. Wilma patted her knee a few times before returning her attention to Moses. Abbie blocked their conversation from her thoughts.

Before long, they turned into a secluded drive that opened into a compound of log cabins several hundred yards from the main road. In the distance was a long, low log building with smoke coming from a chimney at one end. More than two dozen vehicles, most of them pickup trucks, were parked helter-skelter in the gravel area at the front.

"Is that it?" Abbie asked.

"Sure nuff is," Moses said. "The Outfitters' Den. It's the best place in these here parts to bend an elbow because you'll always meet your friends here." He squeezed Wilma's knee. "Let's get a move on, ladies." Wilma yelped and slapped his hand away.

Abbie followed them up the steps, a little surprised to see Moses politely open the heavy door made of upright poles and hold it as the two women entered. In spite of his chauvinistic remarks and his treatment of Wilma, behaving like a gentleman was still important to him, she thought, as her eyes adjusted to the dim interior.

Moses located the rest of the Grasten crew at two tables that had been pushed together in one corner of the large room. Wilma and Abbie followed him through the crowd. Rustic was the only word for the interior design. Wild game heads had been mounted high on the walls, with single trees, horse collars and other ranch and outfitting paraphernalia scattered elsewhere.

A stone fireplace with blazing logs filled the major portion of one end of the room. A long bar made from peeled and stained logs stretched from one end of the room to the other, with a window for food orders at the far end. A band was tuning up on a triangular stage opposite the bar.

Within minutes a waitress arrived for their drink orders. A wave of embarrassment swept over Abbie. "I didn't bring any money, not even my purse," she said, grimly.

"Don't worry," Moses said. "The first few rounds and supper are on the boss. After that, the boozers are on their own."

Abbie requested a gin and tonic, and the waitress left. "I'm certainly not a boozer," she replied. "Tell him thanks."

"Tell him yourself," Moses said. "Here he comes now."

She looked up. An unexpected pressure in her chest left her breathless as she watched the tall blond man approach them. He took off his leather coat and positioned it on the back of an empty chair three seats away, then slid into the chair and motioned to the waitress.

The attractive woman, wearing jeans so tight Abbie wondered how she moved, sidled up to Dane. "Hi, Dane, honey. Can I get you the usual?"

Abbie could have groaned at the waitress's familiarity. Out of the corner of her eye she tried to see his reaction, but Wilma moved and blocked her view.

"Ditch," he said simply.

Puzzled, Abbie watched as the waitress brought Dane a glass filled with amber liquid. Had she forgotten the rest of their drinks? Abbie wondered.

"What is a ditch?" she whispered to Wilma who was sitting next to her.

Wilma laughed. "Hey, boss, the tourist lady here wants to know what's in a ditch."

Abbie shrank back into her chair, wishing she had not been so curious. The rest of the drinks arrived and the answer to her question was left hanging. The band began to play a fast two-step and several of the men left to find dance partners among the women who had gathered at one end of the bar.

"Dance, sweet thing?" Moses asked, reaching for Wilma's hand.

"Sure," Wilma replied and they left the table.

Abbie glanced past the two empty chairs to where Dane was sitting. He was talking to Buck and didn't look her way.

The dance ended and another round of drinks was ordered, but she hadn't finished her first so she declined. Two more dance numbers were played. Abbie was sure she was the only woman in the place who had not been asked to dance.

When the band began to play the next song, a slower romantic tune, and the lead guitarist started to sing in a pleasant tenor voice, the shapely waitress in the tight jeans came to the table.

"I'm on my break," she said. "Dance with me, Dane?"

He shrugged and rose from his chair. Abbie watched with envy as the couple danced, their bodies pressed unnecessarily close. Lowering her eyes, she finished her drink. The liquor tasted bitter and burned as it went down her throat.

Buck came to her. "Dance, Abbie?"

"Sure." She rose, accepting his callused hand. As Buck guided her around the dance floor, she caught glimpses of Dane and the waitress. The woman was looking coyly at Dane while he listened attentively to her every word.

Buck proved to be a competent dancer. At least one man found her a suitable partner, Abbie thought, even if he was the wrong man. The tune ended and he started to lead her to the group.

"I need the powder room, Buck," she said. "I'll find my way back . . . and thanks. I enjoyed the dance."

He nodded, grinning as he tipped his black western hat to her and returned to the ranch employees at the table. Several plates of food were beginning to arrive.

In the women's rest room, Abbie glanced in the mirror. She was as pale as a ghost.

Wilma came out of one of the compartments. "How are you doing? Having fun?"

"No," Abbie admitted, "and after seeing myself in the mirror I can see why. I look terrible, like death warmed over. No wonder no one but Buck has asked me to dance."

"Put on some lipstick," Wilma suggested.

"I can't. I left my purse back at the ranch."

"Want to use mine?" Wilma asked.

"Thanks," Abbie replied. "But I don't know why I bother. No one else will be asking me to dance."

"I overheard some of the fellows from the other ranches talking. They've decided you must be the boss's."

"The boss's what, for heaven's sake?" Abbie exclaimed. "He hasn't spoken a word to me since he arrived. I should have stayed home." She handed the lipstick back to Wilma without opening it.

Wilma frowned. "The boss does seem a little out of it. Moses said he had words with Windy before he left. Moses suspects Windy has a problem with the bottle, if you know what I mean. If the boss had known about it, he would never have hired him."

"But Windy was taking my place," Abbie said. "Is Dane mad at me for leaving? Maybe I should still be there working."

"Don't let either of them lay a guilt trip on you, honey. You're clean because the boss said it was fine for you to go. Now use this tube of color and get back out there. The boss is a fool if he doesn't notice what's right under his nose."

"They're starting to have supper," Abbie said.

"Great, I'm starved," Wilma said. "And it's nice to not have to do the cooking or cleanup after those sheepherders."

Abbie nodded.

"Coming?" Wilma asked.

Abbie shook her head. "I'm not hungry. I'm going outside for some fresh air." She turned away before Wilma could see the moisture in her eyes. Abbie decided she wouldn't subject herself to Dane's continued rejection. Why couldn't he at least have shown a little common courtesy? Was the waitress a more suitable dance partner? The woman had taken the initiative and asked him to dance. Was that the answer? Should she simply ask? But what if he said no? Her mouth tightened at the thought.

Abbie shoved the door open and went outside. A gust of cold air blew past her as she stepped off the porch of the log building and hurried across the parking lot, unsure of her destination. She pulled the shawl snugly around her shoulders, wishing she had stayed home. Home. Did she mean Salt Lake City? Kentucky? Or the Grasten ranch?

She didn't want to think about anything anymore. Feeling numb, she walked to the river running past the complex. Stopping a few feet from its bank, she stood in the shadows of a grove of cottonwood trees, their skeletonlike limbs casting webs across her silhouette in the dusky evening.

Glancing up, she saw the slender slice of a new moon making its appearance high in the darkening sky. She closed her eyes. *Home...homeless...that's my problem, I don't have any place to call my own.*

At her feet was the stump of a large tree, long since cut down. She stepped up onto the stump, elevating herself several inches. The wind gusted again, brushing her skirt against her legs. She crossed her arms and rubbed her shoulders with her hands, trying to rub a little warmth into her body.

The lonesomeness of her plight brought a rush of unbearable longing for companionship, someone to talk to, someone who cared enough to shelter her when she needed it, someone to hold her in the darkness.

"Oh, God, please help me," Abbie murmured, hugging herself and giving in to feeling low. What was the matter with her? She seldom had a problem with depression. Usually her spirits soared, for she felt in control of her own destiny. But tonight that destiny seemed cold and empty.

She heard the sound of footsteps on the gravel behind her and stood perfectly still. Perhaps if she ignored him, the intruder would go elsewhere.

"A ditch is whiskey and water," a man's somber voice said.

She whirled around. Dane stood less than a foot away from her, holding her coat in the crook of his arm. "In the old days, a man would carry a bottle of whiskey in his saddlebag and when he needed a lift, he would take water from the nearest source to dilute it. Sometimes it was from a river or creek, but just as often the only source was a ditch. So the drink has become known as a ditch in some parts of the county."

"You didn't have to come out here to tell me that," she whispered, willing her heart to stop racing.

"You left your coat inside," he said.

The coat fell to the ground as his hands settled on her waist. His eyes scanned her figure. "I've never seen you in a dress," he said. "Have you been hiding that figure beneath those baggy sweatshirts?"

He stepped closer, peering up at her.

"I didn't think my clothing mattered," she whispered, unable to hide the tremor in her voice.

Beneath the shawl, his hands slid up her ribs, his thumbs resting against the swell of her breasts. "You're right. Your clothing doesn't matter because you're a striking woman no matter what you wear. But tonight you look especially stunning."

Her heart thudded against her ribs and she was sure he could feel it beneath his palms. She raised her arms, allowing them to settle on his shoulders. "Thank you. The way you were ignoring me, I didn't think you even knew I was at the table."

He frowned. "I knew you were there, but each time I looked your way, you were staring at the dancers. You were ignoring me."

"I was not!"

His thumbs moved against the fullness of her breasts and she felt her nipples harden. "Why didn't you ask me to dance?"

"I wasn't sure you would accept," he replied. "You've avoided me since I told you that you could stay the full six months. I thought, perhaps you had what you wanted. I was trying to leave you alone and let you have your way."

"You're always so busy," she said. "I don't want to complicate...Dane, I came here to work, not get involved."

"We're not involved...but the idea is tempting."

"What would be the use of hurting each other?" she asked. "I think you could hurt me...if I let you."

"I would never deliberately hurt you, Abbie. It's been a long time since a woman affected me the way you do. Abbie, I've wanted to hold you every time I saw you, but I knew I couldn't, not in front of the others."

She caressed his smooth-shaven face, tracing the broad cheekbones to the edge of his nose and down to his mouth, stopping at the middle of his upper lip. "And I've wanted to touch you, so very much . . . especially when I have to sit beside you at mealtimes and you're only inches away. But you act as if I'm not there. When you come to the lambing tents and talk to me about the lambs, you stare through me until I could scream. You're very good at keeping the discussion strictly business."

She traced the line from his lips to the slight cleft in his chin and along his jaw to the side of his neck where her hands came to rest. "I have this terribly compulsive desire to touch you . . . and tonight, here in the darkness where no one can see us . . . I can. Am I crazy to feel this way?"

"If you're crazy, so am I. But touching is not nearly enough," Dane said as his mouth claimed hers.

Abbie arched against him, her breasts against his chest, her thighs against his thighs. She felt his response, and knowing the effect she had on him filled her with excitement.

Her mouth opened under the pressure of his. Slowly, his tongue tested her willingness to let him explore. He began to kiss her face, touching sensitive spots with his tongue along the way to her ear, then down her neck to her throat.

Her head fell back and he untied the points of the shawl, allowing it to float to the ground. As his warm lips found the first hint of cleavage, she moaned aloud. His fingers opened two of the buttons on her chambray blouse and spread the material aside. The edge of a low-cut lacy bra hindered his questing mouth. Abbie slid her fingers between his mouth and her body.

"Abbie, don't stop me," Dane murmured, his voice ragged as he straightened.

She pulled his face close to hers again, distracting him from her breasts. If he touched them again, she would surely scream out her own need. His kisses had ignited trails of fire in her body.

"Kiss me again," she whispered. "Please." He complied, massaging her mouth and building the passion between them to a dangerous level once more.

Suddenly he stopped, holding her snugly against him until their breathing slowed. "You must be freezing," he said, reaching for her coat and the shawl lying on the ground. "Better put these on." He draped the shawl around her shoulders before helping her into the coat.

He smiled. "You smell wonderful. I like your fragrance."

She laughed. "It's probably a little cologne mixed with sheep shed number five. I didn't have time to shower," she said as she rebuttoned her blouse.

"Then we have something else in common. We both smell like sheep. It's a little like eating onions, I guess." He continued to hold her in his arms. "Some women hate the smell of livestock."

"It's not always romantic," she said, "but I don't notice a thing wrong with the way you smell tonight." She pulled away. "We'll have to accept each other just the way we are."

"Shall we go back inside?" he asked, draping his arm around her shoulders.

"Yes," she agreed, leaning against him in the darkness. "And this time, please ask me to dance."

They dropped off their coats at the table and went directly to the dance floor, unaware of the change in musical numbers or the curious glances being sent their way. Only when the band took another break, did they return to the table.

"Hungry?" he asked.

She nodded. "I could eat a horse!"

"That's the second one this week," he said as they sat in vacant chairs and he motioned to the waitress. "The menu is limited," he warned. "Hamburgers and chicken. They both come with fries and dill pickle."

She smiled at him. "The chicken sounds fine."

"Two orders of chicken," he said to the frowning waitress. His arm was resting on the back of her chair, his fingers stroking her upper arm lightly through the fabric of her blouse.

The musicians resumed playing, the others in the Grasten party abandoned the table as the food Dane had ordered arrived. Abbie and Dane ate in silence, enjoying the privacy of the moment.

"Delicious," she said, wiping her lips with a paper napkin and turning to him. "Will you be deducting the cost of dinner and the drinks from our paychecks?"

"Considering I already wasted a double hamburger order earlier in the evening, maybe I should," he said.

"I was just joking," she replied, smiling at him. "Please don't take my remark seriously. The others would never forgive me for putting such ideas into your head. And how could you hold me responsible for food you didn't eat?"

"My order had just arrived when Wilma came back to the table," he explained. "She said you looked as if you might burst into tears. I couldn't let you stay outside, alone and upset. I told the others to toss a coin for my dinner. I thought that someone had done or said something to hurt you. I was ready to tear the culprit apart."

"You were the last person I expected to see, but I'm glad you came. I was upset, but it wasn't really your fault. I read too much into people's actions sometimes. I let my emotions get out of hand. Now, eat your dinner and let's forget what's happened.''

"Not everything," he promised, his gaze lingering on her lips. He was about to say more but the others in the party returned to the table, and the intimate mood evaporated in the midst of the noisy conversations around them.

An hour later, Dane rose from his chair.

"Morning comes pretty early. Moses," he said, turning to his foreman, "can I hitch a ride back with you? I came with Oscar and Trudy but they want to take a run into Sheridan. I had planned to get a ride with Buck, but he and Andy have found themselves two sisters and aren't ready to leave, so... I'm on foot.''

"Sure, boss, but four in the cab will be a little snug.''

"We'll manage, if Abbie and Wilma don't mind,'' Dane said.

In the truck cab, Abbie found herself perched between Dane's legs while Wilma snuggled close to Moses. Gradually the lights from the Outfitters' Den faded away and darkness engulfed them.

Dane's arms slid around her and she settled against him. His arms tightened slightly. The late hour and a pleasant physical exhaustion brought a cloak of peace surrounding her. She rested her head against his chest and closed her eyes. Within seconds, she was asleep.

Moses glanced at Abbie and then up at Dane. "You be careful with her, boss.''

"Why?'' Dane asked, curious.

"She's different,'' Moses said.

"Yes,'' Wilma chimed in. "She's a cut above most women.''

Dane's mouth tightened. The warnings haunted him for several miles. Abbie's auburn curls tickled his chin and he shifted her head to one side. She stayed asleep, but her hands came to rest on his folded forearms. The tough assertive woman had disappeared. In her place was a woman he wanted to know better, not only to share his business expertise with, but to take to the high country and show her his world. As he recalled the embrace they had shared earlier in the evening, his body reacted immediately. Yes, he admitted, he wanted to make love to this woman, to bring her into his life and give her reasons to stay.

But she had arrived less than a week earlier. They had had angry words more than once. It was unrealistic to jump so far ahead, all because of a few shared kisses in the darkness.

Abbie had her future all plotted out while his was beginning to flounder on insecure financial underpinnings. She was free as a bird in flight while he was tied to his family. She could walk away at any time but he had to stay until the sheep ranch was either his or sold out from under him by his own sisters and brothers.

Memories of the feelings of his mouth on the warm skin between her breasts came to him, memories of his hands on her slender waist, her hands pressing against his ribs. *Damn it,* he thought, *what makes this woman different? Don't they all have breasts and warm skin, mouths that respond, bodies that open and give satisfaction?*

Logic said yes, but the woman he held in his arms made a shambles of his ability to be rational. The moment she had stepped from her motor home onto his property, fate had taken over. Now an invisible thread was drawing them closer, to an intimacy that had all the potential of either bonding them together forever or tearing them apart. He needed time to consider the consequences of his own actions. She had everything, while he had nothing concrete to offer her. And his one brush with marriage had been a total disaster.

Good Lord, how could he be thinking of his failed marriage and comparing Abbie to Lillian when he had only known her a week, only kissed her twice?

It would be better to back off and give each of them time, distance. But it would be impossible to avoid her in the days to come. Three times a day she sat next to him. Their fingers would touch when she passed serving bowls.... He touched the top of her head with his mouth to keep from laughing aloud. Never before had the thought of passing bowls of food brought him sensual pleasure.

He lowered his voice. "Why would I hurt her?"

"You and Lil had troubles from the start," Moses said.

"And you were mean as hell to Lil sometimes," Wilma added.

"Abbie isn't Lil and you're both jumping to conclusions," Dane said. "If Abbie and I happen to get along while she's here, that's our business."

"Well," Wilma said, turning to look him in the eye, "if you do anything to hurt Abbie, you'll have Moses and me to answer to. And don't you forget it, boss or no boss."

"Yes, ma'am," Dane murmured.

CHAPTER NINE

No ONE HAD TIME for personal matters in the next few days.

"The bucks must have gotten their second wind five months ago," Moses commented during breakfast four days later.

A sheep tender could check the drop pens, find them without activity and return fifteen minutes later to see two or three lambs on the ground.

Ewes and their offspring were moved through the jugs quickly, often with only hours to allow the bonding to take place. Some hearty lambs had their umbilical cords trimmed and iodined outside and never saw the inside of the lambing tents. The lambs in the bum pen grew in number. The weather turned cold and nasty but without snow, the worst being a chilling wind that showed no sign of weakening. The heavy gray sky took its toll on the workers' spirits.

"It can't last," Dane warned. Several of the workers glanced out the kitchen windows at the breaking dawn, revealing itself in an eerie rose glow to the east as a rising sun teased the cloud cover but couldn't break through. "It will either clear up or we could have a real killer storm."

Abbie turned to him. "What is a *real killer* kind of storm?"

His harsh expression softened as he admired the sincerity reflected in her features. "Several inches of snow in a few hours, with the wind blowing it into drifts that can bury the lambs. If you're out alone and the snow gets heavy, for God's sake come tell me. We can move some of them to the burned-out lambing shed for shelter. That's why we built it there."

"Why haven't you repaired it?" Windy asked.

The change in Dane's expression sent a chill through Abbie. Still she had been wondering the same thing.

"I've been thinking about just that," Dane said, surprising several of the workers. "The time has come to start doing the repairs. When I went to town yesterday, I bought the materials." He surveyed the men at the table. "They'll be delivered Monday. It will mean extra work for you all, but extra pay as well. See me later if you'd like to help. Otherwise, I'll have to hire some outsiders. I want to finish the project in two weeks, so we can use it when the quarter Finns begin to lamb next month."

Abbie raised her hand.

Dane frowned at her. "Yes?"

"I used to help my uncle on our farm when I was a kid," she said. "I know quite a bit about carpentry. I've built two of the looms I have stored down in Salt Lake City. I'd be glad to help."

Dane looked away. "We'll see. The weather is our first concern now."

His rebuff stung. He had pierced her tough emotional armor with arrows of passion, but apparently he had no desire to pursue what had started the night of the dance. She certainly wasn't going to be the one to bring it to his attention. If he was that forgetful, she'd let it be.

She left the table and stopped in the service porch to pull on her coveralls, before going out to the main porch.

Pausing, she stretched, enjoying the rush of energy surging through her body. The time on the ranch had conditioned her body to a new level of healthiness. The nutritious food had added a few pounds, but in the form of smooth muscles. She felt better than she ever had in her life.

Yanking her water-proof boots over her oxfords, she stood up and scanned the area, looking for a ride to the lambing tents.

"Need a lift?" Dane asked, coming down the steps.

"I'm going, too," Moses said, shaking his keys at her.

"Thanks, Moses," Abbie replied, grateful of his rescue. "I'll go with you." She was settled in the truck cab before Moses and Dane had finished their conversation. She sank into the seat and closed her eyes, trying to keep her thoughts away from the man who haunted her day and night.

The door on the driver's side opened and she felt the seat sink under Moses's weight. For a wiry man whose body was almost gaunt, Moses felt unusually heavy.

Her eyes shot opened as Dane stuck the key in the ignition.

"Where's Moses?" she exclaimed. "Moses is supposed to be the driver." Her hand reached for the door handle.

Dane gunned the engine and the tires spun on the icy driveway, regaining their traction when he lifted his foot from the accelerator and they left the yard. "Stay put, Hardesty. We'll be there in a few minutes."

Abbie stared at the road ahead, trying to ignore his sidelong glances.

"What's happened between us, Abbie?" he asked, his voice soft and warm in the privacy of the cab.

"Nothing," she replied grimly.

He took a deep breath and exhaled slowly. "I know, and that's the trouble, isn't it?"

"It's no trouble. We're busy. There's lots of work to do. I've been here almost two weeks. I hope you're satisfied with my performance so far. If you regret the few times . . . we let the situation get out of hand, I'm sorry. Tomorrow is my day off and I'll be in my motor home weaving, so I won't be in your way. I'm glad you've decided to rebuild the lambing shed. I know it will be put to good use. Well," she concluded, her hand grasping the door handle again, "we're here and there's a lot of work to do. Thanks for the lift." The instant the truck rolled to a stop, she was out and gone.

The day passed quickly. Abbie hardly had time to catch her breath. She volunteered to stay over the noon hour while the others ate. When they returned, she drove to the house and had a quick bite with Trudy. The sandwich she tried to eat turned to sawdust in her mouth.

Snow began to fall at dusk, and once again Abbie volunteered to eat late. "I'll stay until the night lambers come on," she said, avoiding Dane's menacing stare. "I'm off tomorrow," she added, "so a few more hours now won't bother me."

Her co-workers left her alone with the ewes and lambs and her thoughts. As she became engrossed in the work, she pushed Dane from her mind and concentrated on her plans for her day off. Her first goal was to finish the small tapestry on the loom. It was ugly, clearly the ugliest work she had ever done, but the design had been suggested by a client whose sense of color and design was sadly lacking, although her bank account was full.

Abbie smiled to herself, wondering if perhaps she might manage to forget to sign the piece. As she finished her work, Windy and Blackie arrived.

"See you, boys," she called, waving to them as she ran through the darkness to the truck. The snow was falling more heavily but seemed to be melting as quickly as it settled on the countryside.

THE UGLY TAPESTRY was finished and removed from the loom in midafternoon. Now, with several hours left of her day off, Abbie could begin to prepare a very special tapestry.

The cartoon had been modified several times. Once she had become so frustrated that she had wadded the graph paper into a ball and thrown it across the room, but in the end she had retrieved the paper and copied the sketch.

This tapestry would become the perfect memento of her stay at the Grasten Sweetwater Livestock Company. In the foreground was the focal scene; the man who ran the operation with an iron fist and his trusty blue pickup truck, done in subtle tones to allow the viewer to draw his or her own conclusions as to the man's physical appearance. By his side were the dogs who had sheep tending in their genes. In the distance the beautiful two-story house stood regally among the trees. Off to the left and beyond the house she had added a tiny depiction of the lambing shed with a scattering of white dots to represent the sheep she imagined to be there.

As she selected the yarns she would use, Abbie allowed her thoughts to return to the previous Sunday evening, when everything had seemed so right, when Dane's kisses had held such promise.

Some of the colors she needed were not in her supply bags. She dumped the sacks of skeins and scrap balls onto the bed and searched through them. Three special shades of blue for the sky were nowhere to be found.

Could she had left some of her yarn behind in Salt Lake, stored away by mistake?

She straightened, rubbing the small of her back as she tried to recall if she had ever had such shades. If not, she could always make them. It would take her a few weeks to work the tapestry up to the point where the sky came into the weaving. By then, the weather would be spring-like and warm enough to bring out her pots and try some dyeing outside.

The dinner bell rang, and she ran to the kitchen door and found Trudy. "I'm in the middle of something," she said. "I made some soup. I'll finish it while I clean up from my weaving. Give everyone my excuses." She hurried back to the motor home as the trucks rolled to a stop about fifty feet from her door.

She peeked out the window. Dane was the first person she spotted. He turned once and looked toward the motor home. Inside, she drew back from the window.

He stared at the motor home for several seconds before turning away, his head and shoulders hunched against the wind that was blowing lacy riffles of snow across the yard.

After he disappeared into the house, she slumped into the bench seat of the eating area. She was hiding from him; there was no other excuse for her actions. She was hiding from a man whose inner strength and character had gradually revealed itself as she worked with him day by day, hiding from a man who had grown more attractive with each passing hour. Had she proved the adage that handsomeness was in the eyes of the beholder? Each time she looked at him, she longed to do nothing else.

She was also hiding from a man who didn't want to be bothered with her, and hiding from the discomfort of having to sit by his side three times a day, pretending to be indifferent.

Even though she was probably just infatuated, the pain of Dane's passive rejection had left a wound in her heart as difficult to heal as the spurning by a first love. Could this be love? No. Love would be wonderful, reciprocal, enthralling, tender.... If this was the beginning of love, it must be ended immediately. She had no time for loving a man like the complex Dane Grasten.

THE NEXT MORNING, Abbie awoke, confused by something she couldn't identify. At first she thought it was the silence of the subfreezing night. When her sleep-drugged mind cleared, she heard the wind. Its force shook the usually stable motor home, rocking it gently from side to side.

Crawling from bed, she peeked out the window above the sink but all she saw was white. In place of the normal peace of a settled snowfall was the unearthly glow of a half moon unable to cast its light on the ground. She squinted out the window, shaking her head. The snow wasn't falling, it was blowing horizontally.

Abbie ran to the door to open it and was shocked by the frigid blast of wind that blew snow into the vehicle. The door dragged on the snow outside, and Abbie stared down in disbelief. She hadn't expected the snow level to be higher than the bottom of the door. The door was at least two feet above the ground, and all the exterior steps to the ground were buried.

She tugged the door shut again. Glancing toward the house through the blizzard, she searched for a lighted window. If the "killer storm" had hit, wouldn't everyone be up and about? Why hadn't someone come knocking on her door? Surely they knew she was willing to help. Perhaps Dane had already gone to the lambing area. When she scampered into the camper's driving seat to see outside, a heavy blanket of snow on the windshield obscured her view.

Something was wrong. The insulating blanket of snow had blocked all the normal sounds of life on the ranch. Images of the newborn flashed before her eyes. Her lambs...her bum lambs without mothers to protect them from this harsh storm...the ewes who might be lambing in the drop pens, their newborns out of sight in the deep snow...

As she raced into her clothes, her thoughts centered on Dane. First she would make sure he was up and outside, then she would help him however she could.

Grabbing a pair of insulated coveralls, Abbie stepped into them, zipped them up and rushed out the door. Unsure of her footing, she fell to her knees in the snow.

As she got up, she realized the snow was deeper than she had first thought. It came above her knees, making normal walking impossible. Picking up her feet, she stepped high and worked her way through the drifts toward the house. Every room in the house was dark. Dane's blue truck was only a mound of snow where he had parked it the evening before. Why wasn't he up? Panic sent a burst of adrenaline pumping through her.

Because of the round-the-clock activity at lambing time, the door was usually unlocked, and now, in the early hours of predawn, she stomped her boots and entered the kitchen.

Blackie and Windy were on night duty. Why hadn't they sounded the alarm? She turned on the kitchen light and ran across the room into the darkened hallway.

Some inner voice told her Dane's bedroom was on the first floor. Not wanting to cause a false alarm, she began working her way down the hallway. The first door led to a large room with paneled walls, obviously a den. When she opened the next door and turned on the light, her eyes widened. The pattern of tumbling baby blocks on the pastel blue wallpaper denoted its unfulfilled purpose. A twin bed and matching dresser were the only pieces of furniture in the room.

With no time to satisfy her curiosity, she closed the door and hurried to the end of the hallway. Only one door remained.

Abbie threw the door open and turned on the light. Her eyes sought the bed. Dane lay on his back, his bare arm thrown across the pillow lying on the unused side of the king-size oak bed. She ran to the bed and sat down on its edge.

For a few seconds, time stopped as she stared at him. His blond hair curled around his ears, softening the harsh planes of his face, now placid in deep sleep. His mouth was relaxed, bringing a fullness to his lips that gave them a look of sensuality. He was beautiful...no, handsome and rugged...yet beautiful, too. Her eyes roamed across his naked shoulders to settle a few inches down his sternum. A scattering of curls covered the flat portion of his chest. Her gaze was drawn downward, but the comforter was twisted around his waist.

The urgency of the reason for bursting into his bedroom brought Abbie's sensual meanderings to an abrupt halt. She touched his hand gently, not wanting to startle him. Still asleep, his fingers reached out and snared hers. She tried to pull free.

"Dane," she whispered, "wake up...please."

He mumbled and his other hand found her waist. His brows furrowed as he fingered the coarse fabric of her coveralls. When his eyes opened, his puzzled expression made her smile.

"Abbie?" He relaxed into his pillow, his sleepy gaze roaming her face as he gradually awakened. "I've dreamed about you coming to me, but not dressed like this."

Suddenly he sat up, sensing that parts of his fantasy puzzle didn't fit. The bed covers fell to his hips. His attention was glued to her face. "What's wrong? Why are you here?"

"Snow," she whispered.

"Snow? Where?"

"Everywhere," she gasped. "It's so deep, I . . . could hardly make it . . . to the house. Oh, Dane." Her fingers tightened on his hands and she began to tremble. "It's terrible . . . so deep!"

He pulled her closer. "You mean . . . outside?" he said sleepily.

"Yes," she replied, "I don't understand why Windy didn't come and get you. Oh, Dane, it must have been falling heavily for hours. Your truck! I don't know how you'll be able to drive it. The snow is past my knees," she said pointing to the thin white coating still clinging to her coveralls.

He released her hands and one long muscular leg snaked out from the covers as he began to rise. "The lambs—they'll die if we don't get them to shelter. My God!"

She backed away, staring at his nakedness as he left the bed. Dane ignored the impropriety of her presence. As he reached for his underwear, he waved a hand to her.

"Wake the others," he directed. "They're upstairs. Hurry!"

She ran out the door as he reached for his jeans. By the time she returned from banging on everyone's door and shouting the alarm, he was in the kitchen, one foot propped on a chair as he tied the leather laces of a pair of Sorel boots.

"Let's go," Dane said, motioning for her to follow. On the porch, he stopped abruptly, unable to absorb the depth of the snow on the ground. "Oh, no," he murmured, shaking his head slowly from side to side as he evaluated the situation. The first rays of true sunshine appeared in the east, signaling the end of the storm.

Abbie agonized for him as he stood stock-still, his features grim in the shadowed light from the kitchen. She moved closer and reached for his hand to stop the clenching and unclenching of his fist. His fingers closed in a vise grip around hers as he began to work his way down the buried steps, pulling her along behind him.

"The Jeep has a plow in the front," he said. "We'll break trail for the others."

They were out of breath by the time they reached the old four-wheel-drive Jeep and began to brush the snow off the hood and windshield. He climbed inside and started the engine. When she joined him, he shifted into low gear and began to rock the vehicle back and forth to allow him space to use the plow.

The others were on the porch. Moses waved his acknowledgment of Dane's strategy. As the Jeep began to shovel the snow aside and slowly make progress toward the road, the others readied their vehicles for travel.

The going was agonizingly slow, with Dane muttering expletives under his breath several times when the Jeep became stuck. An hour had passed when they arrived at the lambing tents.

"Oh, God!" Dane groaned as he and Abbie climbed out of the Jeep and surveyed the area.

"I can't see the lambs!" Abbie cried. "Where are the lambs? My bums! Are they all right?" She ran and stumbled to where she thought the pen should be, but the drifts had covered the top rails and she lost her bearings.

Dane helped her to her feet. "Where the hell are the two night lambers? They had better have a damn good explanation." He trudged his way toward the hospital tent, its sides visible for a few feet beneath the canvas roof, where the men working the night shift often gathered.

Inside, Dane stopped short and Abbie ran into his rigid body. She sensed his rage when she touched his arm. When she peered around his side and spotted the two sleeping men, she understood his anger. An empty whiskey bottle lay on its side near the first jug. Windy was curled up on his side in a jug filled with straw bales, snoring peacefully. Blackie Swensen had propped himself up against the gate of a jug containing a ewe and twins. One curious lamb was sniffing at the man's knitted cap.

The room shook with Dane's thundering voice. Blackie jerked awake and spied the sheepman standing over him.

"Hi, boss," he slurred. "Up early, ain'tcha?" His head fell forward again. Windy didn't move. Dane kicked at Blackie's leg and the man stirred again.

"You're both fired," Dane shouted. "You have an hour to get off the place." He kicked Blackie's rump. "Take your drunken friend with you and don't ever set foot on this property again, or I'll sue you both for every single one of the lambs I've lost. Now get out!"

He stomped out of the tent. The other employees were standing near their trucks, bewildered by the sight surrounding them.

Moses took charge. "Get the shovels and dig out the lambs, and be careful. They could be anywhere."

For the first time Abbie realized Wilma and Trudy were there, willing to work side by side with the men to find the buried lambs. Moses passed out broad shovels and several sheep hooks. The workers paired off and began walking carefully, feeling with their boots as they went. Ewes were nuzzling the snow nearby and the workers started their work in the logical places first.

Abbie watched as Trudy motioned to a particular spot and Wilma searched the ground, finally bringing up a struggling lamb. But Oscar and Buck retrieved a dead lamb several feet away and the extent of the tragedy began to register on Abbie.

"My bums," Abbie mumbled. "Where is the bum pen?" she searched for the pink flag she had hung on the gate post a few days earlier. Never would she have thought the flag could point to such devastation. When she finally had it in sight, she tried to run to it, but her speed was slowed to an snail's pace. After what seemed like a lifetime, she reached the gate and pried it open.

She dropped to her knees and began to dig with her hands, making a tunnel into the shelter area of the pen. Tucked into the corner at one end, up against several bales of hay, she spotted eight lambs huddled together. She screamed for help.

"Take them," she cried, carefully passing each lamb to Wilma who in turn passed it to the next pair of waiting hands. Seven lambs were rescued, but as she reached for the eighth one, it didn't respond. She cradled the dead lamb in her arms and she stood and handed it to Wilma.

Wilma confirmed its condition and tossed it into the snow.

Abbie had no time to react to the harshness of Wilma's action as she mentally counted the lambs she had cared for just two days earlier.

"I had fourteen on Thursday," she said.

"I added two yesterday," Wilma said. "Let's find them."

The three women began searching the area for the other lambs. Trudy found two near the feeder, frozen. Shaking her head in sorrow, she dropped them near the first carcass.

"I'll find the others," Abbie, cried, dropping to her knees again and clawing into the drift near the other end of the shelter. Panic set in as she fought the snow with her mittens, using them as twin shovels until they became so packed with snow they were useless. She tore the mittens off and threw them behind her, without wasting more than a few seconds, crouched on her knees in the snow and began to scrape again with her bare hands.

A clump of impacted snow fell to the ground, exposing a small cavern in the shelter. "I've found them," she called. "They're all here together." She dug out the opening until she could push herself inside. In the dim interior, she refused to accept what lay a few inches from her knees.

Numbly, she handed out five lifeless bodies. Hands relieved her of her burden. She clutched the sixth dead lamb to her chest and scooted out the opening.

Dane took the carcass from her and handed it to Trudy who added it to the growing pile of dead lambs.

Abbie could no longer hold back the tears she had suppressed for hours. Unleashed now, they gushed down her cheeks. "Why?" she sobbed. "Why did they have to die? I fed them and took such good care of them, and now most of them are dead. They were my bums and I should have checked on them. If I'd only. . ." She gazed up at Dane, searching for an answer that made sense out of the devastation surrounding her. "Why?"

"Oh, Abbie," he whispered, pulling her into his arms, "there's never an answer for something like this. Please don't cry, please." The tighter he held her, the harder she cried.

"Honey, don't. . .please. . .oh, hell, cry your heart out, and cry for me, too," he murmured against her forehead, holding her until there were no tears left to shed.

When she had regained a semblance of composure, Abbie pulled away and returned to the task at hand, working mechanically while Dane coordinated their search.

As the day progressed, the snow began to melt. The bright sunshine made a mockery of their work, as snowbanks caved in from the heat. Dinner was a brief somber break for sandwiches and thermoses of soup, then they continued their search.

By late afternoon, Dane was able to estimate the damage. Just under half the new lamb crop had been lost, along with fifteen ewes who had lain down on the ground to give birth and hadn't been able to get up again.

As Abbie's weary body gave in to a few minutes of rest, she watched the others working nearby. Such dedication to the land and livestock, and for what? To be wiped out by two drunken irresponsible men and a freak storm?

Dane came to her side. "Why don't you call it a day, Abbie? You've been here since before dawn. Go home and rest."

She looked at him. "So have you."

He laid a hand on her shoulder and turned her in the direction of his blue truck, then handed her his keys. "Drive home. I'll ride back with someone. You're about to drop. Go. I'm the boss, and I insist."

She walked away, the droop of her shoulders tugging at his heart. "Drive carefully," he murmured, as the truck disappeared behind a six-foot snowdrift.

Two hours later, he called a halt to the work. "We can't do any more good today. We'll tackle the upper pasture tomorrow and see how the earlier lambs have faired. What's done is done. They're older and stronger. Perhaps they've found shelter in the willows." He turned to Wilma and Moses. "If you two will stay here until ten, I'll come relieve you. Oscar, you and Buck, set your alarms for two in the morning and take my place. I'll call the employment office tomorrow and try to find replacements for those two derelicts. Anyone see them leave?"

Andy nodded. "They were working their way to the Sweetwater Road two hours after you found them. With the road the way it is, they'll have a long walk ahead of them."

"I don't give a damn," Dane replied through clenched jaws. "Can I hitch a ride with you, Andy?"

Two other workers climbed into the back of the truck, and soon they were creeping back toward the main house. As they neared the burned-out lambing shed, he spotted his blue truck.

Damn Abbie, he thought, *she must have ignored my orders.* "Let me off, Andy."

"Sure. Is Abbie inside, boss?"

Dane nodded. "I'll get her and drive the truck back to the house. She was pretty upset by all this."

He hopped from the vehicle and followed the tracks of the blue truck to where Abbie had parked it. Signs of the rear tires spinning were easy to read in the snow and ice.

She was nowhere in sight. Cautiously, he pushed open the door of the giant shed.

"Abbie?" he called, but no one answered.

He began to search for her, glancing into every jug along the aisles on his left, then rerouting his footsteps to the other side of the shed to check out the larger pens he'd designed for the ewes to deliver, his maternity pens.

As he searched for Abbie, he recalled how his former wife had ridiculed the design. She had accused him of caring more for his pregnant sheep than for her. Not until the night of her arsonist act, had he learned of her own pregnancy and how much she had despised her condition.

He had suggested the floor plan to his father shortly after returning from college in Idaho. His father had agreed that the time was right for modernizing the lambing facilities.

The pens could be disassembled after lambing so the building was open and available for the shearing, which took place after lambing and before moving the animals to the higher range for summer grazing. In the coldest weather, the building could be heated with three double-barreled oil-drum stoves and used for mechanical repairs of the farm equipment. It had been designed for multipurpose use and was seldom empty for long throughout the year... until the fire.

A few years later, Dane and his father had added thirty more feet at one end for an office and a hospital wing. The exterior was made of logs slabbed on three sides, with insulation for winter and large windows for ventilation in warmer weather.

Dane had designed and installed a gravity flow watering system that provided fresh water to each jug. He was especially pleased with that improvement because it replaced the tedious task of hauling water to the tents and pens at the old facility, a job that had been his since his youth. One spring day, a few months after his twelfth birthday, he had promised himself that his own sons would never have to haul water. Yet now he had neither a working gravity system, nor sons to appreciate his plan.

The building had been a showcase of progressive sheep-raising technology and they had thrown a barbecue the summer it was completed, inviting all their neighbors and friends. Ironically, he had met Lillian Rogers at that same celebration.

Their stormy courtship had lasted a year. One summer day when she stirred his hormones to the explosion point, he had asked her to marry him. Their marriage had been as stormy as their courtship, with a treadmill of fights and arguments that would end in passionate reconciliations filled with carnal satisfaction and promises to try again. The promises had ended in the ashes of the fire deliberately set by Lil, ashes from the charred beams that now stood around him on three sides, ashes long since mixed with the dirt from the earthen floor of the building.

Dane dismissed the memories. Abbie was his concern now. Abigail Hardesty, whose care of the sheep and dedication to the bums had remained constant from the first hours they had worked together, whose sense of responsibility had brought her to him in the darkness in his bedroom, where he had spent many a night lying awake thinking about her.

"Abbie?" He stepped over a charred fallen rafter and into the burned-out section of the shed. Rays of the late afternoon sun cast an exotic pattern of light and shadows on the snow-covered floor, hiding portions of the side sections in darkness. He peered into the distant corners of the building. "Abbie. Please, Abbie, answer me. I need to know you're safe. Abbie?"

He caught a movement to his left and saw her straighten up from her perch on the edge of a jug.

"Dane?"

"Yes, Abbie, I've come for you."

CHAPTER TEN

ABBIE RAN TOWARD Dane and he met her halfway, sweeping her into his arms as she fell against him.

Surprised at the strength of her embrace, he savored the feel of her arms around his body as she buried her face against him. He massaged her trembling shoulders, yearning to find a way to ease her misery.

"Why, Dane? Why did it happen?" she asked, pulling away slightly. Before he could reply, she buried her face against his coveralls again.

"There's no answer, Abbie," he tried to explain. "We can only accept it and move on. It happens."

She jerked away and frowned up at him. "Don't you get angry? They're your sheep. Don't you want to rage and scream...and cry?"

"Of course, and yes, I've raged and shouted," he replied. "I haven't tried crying. Perhaps I should...would help?"

Her eyes were red and glistening with tears, her face red and blotchy. He still found her lovely.

"Abbie, this isn't the first time we've suffered a loss." He stared past her head to the shadows beyond. "It may very well be the worst, but it's not the first and it won't be the last. If you want to be in this business, you accept the hard times along with the good times. This is one of those hardships that tests our ability to

"But it's so unfair, so senseless," she cried. "Those poor little lambs couldn't do a thing to help themselves." Her features twisted in sorrow. "Was it fate that allowed some to live and some to die? My Aunt Minnie would have called it God's will, but I don't believe that."

"Good," he said, touching her flushed cheek with his hand. "I wouldn't want your faith tested and found wanting."

His comment made her smile, briefly. Her eyes soon filled with tears again.

"Abbie, please don't cry anymore," Dane murmured, brushing a stream of moisture from one cheek "Perhaps I've learned to compartmentalize the differe parts of this business. I thoroughly enjoy lambing ti but most of those cute little lambs are destined slaughter this fall. It's their fate. Those expensive chops people order in fancy restaurants have to from somewhere."

"That's a terrible thing to say," she murmure

"But true," he replied, his fingers trailing temple. "Don't think about what's happe something new and wonderful that will take off this day."

"What?" Abbie asked, searching his fe source of his own strength to cope with th

"This," he whispered as he drew her cl again. His hands gripped her cheeks as h her mouth to open to his kiss, but when hers she met him willingly. Fiery desir kiss deepened. Between them, her ha per of his coveralls and she lowered reach, then slid her arms inside a body.

"Oh, Dane, you make me forget." Her hands massaged his back through the flannel shirt.

"Then kiss me once more," he said, "and we'll forget together."

She raised her lips to his. He tried to bring her closer. Slowly he raised his mouth from hers, smiling as he gazed down at her enraptured face.

"We're tangled worse than a couple of octopuses," he said, chuckling in the stillness of the building. "Let's go home."

She nodded and withdrew her hands from inside his coveralls. He took her hand, leading her out of the shed and to the pickup.

"I got stuck," she admitted. "I didn't know how to use the four-wheel-drive gears. It was the final straw and..." Her eyes began to fill with tears again.

He gave her a boost into the cab. "We'll be out of here in no time." He went to the driver's side and climbed in, starting the engine as he turned to her. "Are you all right?" She nodded.

Rocking the vehicle back and forth a few times loosened the tires from their icy tracks and soon Dane and Abbie were in the front yard.

Through the lighted windows of the kitchen, the other workers were gathering around the table.

"Ready for supper?" he asked, turning off the ignition.

She shook her head. "I don't feel like joining the others tonight. I'd rather eat alone."

"Change into something comfortable and I'll bring you a tray."

She watched as he hurried to the back door of the house. Inside the motor home, she pulled down all the window shades before undressing. She slipped into a pair of mid-thigh-length white satin pajamas, and pulled on the green velour robe, tying the belt tightly around her waist.

A few minutes later, she heard a light knock on the door.

"Come in," she said, holding the door open.

Dane entered, carrying a large tray with two covered plates. As he set the tray down on the table, he turned to her. "I thought you might like some company while you ate."

"I would." She sat on the bench across from him.

He shed his leather coat. A short-sleeved yellow knit shirt had replaced his work shirt. Its style gave him a casual urban look that quickened her pulse.

"Your shirt is out of character," she said, as he sat down.

"So are the pajamas," he said.

She glanced down and found the front of her robe gaping. She tugged the sides of the robe together over her knees.

"Don't worry," he said, taking a bite of food. "I've seen women's knees before."

"But not mine," she replied.

"No, not yours, but they are as pretty as I knew they would be. Have I told you how lovely you are, Abbie?"

Some of the haunting grief faded from her eyes. "Once," she murmured, "that first night . . . outside."

"Yes," he replied, savoring the memory. "When you brought me the pup. He's doing fine."

"I know," she said. "I stop to see his mother and the puppies each morning before I come to breakfast. I'm glad something is turning out all right."

"Most clouds have silver linings, Abbie. Sometimes you just have to search a little harder to find them." He motioned to her untouched plate. "Now eat something."

She took a few bites, but her eyes were drawn back to his face. All she could think about was the wonder she had experienced in his arms.

When she took another bite, the food stuck in her throat. She looked up and found him staring at her. Recollections of their time in the burned-out building hung heavily between them.

"I'm not hungry," she whispered, rising from the bench. She glanced toward the rear of the motor home. "I want to lie down," she said.

"Then I'll leave," Dane said, standing up.

"No," she said softly. "Would you ... lie down with me?"

"Why, Abbie?"

"I want to be with you. You make me forget." She crawled onto the bed and turned to him. "There's no graceful way to get in. It's really quite spacious once you're inside."

He joined her on the bed. "And now?"

"Lie down," she said, offering him a pillow from the stack in one corner. She stretched out alongside him. Sweet prickles of desire ricocheted through her body when his hand came to rest on the flat of her stomach.

She rolled against him and her arm slid around his waist.

"This may not be such a wise thing to do," Dane said, his fingers tracing the satin edge of her robe.

"You don't want to be here?" she asked, looking up at him.

"Yes, but ... I don't want you to regret what might happen."

"I take full responsibility for what's happening," she said, touching the knit of his shirt. "I don't want to...think about...today." Reaching out, she switched off the lamp and turned the bedchamber into subdued shadows.

"Is the door locked?" he asked.

"No."

"Perhaps it should be," he suggested. "I wouldn't want anyone to stroll in on us." He left the bed.

When he returned to her side, she caressed his arm. "Hold me, Dane, I don't want to be alone tonight. I want to touch you and have you touch me." She drew one knee up and the green robe fell open.

The sensual movement was his undoing. His gaze swept her body. "Abbie," he murmured and his hand tugged on one end of the belt. When the belt fell away, his hand disappeared beneath the pajama top.

"Oh, God, Abbie," Dane groaned, pulling her closer, turning onto his back and supporting her body with his own. "I'm sorry you had to be part of this day. I wish I could have spared you."

She shook her head. "No, I was where I belonged, but..." Her voice broke and she buried her face against his shirt, moistening the material with her tears.

His arm tightened around her shoulders. "Please don't cry anymore. Just think about us, here in this quiet place, with nothing to disturb us." His hand began to move back and forth across her skin.

He watched the dilation of her dark pupils and became aware of her shallow breathing, and knew she was vulnerable. The only thing that mattered now was the promise that lay ahead. He wanted to love her, to share passion and fulfillment and knew she wanted the same. His fingers moved and she inhaled sharply.

The warmth of his hand ignited a flame. The day's events were erased, replaced with visions of intimacy with this special man under whose touch her body was coming alive.

Dane's hand move higher until his fingers met the swell of her breast. Fire raced across her skin as she waited, urging him on with the subtle movement of her body against his. Until this moment she had been unaware of the depth of her hunger, but now she knew her body's needs could be assuaged only by him.

He found her nipple, its own erection as rigid and ready as his own. Her breathing grew short and erratic.

"I can't just hold you, Abbie," he said. His head dipped to her throat, his mouth savoring its texture as his hand continued its exploration.

"I know," she replied, her hand caressing his cheek. "Give me something to remember that can't be taken away. Make love to me. Let's forget who we are for a few hours and just love each other." Her fingers traced the line of his jaw. "Share your strength with me, just this once. That's all I ask."

She touched his upper lip and he kissed her fingertip.

"Sit up," she suggested. When he did, she rose to her knees and tugged the shirt up and over his head. She dropped the shirt onto the bed and sat still, admiring his torso. He ran his fingers through his tousled hair and tried to smooth it.

He pushed the robe from her shoulders and reached for the buttons of her top. Motionless, she waited as he worked the four pearl buttons apart and slid the satin material from her body.

As his gaze roamed her breasts, admiring their fullness and symmetry, a sense of womanly pride filled her. She felt her nipples harden. She wanted him to take them in his mouth and taste them but couldn't bring herself to tell him so.

"Abbie, love," he whispered, his voice hoarse as he eased her back onto the bed. Her hands sought and held his head, guiding him as he touched one nipple lightly with his tongue, tracing a moist circle around the delicate rose areola, nipping at its crest, and finally taking it into his mouth and sucking gently.

In the twilight of the bedchamber, he finished undressing her. "I've wanted to be here with you each and every night since you came," Dane murmured. "I've imagined how you looked naked. I lay awake at night, unable to sleep, wanting to come to you, wondering if you might be awake, too. Would you have welcomed me or turned me away?"

Her answer was in her touch. She tugged at the top snap on his denim jeans, slowly undoing each fastener until she freed his body and tossed the jeans aside.

He groaned aloud as her hands grew bold and confident.

"I saw you this morning," she whispered. "When you left your bed. I watched you and...found myself..." She stopped in midsentence when he drew her close again, his hands memorizing each curve of her hips and thighs.

"Yes, love?"

"I wanted you to think of me as more than your intern."

"I have, from the first moment I saw you," he admitted.

She held her breath when his hand slid between her legs, but as his fingers sought and found the moist core of her, she arched against him until the tremor subsided.

"I want to touch you, too," she whispered. "Here." Her hand caressed his ribs, counting each one aloud.

"And here." Her lips touched his nipple, bathing it with the tiny, taste-sensitive tip of her tongue. "And here," she murmured, her mouth still close to his skin as she placed tantalizing little kisses on his stomach. Her curiosity moved to the trail of blond hair that grew down his chest, skipped across his navel to broaden and surround that special part of him, turgid and ready to take its rightful place in her body.

Lightly, she surrounded him, caressing him until he moaned and eased her hands from his body.

"I want to touch you, too, my darling Abbie," he said, "but touch you deeply, to show you how good it will be between us, to satisfy you, to feel your body beneath mine and have you move against me, to feel the heat of you surround me and..."

She laid her fingers against his mouth. "Don't tell me...show me," she whispered.

He paused, filled with wonder and admiration. Her body was perfect, her skin glistening in the glow of the lamp behind them, her auburn hair reflecting the fire he sensed within her, her green eyes shining with desire. Her breasts were full and responsive and he had savored them eagerly. His hand reached out to trace her rib cage downward to the rounded slope of her hip.

The flatness of her abdomen intrigued him and he rested the palm of one hand a few inches above her pubic bone, knowing that hidden beneath that bone was a womb he wanted to bathe with the life-giving fluid of his soul.

Slowly, he lowered himself to her and she arched to meet him, gliding his entry through the hot moist passageway to its destination. Before he had settled against her, she began to move, her hips pushing against him.

"Lie still, Abbie," he whispered.

"I can't," she murmured breathlessly, her body consumed with passion. "I want this to last forever but I can't help myself. It's happening too fast. Do you feel it, too?"

"Yes, love, yes," he assured her, "I feel it, too. Let it happen, sweetheart, let it happen." He began to move, his thrusts becoming stronger as the sensations grew, pulling from the depths of his body to surge out of control. Her body writhed beneath him, her hips meeting his in an age-old rhythm of lovers.

He slid his arms beneath her as she began to moan, her voice calling his name softly as a trembling took control and he felt her convulsions tighten around him. In his own ecstasy, he rolled her over to lie on top of him, his body driving into her with a more powerful force than he had ever experienced before, a force that had come surging from a secret hiding place, waiting for this special woman.

Out of nowhere she had come into his life, to lie with him now, giving herself to him freely. As the world passed then exploded inside him, he drew added satisfaction from knowing she had been his companion on the journey.

His breathing gradually settled. She stirred but didn't speak and he was glad. They had failed to prolong this act of making love, but he would try to keep the world away for a little longer now. He rolled onto his side, still holding her closely against him. Their mingled perspiration gradually changed to a chill. He felt behind him, found a fluffy comforter and pulled it over them.

Nothing would take her away from him, not for a while. He would hold her and protect her, shield her from the sadness of the day until her heart had time to heal. In a way, he was responsible for her grief. If he had sent her packing at the end of the third day, she would have been spared. But if he had sent her away, she wouldn't be in his arms now, her warm body lying against his, her hand resting on his chest.

Gently, he cushioned her head against his shoulder as he gave in to the exhaustion that settled over him, numbing him like the intoxication of a fine wine.

WHEN ABBIE AWOKE, her face was buried against Dane's shoulder, his face in peaceful repose inches away. Pleasurable images of the evening were followed immediately by the impact of what they had done.

She had committed the one act she had vowed she wouldn't. Making love to the man who held her future in his hands would surely become a factor in their relationship.

In spite of the explosive passion they had shared, she regretted their intimacy. Even the simple act of leaving the bed and dressing would be awkward. Worse would be getting him out of the motor home. Her heart began to race as she searched for solutions to a problem that should never have been created.

She began to ease away from him, but the draft that came rushing in beneath the comforter had him instantly awake. Her eyes were drawn to Dane's face and she found herself unable to look away. Would he have the same regrets when he saw her leaning over him? Unexpected tears burned her eyelids as his blue gaze met hers. She dropped her head back to the pillow.

"Oh, Dane, what have we done?" she whispered.

He raised himself on one elbow and his free hand came to rest between her breasts. Her body came alive under his touch, and her desire to withdraw disappeared. His hand moved upward to settle against her throat, his thumb on her chin while his fingers splayed across her cheek and ear and into her short hair.

"What have we done?" he said, repeating her own words. "We've made love. We've given pleasure to each other. We've pushed away the horrible reality of the day for a while." His lips brushed hers, lingering for a few seconds. "We've given to each other...and taken from each other, too, but without reserve or strings."

"You make it sound wonderful," she said.

"It was." He dropped to the pillow and drew her close again.

She gave into the pleasure of his embrace. "But it was wrong," she whispered.

"Wrong?" His voice hung heavily in the shadows of the bedchamber. "No, I don't think so." His lips brushed her forehead. He inhaled sharply. "God, Abbie, I've never wanted a woman as much as I wanted you tonight. We've know each other two weeks, yet I feel as though I've known you forever. I'm caught in a web." He nibbled her lower lip before kissing her fully on the mouth. "Have you been weaving me into your dreams?"

"I seduced you, didn't I?" she asked.

He chuckled. "I think so."

She pulled away and rolled onto her side, turning her back to him. When she felt his fingers caressing her skin, she knew it was the wrong move to have made.

"You have the smoothest skin I've ever touched on a woman," he said, laying a soft kiss on the wing of her shoulder.

"And have there been many women?" she asked.

"I'm thirty-eight years old, Abbie. Of course there have been women. I've never kept score."

She stiffened. "I've never kept score, either," she said, turning back to him.

He gazed down at her for a moment, his face a mask. "Are you on the pill?" he asked.

The bluntness of his question strengthened her defense. "Does it matter?" she asked.

He frowned. "Of course, it matters. I'm a responsible man. I want to know if there is any danger of . . ."

"Don't fret about such matters," she said grimly. "You're in no danger of becoming a father." She found no reason to elaborate.

"Good," he said, "neither of us would want to be bound together by a child conceived under these circumstances."

"Of course not," she said. "I have plans. You have this place. Any relationship we might have would be short-lived."

He dropped back to the pillow, pulling her with him. "Then let's enjoy it while we can. Tell me about your plans when you leave here. Where will you go?"

She toyed with the curls running down his stomach. "I don't know. I've been alone most of my adult life. But I'll know the place when I find it." She ran her finger back and forth across the narrow line. "And what about you? Moses told me you were married once. Why not again? Don't you want children?"

"At least I took the plunge once," he replied noncommittally. "What about you? Don't you want a family? A woman has more to be concerned about as she gets older than a man. Her biological clock begins to wind down sooner."

She lay in his arms, thinking about the parallels in their lives. They had each chosen to make their way through life alone, independent, yet here they lay together, sharing very personal feelings about their pasts.

"You're very quiet," he said, his hand brushing up and down on her arms. "What are you thinking about?"

"Families."

"Can you elaborate?"

She sighed. "My cousin Eileen and her husband, Duncan...they were always so happy, but they've had only eleven years together and the past several have been darkened by his illness. He has multiple sclerosis."

"Isn't eleven better than none?" he asked.

"I suppose," she replied. "What about your own marriage? How long did it last?"

"Two and a half years."

"Do you feel the same way about it? That two years were better than none?"

"Some marriages are destined to fail. Mine was one."

"Why?" she asked.

"We differed on so many things," he replied. "Lifestyles, responsibilities, wants versus needs, how to spend what little free time we had, whether it's best to spend or save, cooperating and helping each other...and lots of other differences."

"Why did you marry her if you had nothing in common?" she asked.

His gaze flickered over her features. "I guess you could say the only thing we really had in common was sex...and it was our final undoing."

"I don't understand."

"She became pregnant."

"But that should have been...wonderful...shouldn't it?"

"Not to a woman who didn't want children."

"But what...what happened to the baby? I had no idea you were a father. I haven't seen any photos of..."

"I have no photographs because I'm not a father." His hold on her arm tightened.

"What happened?" she asked.

"I'll tell you some other time," he replied, his hand suddenly dropping away.

"I'm sorry," she said, propping herself up on an elbow. "I guess it's never a good idea to talk about past lovers at a time like this." She touched his cheek, and his gaze swung toward hers. "When I first woke up, all I could think about was getting you out of here, but now...I want you to know I have no regrets."

"Nor I," he agreed. He buried his hand in her hair.

Slowly, her mouth came to his. This time, she initiated the kiss, wanting it to become proof of their restored passion. She sensed Dane's withdrawal. "What's wrong?" she asked.

He glanced at the clock nearby. "I should go," he said. "I promised Moses and Wilma I'd relieve them at ten at the lambing tents. There's still lots of cleanup that can be done. It's nine thirty-five already."

He slid from the comforter and off the bed. Abbie closed her eyes, listening to the rustling sounds of his dressing and wishing she could turn back the clock a few hours.

Suddenly he was kneeling on the bed and rolling her over. Her arms slid around his neck as his lips claimed hers.

The kiss roughened as his tongue plundered her mouth. She responded, and as the kiss deepened, her fingers ran through his blond hair. His mouth moved to her throat, and for an instant she wondered if he had changed his mind about leaving.

He eased himself away. "I'd give anything to stay here, but it wouldn't be fair to Wilma and Moses. At their ages, they need their rest. Think of me when I'm gone?"

She nodded and felt the unexpected burning of tears in her eyes. "Maybe."

She sat up, tucking the comforter around her breasts as she watched him put on his coat and walk toward the door. He paused, his hand on the knob, looking back at her. Then he was gone.

CHAPTER ELEVEN

MEMORIES OF THOSE passion-filled moments swept away the bitter taste of loneliness as Abbie relived the miracle of their union. But, when the scene had played to its end, she was left with the dismal reality of being alone again.

She sighed, giving in to the tears she had suppressed ever since his departure. She had accomplished her goal. The tragedy of the snowstorm and the loss of her lambs had been forgotten during their lovemaking. Drained by the day's events, she finally slept. When the alarm awoke her, Abbie dragged herself from under the covers and dressed. In spite of her limited sleep, no one could ever accuse her of not being conscientious about her assigned duties, she thought.

She made her way to the house for breakfast, speculating on what they would find in the light of a new day. Perhaps the older lambs had survived. Two weeks before the storm they and their mothers had been moved to three fields over the ridge in a small valley to the south of the lambing area.

As she slid into her seat, she noted Dane's chair was vacant.

Moses motioned to the empty chair at the head of the table. "The boss is still out. He relieved Wilma and me at ten and then stayed through the next shift. I was out early this morning. It's looks like a battlefield out there, with casualties everywhere. Ouch!" He jerked around toward Wilma who had flicked his neck with the dish towel.

"That's enough of that kind of talk at this table," Wilma said. "Here comes the boss now, so let's have more eating and less yakking."

Even while he was out of sight, Abbie sensed Dane's presence. When he entered the room several minutes later, she followed his movements until he dropped into his chair.

"Don't hold the meal on my account," he said.

Abbie felt his eyes on her before he looked away, but she sensed a change in his manner. *What did I expect? A breakfast kiss?*

"Stop!" Wilma cried, and gave a rapid-fire blessing of the food. "This motley crew needs all the divine intervention it can get today," she said. "Now you can eat, you heathens."

Moses took several pancakes, slathered each one with butter as he stacked them, then poured maple syrup on them. Abbie glanced at his plate, sure it could not hold another drop.

"Save a little for the rest of us," Buck complained, "and pass it around."

"Sure thing, no need to complain," Moses said, handing the glass container to Abbie. "How was it going, boss, when you left . . . ?" He stopped in midsentence when he caught sight of Dane's face. "Lord in heaven, boss, you look like death warmed over. Have you given up shaving again?" Moses laughed heartily and the others grinned obligingly.

Abbie passed the container to Dane. "Take it," she said, without looking at him directly. Their hands touched for an instant before she could release her hold.

"I've been up since yesterday morning before dawn," Dane said, accepting the pitcher of syrup from Abbie, irritated at her refusal to acknowledge him.

"You disappeared before dinner last night," Oscar said. "We thought you'd found a place to get some shut-eye."

Dane concentrated on his three pancakes. "I managed to catch an hour."

He glanced toward Abbie and caught her fidgeting in her chair. Was she afraid the others had somehow learned of their tryst? He certainly didn't believe in making love and then bragging about it the next morning.

He had spent the night thinking about her, and only one portion of their night together had bothered him: the scoring of lovers. He had been so confident that her passionate response had been unique. Perhaps it was only male vanity, but learning she had probably had many men had sent an icy chill through him.

Yet, now as he met her steady gaze, he knew something very special had passed between them in the privacy of the motor home. Her prior love life was a personal matter, just as his own was. They owed each other no explanations.

She rose from her chair, leaving most of the food untouched on her plate. "I'm walking to the lambing tents this morning."

"Something bothering you, honey?" Wilma asked.

Abbie shook her head. "No, I just need some time alone, to think about . . . things."

MOSES OFFERED HER A RIDE when she was within a quarter mile of her destination.

"We're to check on the older lambs," he said. "We'll drive. I have a good feeling about them. Then we'll meet the boss and help with the feeding."

"I thought he was going to bed," Abbie said.

"After he knows how all the stock fared from the storm."

"Can't he delegate the work?" she asked. "He acts as though he's indispensable. He's not Superman."

Moses scratched his forehead. "You're right there, but he feels the pressure of his promise to his folks and doesn't want to disappoint them. This lamb loss is going to make a deep dent in the profits forcast for this fall. His folks' retirement depends on the profits. He runs the place for them, ya' know?"

She clutched the door handle as they bounced over a rut buried in the snow. "He doesn't own this place? I assumed... Well, never mind what I thought."

"He runs twenty-six sections for his pa and ma and owns another ten sections outright for himself."

"That's a lot of land," she exclaimed.

"Not in these here parts," Moses replied. "It takes a lot of land to run the bands. When the summers are dry, that ol' sun can cook the grasses like a gas oven and make them bone-dry in weeks." Moses glanced her way. "You like it here, Abbie?"

"Very much."

"And the boss? How are you getting along with the boss? The two of you were acting kinda strange this morning, like you were sharing a secret that had turned sour. Want to talk about it?"

She shrugged. "Dane is... well, he isn't an easy man to know. He's very private sometimes."

"But you sort of like him, too?"

"I could."

"Hot doggie!"

"Moses," Abbie said, turning to him, irritated by his unabashed grin. "Don't make a mountain out of my answer. Dane and I...there's an attraction, but he said something that's bothered me. Have there been a lot of women in his life?"

"Do you want to know if he messes around?"

Her mouth tightened. "Does he?"

"There's that good-looking waitress in those skintight jeans at the Outfitters' Den. They were a pretty hot number a few years back," Moses said. Then he paused, making Abbie wonder if there had been too many women to count.

"That's all right," Abbie said, "his affairs are no concern of mine."

Moses shook his head. "I don't think any of them would qualify as a full-blown affair. Probably just casual dillydallying around when the moon is right. You know how a man can get when them hormones of his'n get stirred up. It ain't normal for a man to be alone all the time. Why are you asking?"

Abbie dropped her gaze. "He made a comment once, about not keeping score. I was wondering...if there have been lots of women since his first marriage. And if he has so many women panting after him, why hasn't he remarried?"

"Your tongue is sharp this morning, Abbie," Moses said, looking surprised by her cutting words. "It ain't like you. If you want to know about his love life, just ask him."

Her lips narrowed. "Is he still in love with his former wife? I asked him about it, but he didn't want to talk about her. Is that why he's never remarried?"

"Nah." Moses grinned. "He just hasn't found the right one to justify getting hitched up with. I doubt there was any genu-wine love between him and Lil, just a whole lot of fire and passion. You know how that goes."

I certainly do, Abbie thought. Moses concentrated on the icy trail of a road to the crest of the hill they had been climbing.

"How about you? Got a beau?"

She shook her head. "No. I lived with a man for a few years in Salt Lake but we broke up. That was over before I returned to college. He was the only man I've ever been involved with until..." Her voice quivered and she clamped her mouth shut.

Moses patted her clenched fist. "That's all right, Abbie. Just don't misjudge the boss. I've known him since the day he was born, and I'm right proud of him. He's a man with more than his share of grit, and he's got a heart in his brisket as big as a saddle blanket. He's got a tight lock on it and you'll have to find the right key to open it. If you had asked me years ago, I would have bet a paycheck that by now he would have a half dozen little towheaded carbon copies running around the place." He shook his head. "He's a purty decent-looking feller, ain't he?"

"He's very handsome... when he shaves," she said, smiling.

"Wilma and I thought you might be able to see beneath those coveralls," Moses said, laughing.

If you only knew, Abbie thought, as a fleeting image of him lying naked on her bed flashed through her mind.

"We'd best get on with our job before the boss finds us here yakking about him," Moses said. "Let's see how those little lambies are doing. I'll bet they're nuzzling up against their mommas and suckling away."

His guess was right. When he braked at the crest of the hill, the fields in the valley were dotted with ewes and lambs, the lambs frisking about in the melting snow while the ewes grazed.

Abbie gasped, wiping unexpected tears from her cheeks. "I've only been here once, that day I helped feed. They've grown so much! I was sure they would all be dead." She turned to Moses. "How did they manage to survive?"

"Sheep tend to move with the wind," he said, surveying the scene below them. "My guess is that when the storm came up, the ewes worked their way down the hillside to the willows near the creeks and the lambs stayed by their mommas' sides. When the brunt of the storm hit, the trees and bushes provided a natural shelter from the snow. It looks real good from here, but let's check it out before we report back." His brows furrowed. "You really take to these sheep, don't you? People either hate them or love them. Unfortunately, more lean toward the former."

She shook her head. "I enjoy this work very much, more than I'd thought possible. If I don't watch myself, I may get very possessive about each and every one of them. Please don't tell Dane. When I'm working with an ewe and she looks me right in the eye, I feel as though I can communicate with her. There's more behind those blank faces than a person would think. When a ewe lies down in labor, I actually hurt for her. Sounds crazy, doesn't it? And how could anyone not enjoy working with the lambs?"

"We're in the minority," Moses said, "but welcome to the club. Now let's get busy and count the damage. The boss will be in a snit if we raise a false alarm."

She smiled. "We wouldn't want that."

Moses shook his head. "He's been hard to live with ever since he canned Windy and Blackie, and last night when he came out to relieve Wilma and me, he was as much fun as a baby with a bellyache. I finally accused him of growling worse than that old male sheepdog when the female is in heat. He shut up about then and we came home, leaving him to complain to the ewes."

"Moses, you get a little earthy at times. Perhaps he's coming down with something," Abbie said.

"Could be," Moses agreed. "We've had two bouts of the flu pass through the crew. But you know," he said, turning to her again, "he's been getting crankier, especially since you came. Still, that ain't no call to be short with any of us." Moses squinted at her. "I hope he hasn't been too hard on you. You let me know if he starts making your life miserable, too."

"I can hold my own with him," Abbie assured him.

"Well," he said, dubious about her confidence, "don't you take none of his guff. Normally he's all heart above the waist and all guts below, but lately he's acted like he has a hernia. Maybe it's having you three women around. He's a man who had to stand up before he was weaned, and that has left its mark on him, but he's a fine decent man. What he really needs is a good woman." He sent her a side-glance.

"He can find a woman in any bar," she said, squaring her shoulders and concentrating on the road.

"He ain't a drinking man and I don't mean that kind of a woman." Moses snorted, shaking his head. "I mean one who will stand by him in the tough times and hold his hand when he needs it. A man needs his hand held once in a while. A man needs a reason to smile and laugh and have fun, too, and it takes a special woman to make a man like the boss laugh. When you stepped out of that motor home of yours I thought right then and there he was in for a surprise. Yes, ma'am, that Doc Christensen has sure played a good one on that hard-as-nails boss of mine this time around." He turned to her. "So what happened? Why haven't you two hit it off better?"

Abbie sighed. "Moses, you shouldn't play match-maker. First of all, I've only been here two weeks, and secondly, if you and Dr. Christensen are in collusion, you're wasting your time. Dane and I... Sometimes we've been able to really enjoy each other's company, but then he says something or misunderstands what I say and..." She turned away.

"You mean like comments about not keeping score?" She nodded.

"And what did you say to him?"

"That I didn't keep score, either."

"So maybe he mistook your meaning, just like you did. Oh, Abbie." He shook his head. "You each think the other has had so many lovers you can't count them?"

"Probably."

"You know that ain't true for him," Moses said. "I'll just go to him and explain what you told me and..."

"No!" she cried. "Matchmaking usually boomerangs on everyone involved. I don't want to get hurt. I'll be leaving at the end of my internship. Getting involved with Dane would be detrimental to all my plans. He's got this ranch to keep him busy. Don't you agree?"

"Maybe so," Moses replied. "But his relatives have been making waves about the place. They want his folks to sell. I don't know what he would do if he lost all this."

She frowned. "Is there a chance of that actually happening?"

He shrugged. "You never know a person until you have to share an inheritance with him."

"But his folks are still alive. Can't they refuse?"

"They could, but they're real nice people and might want to try to keep all the kids happy. The boss might be the one left holding an empty bag."

"That would be a crushing defeat for him," she murmured.

"Sounds like you care more about him than you're willing to admit," he said.

"I could, if things were different," she admitted.

Moses turned and grinned at her. "You two sure make a sharp-looking couple. Wilma thinks the same way. We watched the two of you dance and when you snuggled up against him and he smiled down at you, why it made this old ticker skip a beat or two." Moses flapped his hand several times over his heart.

She smiled at his effort at comic relief. "You use that romantic flair on Wilma instead of Dane and me," Abbie advised. "Wilma is a wonderful woman and she thinks a lot of you."

Moses pushed his cap back on his head. "Wilma and me, we go back a long ways. My Pauline died of cancer several years ago. We had been married forty years. Wilma was her best friend for the last twenty. I always did think a lot of Wilma but I would have never laid a hand on her. I don't believe in this modern-day fooling-around business when a person's married. But Wilma's changed these past two years. By damn, if I don't think she's getting purtier in her old age."

Abbie laughed. "Wilma isn't old and neither are you. Don't you think Pauline would have wanted you two to be happy?"

Moses's features softened as he stared at a distant snow-covered mountain. "Sometimes I feel a stirring in this old body when Wilma lets me have it with that dish towel. Ain't that a crazy reaction for a man to have?''

"Not when it might be hiding love," she replied.

"Love? Me?" Moses scratched his head again. "Dunno, but it's something to think about." He straightened. "But I thought we were talking about you and the boss."

"Dane and I can take care of ourselves," she assured him. "Now, don't we have work to do?"

For the next hour, they concentrated on finding any lamb carcasses that might still be buried in the remaining snowdrifts. There were less than a dozen.

They drove back to the lambing tents to find Dane waiting. When they got to the haystacks, he handed her the keys.

"You drive, Hardesty," he said briskly. "Moses and I will do the spreading. Watch for my signals."

"Does the rider still get to open and close all the gates?" she asked.

"Of course," he said, tipping his cap to her.

When only three bales from the second load of hay remained in the rear of the truck, Dane signaled for her to stop and he and Moses jumped to the ground. Moses climbed into the cab from the passenger side and slammed the door. Before she could spot Dane, her door opened and he stepped on the running board.

"I'll drive," he said. "Move over so I can get in."

Confused and hurt by his continued aloofness, she slid away, but the standard gearshift left no room for her legs.

"Straddle it," Dane said. He tossed his work gloves onto her lap. "Hold these."

His brisk manner irritated her. "Anything else, *boss*?"

Moses laughed. "Give up, you two. Stop the bickering and kiss and make up. It's a lot more fun."

Abbie clutched Dane's gloves as they continued to bounce along the rut-filled dirt road. Her fingers stroked the buckskin leather. "Where are we going now?" she asked, knowing they were still headed south.

"There's more to this place than sheep," Dane said, "so we need to check out the rest of the stock. The horses are a few miles from here and the dry cows are up that road." He motioned to the left. "We'll give them some hay."

"I rode when I was a kid," she said, "and a few times since moving west. I like horses."

"These are working horses," he said. "Not playthings for young, upwardly mobile professionals who might..."

"You have a chip on your shoulder today," she said. "It's not the least bit becoming. Why am I going with you? Shouldn't I be back at the lambing tents?"

"You signed on as an intern. That means you do anything I say." Dane glanced down at her hands holding his gloves, and for a fleeting moment he remembered how her hands had felt on him. "I'm willing to show you the total operation if you want to learn. When you leave, you'll know just what to expect when you find that perfect place you're looking for. Is that satisfactory?"

"Of course, but I have the right to refuse if..."

They hit a deep rut and she found herself jostled against him. Her hand pressed against his thigh until the truck found its traction again and regained level ground. She jerked her hand away, clutching the gloves tighter than before.

"Are the horses used for cutting?" she asked.

"A few are, but most of them are used by the sheepherders when they move the bands to the mountains for the summer."

"Oh," she muttered, glancing at his face. "Will I be doing that?"

"Perhaps."

"But I wouldn't know what to do all by myself," she said.

"You'd be with someone else while you're green," he replied.

"Do you go with the bands? During the summer?" she asked.

"Yes, when we're shorthanded or when we're training someone," he said. "A few people remain at the home place, but everyone is expected to go where he's needed."

"Can you cook, Abbie?" Moses asked. "Trudy leaves the end of May and we're on our own again."

"What about Wilma?" she asked.

"Wilma will go to the mountains," Moses said. "She belongs outside. She's all woman, but she's not very domestic." He smiled and Abbie wondered if he had forgotten they were with him. "She sure can cook up great food over an open fire. She's a special woman, that Wilma."

They stopped on the top of a hill. "Want to get out and stretch?" Dane asked.

"Sure," she replied. Abbie climbed down and walked down from the truck, leaving the men alone. She spotted an outcropping of rocks a few hundred yards away and jogged to it, enjoying the invigorating rush of air into her lungs, the pounding of her heart as she reached her destination. Climbing to the top of the rocks, she discovered a flat section, its matching half laying farther down the mountainside as though a giant hand had toppled it.

She straightened, putting her hands on her hips as she surveyed the countryside. The mountains in the distance were blue at their bases with snow covering each jagged peak. The native vegetation looked microscopic, creating fine lines of darker blues and purples.

Valley after valley could be traced by following the creeks marked by their ever-present line of willows. The creeks meandered through the natural low points of each valley, on their way to join Springbrook Creek, which emptied into Sweetwater Creek near the Grasten house.

Inhaling deeply, she closed her eyes and lost herself in the peaceful quiet of the moment.

A pebble skittered down the rocks behind her. Her heart skipped a beat. She knew Dane had joined her.

CHAPTER TWELVE

"THIS PLACE IS SPECIAL to you, isn't it?" she asked softly.

"Yes," Dane confirmed as he took a step forward.

"It's beautiful but fearsome, too."

He didn't reply as he came to stand beside her.

"I can understand how a man could love this country," she murmured.

"And a woman?" he asked.

She paused, choosing her words carefully. "A woman would have to really love a man to live here. I think this country could be very harsh for a woman, killing her with its desolation and loneliness if she wasn't happy, if she wasn't truly part of the man's life, if for some reason he shut her out. But for the right man and woman, this place could be very special. Being here makes me feel as if I could reach up and touch a bit of heaven."

"Abbie?"

"Yes?" she asked, quietly. A shudder ran through her.

"Look at me, please."

She shook her head, continuing to stand straight and tall on the precipice.

"Abbie, Moses has a big mouth."

She whirled to him. "What we talked about was confidential. He had no right!"

"Perhaps not, but it's too late now," he said.

"Well, it doesn't make any difference."

"You're right. What Moses told me has no bearing on what I'm going to say." He reached out and took her face in his hands. "I want to apologize about last night."

"I've never had a man apologize for making love to me before."

"No, you don't understand. I'm sorry for...taking advantage of your distress, for snubbing you this morning. I brooded all night, thinking about what you said. Oh, hell, it wasn't the other men you've been with that angered me. It was your insinuation that I was no different from them."

She looked up at him, her eyes glistening. "You're wrong again, Dane, you're very different. I've only made love to one other man in my entire life. Being with you has erased all my memories of him because this was... was..." She turned away, unable to describe the ecstasy she had experienced with him.

"Dane, regardless of how or why it happened, making love was wrong. It complicates our relationship. I know very little about you and you know next to nothing about me."

"You're right," he said, "but we can take time to rectify that. We can be friends. I'll teach you everything about the sheep business, just as we agreed. We need you here this summer. I was afraid you might decide to go."

She shook her head. "I'll stay. But you must promise to keep everything between us strictly business." She gazed off into the distance, admiring the land below them.

"Of course." His hand came to rest lightly on her shoulder.

She leaned back against his hard chest. "I missed you after you left me last night," she murmured.

"And I missed you," he said. "I'm sorry I hurt you this morning." He squeezed her shoulders. "It will never happen again, I promise."

The horn of the truck sounded behind them and she pulled away. She looked up into his eyes. "Just don't ever get the idea you can come to me or I'll come to you, like we did last night. Is that clear?"

As THE DAY PROGRESSED, ranch routine began to return to normal. The men tended to the remaining casualties. Abbie assisted Wilma with a new pen of bum lambs orphaned by the storm.

To her disappointment Dane was absent at both dinner and supper.

Abbie hurried through the last meal of the day and locked herself in the motor home, determined to concentrate on her weaving. Hours later, as she undressed for bed, Abbie heard a soft knock. Recognizing Wilma's voice, she unlocked the door.

"Come in, Wilma," she said. "It's late and I don't feel much like socializing."

"I know, honey," Wilma said, "but I was talking to the boss about you and..."

"I don't need your intervening for me, Wilma, any more than I need Moses," Abbie said.

Wilma looked stricken for a few seconds.

"I'm sorry," Abbie said, "I'm not in the best of moods."

"Moses said you'd been grumpy today," Wilma replied, "and I don't hold a grudge. The boss was going to tell you himself, but he was bushed and went to bed early this afternoon."

"Tell me what? I worked with him all morning," Abbie said.

"I like the night shift but Moses can't stay awake. That old man is getting so decrepit, he needs special treatment." Wilma's features softened.

"You like him, don't you?" Abbie asked.

Wilma shrugged. "He knows how to get on my better side, I reckon. We go back quite a few years."

"I've noticed how you keep an eye on him," Abbie teased. "You give him the largest portion of dessert."

"The man is thin as a willow stick," Wilma huffed. "He needs a lot of fattening up. He's the thinnest old goat I've ever known and I'm afraid he'll blow away during a wind storm if I don't give him an extra ration now and then. If I'm willing to look after him a little, can it hurt?"

"I think he loves it," Abbie said.

"So do I. I worry about him and the boss rattling around in that great big empty house in the off season. They take turns poisoning each other with their cooking. Lord, I'd like to live here year round but the boss says he can't justify it. I'd work for nothing just to know they were all right and eating properly." She smiled. "But that's not really why I came to talk." She accepted the seat Abbie pointed to. "I was talking to the boss about Moses and I suggested you take Moses's place on night duty the next two weeks."

"Why me?"

"Now that Blackie and that no-good friend of his are gone, we're short-handed." Wilma beamed. "The boss says you're a natural, and although you still have a lot to learn, he said you were quick to catch on, that you pick up things the first time."

"I try not to make the same mistake twice," Abbie murmured. "When did you talk to him?"

"After dinner today," Wilma said. She laughed. "He was teasing, but he said you were like the dogs, always under foot, and that he was tired of seeing you around everywhere he turned. He said he would be glad to get rid of you for a while."

OTHER THAN THE SOUNDS of construction activity at the huge lambing shed, Abbie found herself adjusting easily to working nights and sleeping days.

Working through breakfast, she ate after the others had left, slept through dinner and snacked during the evening hours at the loom. With careful planning she had become adept at avoiding Dane. As long as she didn't see him, she didn't feel the surge of desire that came from out of nowhere to inundate every nerve and cell in her body. Out of sight, out of mind, was her motto, and the best ways to make it true were to stay busy and stay alert.

"WHO KNOWS ABOUT this ewe?" Dane asked, squatting in the jug to get a better look at the ewe and lamb. The lamb, its back humped and its head down, bleated weakly as Dane picked it up. Gently, he handed it to Evelyn, the teenage girl from the neighboring ranch he had hired to replace Windy.

"Should I put it with the bums?" she asked, cuddling it against her coveralls.

"Yes, but give it a few ounces of colostrum first and mark it with masking tape loosely around the neck," Dane replied. "I doubt if we can bring it back. This ewe had mastitis. See how she keeps her leg away from the bag? It's hot and inflamed and her milk is full of curds. When did she lamb?"

"During the night, I think," Evelyn said. "No one left a note about her. Maybe they didn't notice how bad she was."

"Only a blind person would have missed this," he snapped.

"I didn't know," Evelyn said, clutching the lamb to her bosom as she stepped away.

"I'm sorry, Evie," he apologized, standing up again. "I didn't mean to take it out on you. You're doing fine, really. I was on my way to the house, anyway. I'll talk to Wilma and Abbie."

"They'll be asleep," Evelyn said.

"Then I'll wake them. Someone was negligent to not have seen this. If the ewe had been given a shot of penicillin when she was first brought in, this wouldn't have happened." He stepped over the top rail and into the aisle again. "Find Moses and tell him to give her 500,000 units of penicillin and if she doesn't respond give her another dosage. And mark her for culling out. Her bag will be permanently damaged. Use that dark blue chalk and put two big circles on her back. She'll be sent to market. It's a shame. She was a good ewe."

Still angry over finding the sick ewe, Dane braked to a stop several yards from the kitchen porch and glanced toward the motor home. Abbie had been avoiding him since Wilma had talked him into switching the schedules. *Damn Wilma...damn Moses for pressuring him...damn Abbie for becoming a distraction even when she was out of sight. Damn the whole damn world!* How could the woman live on his property, work for him, without his ever catching a glimpse of her? he wondered.

He suspected he was grasping at straws as an excuse to see her. Just when he had begun to feel that they were on common ground, she'd gone into hiding.

As he climbed from the truck, he turned to the motor home again, and caught movement inside. He glanced at his watch. Ten in the morning. Why wasn't she asleep? Through the screens on the windows, he watched her move back and forth inside. What the hell was she doing?

He strode to the Winnebago and pounded on the door.

"Come in," Abbie called but the door didn't open. He reached for the handle and opened it, stepped up and inside. The latch didn't catch and he turned, irritated at being unable to close the door. Finally, it caught and he stepped up the final step.

Something snagged his cap and flipped it to the carpeted floor. He turned and found himself tangled in blue yarn. Feeling like a fly in a spiderweb, he brushed the strands away, but they seemed to snare his hair and his hands. He took a step backward and stumbled down the interior step. The latch released and the door flew open, sending him crashing.

He lay sprawled on the frosty ground, gasping for air and waiting for the ringing in his head to stop. He heard a muffled giggle and looked up.

Abbie stood on the same step that had been his downfall, wearing the most indecent pair of cutoff jeans he'd seen in a long time. The frayed material brushed the upper flesh of her thighs but the side seams had been slashed all the way up to her... Her giggling sounded again and his eyes drifted up past a form-fitting knit midriff top. It was little more than a strip of stretchy fabric across her breasts, its sage-green stripes matching her eyes.

Her eyes. As his gaze lifted to her face, he saw the laughter in her dancing green eyes. She was holding two hangers with a strange arrangement of yarn. The various shades of blue jiggled in her grasp as her giggle changed to a full chuckle.

She laid the yarn down out of sight inside the motor home and came to his side.

"Are you hurt?" she asked, tugging at his arm.

"No thanks to you, Hardesty," he said, slowly rising to his feet and brushing the debris from his coat and jeans as he regained his dignity. "Do you always booby-trap the place when you don't want someone to get in?"

"I didn't expect company," she said.

"Well, I need to talk to you," he said, feeling her hands brush his backside.

"Then come in," she replied. "It's a mess inside. I'm dyeing yarn."

He followed her up the steps and into the vehicle. As he surveyed the interior, he spotted two large pots on the stove. Steam drifted upward. Several clothes hangers were suspended from the cupboard knobs, each with a long loose skein of yarn tied in several places.

"Sit down," she said.

"Where?"

She gathered up several of the hangers and moved them to the rear of the vehicle, suspending them over a bar she had rigged across the bed. "Sorry, but I told you I didn't expect company. I wanted to dye outside, but the weather is still too cold. It got warm in here so I changed into something more comfortable." Her hand brushed down her front. "I don't usually dress this way, but dyeing is a messy job and I got so hot and..." She grabbed a shirt and pulled it on, buttoning the front as she slid into the driver's seat and motioned him to the passenger seat in the front of the motor home.

He accepted her offer. "I thought you'd be asleep."

"When I'm through dyeing," she replied. "The skeins can dry while I sleep this afternoon. Don't worry, I'll be ready to work when my shift starts. Now, what did you want to see me about? Have I done something wrong?"

"Yes."

"What?" She straightened, her mouth tightening.

"The ewe with mastitis."

"What ewe with mastitis?" she asked. "We didn't bring in any ewe with a problem like that. I'd never just ignore a ewe with mastitis and neither would Wilma. You know that!"

"Someone did," he retorted.

"Well, don't accuse me unless you know I'm guilty," she exclaimed. "I do my job well." She glared at him. "Don't I?"

His anger and frustration evaporated. "Yes, you do. But there's a ewe out there with mastitis and someone brought her in. If not you or Wilma then who?"

"I don't know," she said. "Buck was up and about before dawn, so were you. I saw you driving south about—" she glanced at her watch "—about six."

"I didn't see you," he said, frowning at her. "In fact, I haven't seen you for a week. If it wasn't for this motor home, I wouldn't know you were here."

"I keep tabs on your whereabouts," she admitted, "so talk to Buck or maybe yourself..."

"Are you insinuating that *I* did it?" he asked.

"No, but neither did I," she insisted. "Why don't you question the others before you jump all over me? Now, if you're finished, I have work to do, personal work on my own time." She left the driver's seat and took up a new post by the door.

Reluctant to leave, he felt for the lever beneath the seat and swiveled around. "What are you going to do with all this blue yarn? It doesn't match. Couldn't you get it right?"

She glared at him. "It's exactly the way I want it, and I worked hard to get it shaded just right, so don't you condemn it out of ignorance."

"Ignorance?" He stroked his chin as his gaze swept down her body, gliding over her shapely bare legs to her sandaled feet, before returning to her face.

"You may know sheep, but I know how to dye yarn," she said. "Give me credit for knowing a lot more than you do about what can be done with those fleeces your darn sheep produce. I can spin and dye and weave and make money by selling my finished tapestries. Can you?"

He studied her defiant stance. "I guess I am ignorant about you, Abbie. I'm sorry. I don't understand the steps you go through when you weave your...tapestries." He studied the row of skeins with renewed interest. "Some of the shades remind me of the sky when a storm is brewing and..."

Her shoulders eased and she smiled. "Thank you. Your impression is correct. Most of them are for the sky in a new tapestry I'm working on. The rest will go into my inventory, to be used later when I need them." When he didn't move, the stiff set of her shoulders returned. "Now I really need to get busy and clean up this mess."

Her coolness was irritating. He left the seat and walked to the door. He stared down at the top of her head. A strange odor filled the air. "Your hair smells like wet wool and the steam has made it curlier."

She touched her hair.

"You've got something stuck in it," he said, plucking a piece of undyed combed wool from a curl. Her hand touched his.

She jerked away. "Please leave," she murmured.

"I haven't seen much of you lately," he said, his voice soft and caressing in the closeness of the motor home.

"I . . . I've been busy."

"Busy avoiding me?"

She didn't reply.

"Abbie?" His hand touched her cheek.

"Please don't, Dane," she whispered.

"I've missed you, Abbie," he said. "The place isn't the same when you're in hiding."

"Oh, Dane, don't say that." Reluctantly, she met his eyes.

It was a mistake. For a week she had avoided him and in that week had tried to convince herself he didn't matter, but now, as his blue eyes reflected the depth of his feelings, her self-control shattered. Her hand settled on his waist.

"I'm sorry I accused you," he said.

"I shouldn't have laughed at you," she replied, "but you're always so in control. Seeing you lying at my feet just struck me funny." Her hands moved up his sides. "I'm glad you didn't hurt yourself."

His fingers toyed with the gold loop in her ear. "Do you wear these all the time?"

"Unless I get dressed up," she replied. "I have a gold locket I wear sometimes with them. My aunt gave one to me and one to each of my cousins one summer. She gave me the earrings for graduation."

His fingers trailed across her neck, sending s shiver of delight through her.

"Dane, please, I still don't want this."

His mouth replaced his fingers. "I know," he whispered near her ear. "I'm leaving . . . after I do this," and his mouth found hers. His hand slid down her back and under the shirt to splay across her bare midriff, pressing her against him. Her arms went around his neck as she succumbed to the need to be with him, to know that he wanted her even while his cool outward manner spoke otherwise. There was nothing cool or detached about his hands as they slid up her sides and under her top, pressing the outside fullness of her breasts.

"You're a hypocrite," she said when he withdrew.

"So are you," he replied.

CHAPTER THIRTEEN

ABBIE WATCHED HIM walk across the yard to the house, her emotions in turmoil, the week's carefully built wall of denial destroyed by one brief embrace.

Later, dressed in jeans and a sweatshirt, she slid into her rightful seat at the table. A wave of contentment washed over her, making her glad she had decided to prove her innocence in the matter of the ewe by her presence at dinner.

As Trudy gave the blessing, Dane's hand reached out to hers beneath the tablecloth and squeezed, then withdrew.

"Boss," Buck said, as the first serving bowl was passed, "I'm the culprit Moses said you were looking for, not Abbie or Wilma."

"What?" Dane exclaimed.

"It's true, boss. They were checking the second drop pen when I cut through on my way to find some tools I'd left out last night. A ewe had just had her lamb, so I brought them inside the nearest tent and jugged them."

"But you don't work with the sheep," Dane replied, bemused at his mechanic's confession.

"No, and I proved it today," Buck said. "I remembered where I'd left my tools about then and left. Boss, I'm sorry. I just forgot to tell a soul about that ewe. Wilma and Abbie went off their shift right after that and Moses and Evelyn must have assumed the ewe was okay because there was no note from...well, you see how it happened? Take it out of my wages if she's ruined, but don't blame her condition on these two nice ladies."

Dane nodded. "I appreciate your honesty, Buck. Sometimes we jump to conclusions around here. I'm sorry, Abbie, for thinking you were at fault. You're too good a lamber for that."

After Abbie returned to the motor home, she considered the significance of Dane's public apology. His sincerity had touched her, giving her a sense of peace. She still had no intentions of getting involved with him but she no longer had the need to avoid him. When she crawled into bed and closed her eyes, she slept soundly. No dreams disturbed her slumber.

For the next few days, Abbie joined the crew for breakfast and dinner and slept through supper. Dane was busy supervising the repair of the lambing shed and he had little to say at the table.

One noon, as Abbie excused herself to go to bed, she was surprised to see the waitress from the Outfitters' Den drive up. Dane greeted her friendly wave with one of his own.

Moses stood beside Abbie on the porch. "She called and said she wanted to see the lambs," he said. "She's as interested in lambing as I am in learning needlepoint."

"Does she come around often?" Abbie asked.

"Just when she wants to remind Dane she's available," Moses said, shaking his head.

"And she's available now?" Abbie asked.

"Looks that way," Moses replied. "How's it going, Abbie? I don't see much of my two favorite women lately."

Abbie frowned as the waitress accepted Dane's assistance into the blue truck and they drove toward the lambing tents. "We've established a truce." Her shoulders stiffened. "But a truce is better than bickering."

"Don't you worry none," Moses replied. "He don't really take to her. He's just being neighborly."

"I've been here almost a month and at times I feel as though I've lived here all my life, but I don't think I could ever be 'neighborly' to Dane. Perhaps it's just as well that I'll be gone before the first snowfall."

When Trudy rang the bell for the evening meal, Abbie awoke with a start. She peeked out her window and saw that the sleek little red sports car belonging to the waitress was still parked in the yard, alongside Dane's blue truck.

"He's invited her to supper, the rat," she said, trying to forget her disappointment as she crawled back into bed. If the woman in the skintight jeans was indicative of Dane's choice in female companionship, so be it. Abbie had better plans for herself and she wouldn't let her infatuation with Dane Grasten stand in her way. Nonetheless, troubled thoughts prevented her from recapturing the restful sleep she sought.

Hours later, Abbie knew she had a fever. Hoping to fight it, she took two aspirin and dressed for the night shift. Three more days of working nights and her life would return to normal.

She gulped a cup of coffee and hurried out the door to meet Wilma, who was waiting in one of the trucks.

During a difficult delivery of twins, she was straightening a bent foreleg of the second lamb still inside of the ewe when every ounce of her energy drained from her. She lost her grip on the tiny hoofs.

"Wilma, help me," she called weakly. When Wilma arrived, Abbie withdrew. "I can't keep my hold. Can you help?" As Wilma took over, Abbie washed her hands and went to the wood stove. She stood for several minutes beside the fire before she stopped trembling.

Behind her, Abbie heard the first bleating of the lamb, now safely delivered. After Wilma washed up, she joined Abbie.

"Abbie, honey, what's the matter?" Wilma asked, touching Abbie's cheek with the back of her hand. "Why, you're burning up! You shouldn't be out here in this cold if you're coming down with something." She shook her head. "The flu bug hit us pretty hard just before you came. Want to quit early?"

"I'm fine." Abbie withdrew the bottle of aspirin she had slid into the pocket of her coveralls and tossed two into her mouth, then washed them down with a cup of hot coffee from the thermos.

A dry rasping cough grew worse during the next night, but still, Abbie refused to quit. When she checked in the last night of her shift, she waved to Wilma, but only a sickening croak came from her throat.

Later, Abbie reached for the portable branding rack. As she strained to lift it from its holder, it slipped from her hands and crashed to the dirt floor, spilling the number irons in all directions. The red and green paint blended into an ugly brown on the ground.

With her cheeks flaming from fever, she felt the tears start to flow. "I'm sorry," she said, her voice raspy as she wiped her face. She groaned as she knelt to collect the scattered irons.

"What happened?" a deep familiar voice asked.

Abbie slumped, her shoulders sagging. "I had an accident."

"She's sick, boss, but she won't admit it," Wilma said.

Dane squinted at Abbie. "What's wrong with her?"

"I think it's the flu," Wilma said, leaving a nearby jug to join them. "Dr. Peters says it's the real thing this year, true influenza. It's hit the schools. Buck says the bars are half-empty because of it. I guess it has to run its course, but surely the doctor can do something for that cough of hers."

"It sounds like acute bronchitis to me," Dane said.

As if on cue, a fit of coughing attacked Abbie.

Dane knelt by her side, but she ducked her head. He reached out and caught her chin, turning her face to him. "How long has she been like this?"

"Better part of a week," Wilma replied.

Dane helped Abbie to her feet and propped her against a support post. She coughed as he retrieved the irons and put them back into their proper slots, then kicked straw and dirt over the puddles of paint. "Why hasn't someone taken her into town for treatment?"

Wilma shrugged. "She insists she's getting better."

Abbie jerked away from the post. "Stop talking about me as if I'm not here," she cried, unable to control the crack in her hoarse voice.

"Very sexy voice, Hardesty," he said, but when he turned her face to the light, he cursed softly. "Those rosy cheeks are from a fever, not good health. I've seen you looking better."

She tried to pull free but didn't have the strength. He put his arm around her and she leaned against him. If she rested, perhaps she could absorb part of his strength before she excused herself and began the long trek back to the main compound. Once her head touched his chest, she didn't want to lift it again.

"I'll leave now," she said, turning to go. She bumped into the stove as she tried to turn toward the door.

"I'll take her home," Dane said. He helped Abbie out the door and into the truck and soon he had her at the motor home door. "Maybe you should spend the night in the main house," he suggested.

"No thank you," she croaked curtly.

"Then get inside," he said, his patience running low.

He reached for the nearest light switch, stepped around her and pulled all the shades, then went to the bedchamber and began to search the closets.

"What are you doing?" she asked.

"Taking care of a woman who's too stubborn to know when to quit," he said. Finding what he had been looking for, he turned to her. She was leaning against the refrigerator, just inches away, looking paler then before. "Do you have some whiskey?" he asked.

She frowned, as though she didn't understand his question.

"Whiskey!" he repeated. "You need a good dose of antibiotic but since I know of no physician who makes house calls at this hour this far from town, I'll make you a drink. It will help you sleep. Are you really feeling better? If this is better, I would hate to have seen you when you were worse."

A fit of coughing left her wheezing.

"Abbie, answer me. Do you have a bottle?"

She motioned to one of the upper cupboard doors. "There's a fifth of bourbon and a liter of wine up there ... but don't get the idea I'm a boozer. My uncle would have a fit if he knew I had them. He's Bible Belt conservative, but most of his religion is in my Aunt Minnie's name."

He smiled at the lapse in her accent as he turned on the compressor and filled the teakettle. He lit the propane burner and set the kettle down. "I'll fix you a hot toddy."

While he waited impatiently for the kettle to sing, he measured sugar, cloves and lemon juice in a coffee mug, then poured a generous double shot of bourbon. When the water was boiling, he poured in an equal amount and stirred the concoction.

He turned to her. "While that sits, let's get you undressed."

"You just leave," she said, "I can manage from here on."

"You're too sick to know if you're standing up or lying down, but give it a try. There's a pair of flannel pajamas." He pointed to the bed. "Put them on. I'll wait out here. He pulled the curtain across the aisle.

Dane waited while she coughed again, then watched as various pieces of clothing fell to the floor.

"My leg's stuck," she croaked.

Heaven help me, he thought, as he knelt down and stuck his head under the curtain. He lifted one shapely calf and her knee brushed against his cheek. He inserted her foot into the pant leg of the pajama bottom and retreated. "You pull them up," he said, and again he heard the rustling of clothing.

The curtain opened and she listlessly stepped over the pile of clothes, the flannel pajamas hanging on her body.

"Now drink this," he ordered, offering her the steaming mug.

She gulped it down in three long sips. "That was good," she said.

He watched the color rise in her cheeks.

"Could I have another?" she asked.

"I suppose so," Dane said tentatively before he prepared another drink. He frowned as she drank the second toddy in the same manner. "Easy, Abbie, you should sip it. For a nonboozer, you sure guzzle the stuff. It might hit you all at once.''

He caught the glazed look building in her eyes. ''When did you eat last?''

Her straight brows furrowed. ''Breakfast?''

''Are you telling me or asking me?'' he asked, hoping he hadn't given her the two drinks on an empty stomach. He turned her toward the bed. ''You should rest now.''

He leaned against the closet and motioned for her to climb on to the bed. Instead, she leaned against him, pressing her body full-length to his.

''We fit nice, don't we?'' she asked. Before he could reply, she slid her arms around his neck. ''Kiss me,'' she murmured, her whisky-scented breath sweetened by the aroma of lemon.

''Do you know what you're asking?''

''Sure. I promised myself... I'd never let you in here again... but right now I want you to... kiss me.'' She rubbed against him and he fought against his own body's reaction.

''You're tipsy, aren't you?'' he asked, putting his hands on her hips to stop their gyrations.

''Nope, but I'm kinda hot inside. Someone is ringing a bell in my head and—'' she felt her cheek with one hand ''—my face feels like it's on fire,'' she replied.

''You're sick, Abbie, and I should have fed you before I gave you those two toddies. Now, get into bed.''

''Want to come with me?'' she asked, tipping her head backward.

''Don't ask,'' he said. ''Here's a kiss to sleep on, pretty lady.'' His lips touched hers.

She stretched on her tiptoes and clung to him, her mouth pressed tightly against his. Her lips opened and he felt her tongue dart against his closed lips. Unable to resist, he responded with his own tongue, allowing himself the brief pleasure of her uninhibited show of affection.

Suddenly, she pulled away. "I hope you catch whatever I have." She turned and climbed into the bed, falling asleep instantly.

"Oh, Abbie, sweetheart," he said, admiring her sleeping features, "it's a good thing you're sick tonight."

He tucked the comforter around her shoulders. "Sleep," he whispered, "and dream wonderful things."

As he made his way through the vehicle, he spotted her latest weaving project and paused to admire the few inches of design reflected in the colors. "Nice," he murmured, touching the yarn with his fingertips. He spotted several pieces of graph paper and pulled them from beneath the loom. They appeared to be variations of a sketch. His eyes returned to the loom and he bent over to get a better look at the piece of paper just below the warp threads. To Dane's eyes, it revealed much more than the casual observer would ever see.

Returning to the bed, he stood staring down at the sleeping woman. Some force was drawing them into each other's lives. Unwilling to accept the implications of his own feelings, or what he read in her tapestry, he left the motor home, locking the door behind him.

Inside his own bedroom, he undressed and lay down on the bed, but sleep was slow to come. The redheaded woman from Kentucky was becoming an irresistible force to be reckoned with. Sick or well, he found her beautiful; angry or laughing, he found her intriguing; at work or in her leisure, her enthusiasm was contagious. He smiled in the darkness, hoping the spell she had cast on him wasn't successful.

"HOW IS ABBIE this morning?" Moses asked four days later.

"She was feeling a little better when I checked on her last night," Wilma said.

"She should have been brought in here," Trudy said.

"She refused," Dane said. "She's an independent woman."

"Too damned much that way if you ask me," Moses grumbled.

"Nobody asked you, old man," Wilma said. Instead of flicking her towel at him this time, she handed him a platter of eggs with bacon chips and finely chopped green onions.

Trudy laughed. "I wish I could handle food like you men do. I eat half as much and gain twice the pounds. It's not fair."

Dane listened with half an ear to the chatter around the table. The shock of the storm had worn off and the crew was in its usual good humor. Everything was back to normal, except for Abbie's absence.

"Need a ride, boss?" Moses asked as the workers began to leave the table.

Dane shook his head. "I'm going to see Abbie." He hadn't seen her since the night he had put her to bed. By now, he thought, she should be up and about. He had left the nursing to the women and they had said very little except that her cough was hanging on.

He walked across the yard to the motor home and turned the handle. The door was locked. He knocked and waited, hating to disturb her if she was still asleep, but too concerned to leave.

He knocked again. The door opened. The woman who greeted him was a shell of the Abbie who had challenged him in the early days of her stay. As he entered and closed the door, she began to cough. He caught the odor of sickness in the air.

"How are you?" he asked.

She shrugged dejectedly, tugging the lapels of her green robe together.

"Does that mean better or worse than yesterday?"

"It doesn't matter," she mumbled. "I'm going back to bed. I want to sleep." She ran her fingers through her tousled hair and he caught the tremor in her hand.

"What have you been doing when you're awake?" he asked, glancing at the table loom. The tapestry had not grown by one strand of yarn.

"Nothing."

"Why haven't you been weaving?"

She shrugged again. "Why? What I've done isn't any good. Who would want to buy one of those?" She waved her hand at the stack of small tapestries he'd never seen before. "I got them out yesterday. Look at them. No wonder I haven't been able to sell them. They're all trash. I couldn't even give them away." She turned away, slumping against the bathroom door. "I don't hurt anymore, but I feel so terrible I wish I could die."

She turned to him, her eyes glistening like two wet green marbles in an alabaster face. Dark circles detracted from her usual beauty. Her hair hadn't been shampooed in days.

"I don't know what's happening to me," she said mournfully, and a tear worked its way down her cheek. "I've never felt so unnecessary in my life."

He swore an oath as he took her in his arms, massaging her back as she cried against his shirt. "Sometimes people get depressed when they have a bad case of influenza. It's a predictable secondary complication. I'm taking you into town. If the doctor can't fix your depression, she can surely do something for that cough of yours. It's a wonder you don't have pneumonia by now." He pulled back a little. "I'll go call the office. You get dressed and I'll come back in a half hour."

She opened her mouth to object, but he laid a finger on her lips. "No back talk, Hardesty, this is the boss talking. I . . . we miss you at the lambing shed."

"Lambing shed?" The puzzled expression on her face made him smile.

"Yes," he said. "We moved the few ewes who haven't lambed to the drop pens behind the big shed. We've been setting up the jugs and pens for the quarter Finns. They'll be starting to lamb any day. We can't possibly handle all those triplets without you." He smiled, trying to cheer her.

"You finished the construction?" she asked, her expression brightening. "You mean I missed it all?"

He nodded. "I'm ashamed to admit how quickly we did it. I hired several extra hands just to work on the shed. But time was running out. Imagine doing without that building for ten years."

"You have a stubborn streak," she declared.

"Me?" he asked in mock disbelief.

She smiled, bringing a hint of color to her features.

He left her to dress. When he came for her thirty minutes later, she had added a touch of color to her lips. He helped her into the cab of the truck and slammed the door. When he slid behind the wheel and turned the key in the ignition, he grinned. "I haven't caught your flu yet," he said.

"What?"

"You cursed me with it when I brought you home several nights ago," he said. "Remember when I gave you the hot toddies?

"What hot toddies? I've never had a hot toddy...."

"You don't remember?" he asked. "Not about ... my putting you to bed ... or the kiss you gave me ... or anything you said?"

She shook her head slowly. "Only how terrible I felt. Please forgive me if I said nasty things to you. I wasn't myself. But thanks for caring enough to help me and for this special treatment today."

Her smile was payment enough.

WHEN THEY RETURNED to the ranch, Dane led Abbie to the main house.

"You're staying here until you've fully recovered," he insisted, leading her into the bedroom decorated with tumbling blue and white baby blocks wallpaper.

"Help her settle in, Trudy," he said. "She's your patient until her cough disappears and she's ready to go to work again. That's an order. Here are her prescriptions."

"Thank you, Dane," said Abbie, her gaze lingering on his features. "Thank you for ... everything."

He turned away, his emotions torn to shreds.

Dane looked in on her each morning and evening, but usually Abbie was asleep. During the night he would lie awake, listening to the dry, racking cough coming from the next room, and resist the urge to go to her.

Five days later, he awoke several minutes before the alarm was to sound and realized he hadn't heard her during the night. He had grown conditioned to her disturbing his sleep every few hours. Had the prescriptions finally begun to work? What if she'd taken a turn for the worse? He leaped from his bed and jumped into his jeans, fastening them on the run. When he shoved her door wide and stared toward the bed, he stopped short.

The bed was empty.

"Abbie?" He stepped inside. "Abbie, where are you? My God, woman, what's happened?" Soft footsteps sounded behind him and he whirled to find her standing in the doorway.

"Where the hell have you been? You can't just disappear and not tell anyone," he said.

"No one was up to tell," she said, entering the room. "I woke up at four, feeling so grubby I couldn't stand myself. I had to shampoo my hair." She removed the towel she had wrapped around her head and shook out her hair, running her fingers through it a few times. "I feel like a new person." She smiled, but as she dropped to one corner of the bed, her complexion paled.

"That's great, but you're not well yet," he said, reaching for the damp towel. "Here, let me," Dane said as he began to rub her head.

"Mmm, that feels divine," she said, sighing as she leaned against his hands.

He continued toweling her hair until it was almost dry. "Do you have a blow dryer?" he asked.

She nodded.

"Good," he said. "Use it and then get back into bed. You're still confined to the house." He glanced at his watch. "I have work to do before breakfast, and we're moving the Rambouillet and Targhee ewes and lambs to larger pastures today."

"What about the Lincoln band?" she asked. "I've been here for weeks and I've seen them only twice. When do they lamb?"

"Same time as the quarter Finns," he said. "They need extra care at lambing so they fit in well with the quarter Finns. You can help me with them. We have less than a hundred. They're part of a plan I have to..." He stopped talking and rose from the bed.

"A plan to... what?" she asked.

He shrugged. "Some other time. Take care of yourself and don't overdo anything, do you hear?"

The phone rang in the kitchen.

"Do you need to answer that?" she asked.

"No, Trudy is up now and she'll get it," he said, hesitant to leave her.

"Boss," Trudy called, "it's for you. It's your brother Ejner, from Denver."

"I'm coming," Dane called back. Still he didn't leave.

"Dane?"

He turned back to Abbie. "Yes?"

"Thanks for being concerned about me." She took a step toward him. "We've had words, misunderstandings." Her gaze flickered away before returning to his face. "I don't think I'm strong enough to handle the harsh words. They hurt too much. Let's not have any more... unless they're good words."

His face reflected his conflicting emotions.

"We can try?" she added, stepping closer.

"Yes, we can try." As she lifted her face, his lips grazed hers so lightly he wondered if they had touched at all.

"Boss, are you coming?" Trudy shouted.

They stepped apart, neither speaking. Finally, he turned and left the room.

CHAPTER FOURTEEN

THE PHONE RANG at noon and Trudy answered. "Boss, it's your sister Maren." He took the call in his office. When he returned to the meal, his face was grim.

"First brother Ejner, now sister Maren," Moses said. "I suppose Petra and her rich stockbroker husband are next. What are you planning, a regular family reunion?"

Dane growled an unintelligible response under his breath and left the table. He returned to the office and dialed his parents' home in Needles, California. No one answered.

When the phone rang again late that evening, Dane was at his desk, studying the typed pages of the ranch's federal and state income tax returns. He had picked them up at his accountant's office several days earlier, but he'd been too busy to give them the attention they deserved.

He flipped through the pages, stared at the gross and net income figures, then at the taxes paid. There was only one reason for the good numbers. He had paid off the ranch's debt several years earlier and had stayed out of debt since. Ranching was hard work, and if he was going to work around the clock and around the calendar, he was determined to do it for himself and his family, not for some lending institution.

The phone rang again. The caller this time was probably his sister Petra. He was tempted to ignore it. His oldest brother Knud had caught him during a late supper to warn him that trouble was brewing among the Grasten heirs.

"I tried reaching Mom and Dad earlier today but no one answered," Dane had said.

"They're still on their trip to Denmark, remember?" Knud had replied.

"I'm glad they finally decided to go," Dane had said. "They've talked about it constantly since they retired. But weren't they due back last week? What detained them?"

"They had scheduled a month but they called a week ago and said they had made contact with so many relatives that they've extended their trip for three months," Knud explained. "They'll be back in mid June."

"So why the calls from Maren and Ejner?" Dane asked. "Are they trying to pull something behind the folks' backs?"

"Petra is making a case for having a family discussion while they're out of the country. She's behind it, otherwise I doubt Maren and Ejner would have brought up the subject so soon again. We all know this has been brewing for years. I'm on your side, Dane, but don't be surprised at anything the others do."

"And Anna?" Dane asked, thinking of his oldest sister.

"Anna has been outspoken all along, little brother," Knud had replied. "She thinks the folks should have given the place to you outright years ago. That drives the rest of them up the wall. They've grown increasingly greedy lately. I'm ashamed to call them my relatives when they act this way. They think if they can get us all to agree ahead of time, they can lay their cards on the table when Mom and Dad come in June and have their way."

"It sounds underhanded," Dane said.

"Yes, I agree, but Maren and Ejner have concocted this ruse of a family get-together in early May and I want you to be prepared for their real purpose."

"Thanks for the warning," Dane had said, ending the conversation a few minutes later after hearing about Knud's grandson's latest accomplishments.

Now, as the phone rang, Dane didn't lift the receiver. His oldest brother had two grandchildren while he himself was single and childless. Once there had been a promise of a family but Lil had taken care of that a few weeks after the fire.

After another shrill ring, he decided he could no longer avoid the call from the sister he had little affection for. Petra had been the youngest Grasten child and had been pampered and spoiled... until Dane had been born. She had made it clear to him many times that he had been an unexpected accident. Her grudge had remained constant through the years.

"Yes!" he said gruffly, picking up the receiver.

"Is...is Aunt Abbie..." a young boy's voice stammered. "I mean is Miss Abigail Hardesty there?"

Dane cleared his throat and said, "Yes, but she's asleep. She's been very ill. Can I take a message? Who is this? Where are you calling from? Kentucky?"

He listened as the caller explained. "Oh, my God," he murmured. "I'm sorry I snapped at you, Jordan. Yes, I'll tell her. Give me the time and place again, please." He jotted the statistics on a strip of tape from his calculator. "Yes, I'll tell her right away. Tell your mother I'll see that Abbie gets there. We'll leave early tomorrow." He listened again. "Yes, and you try to... Yes, I know you can, but... Yes, son, I'll go tell her right away."

ABBIE WAS BETWEEN sleep and wakefulness, enjoying the moments of floating in and out of a dream too wondrous to leave. She turned on her side and drifted into the fantasy again.

A hand touched her arm and she started. Inhaling deeply, she rolled to her back again and opened her eyes. Dane was leaning over her, shaking her gently.

She thought she was still dreaming, until the harsh expression on his face registered.

"What's wrong?" She glanced toward the door. He had closed it so softly behind him that she had not heard a sound.

"Sit up," he said. When she did, he stuffed two pillows behind her. "We must talk."

Her heart still pounding, she scooted a few inches toward the middle of the bed and patted the edge. "Then sit down."

Dane had always seemed an overly serious man, and she had accepted this trait as part of his personality. Right now the blue of his eyes was darker than ever, and he seemed more grave than she'd ever seen him.

"You had a phone call," he said. "It was long distance, and since you were asleep I took the message." He reached for her hand. "There's been a death."

She shot upright. "Aunt Minnie? Uncle Harry. Oh, no!"

He tightened his grip on her hand. "No, the call wasn't from Kentucky. It was from your cousin Eileen's family."

The color drained from her. Dane's face floated before her.

"The boy, Jordan, called," Dane said. "It was about his father."

"It's . . . Duncan?"

He nodded. "The boy said his mother had to call an ambulance early yesterday. I'm sorry to be the one to bring this news, Abbie. Jordan said he died early this morning of kidney failure."

She slumped against the pillows, trying to accept the finality of his words. "Poor, poor Eileen and Duncan. They had such a wonderful marriage."

"How old was he?"

"Thirty-three. When he developed multiple sclerosis a few years ago, they had hoped and prayed for a period of remission. Eileen always had such a strong belief in prayer. But when I stopped to visit her in March she . . . was reconciled . . . to losing him. She must be devastated." Tears moistened her cheeks. "They were so special. They had the kind of marriage most of us only dream about."

"How do you mean?" he asked.

"They loved each other so very much," she said, wiping her cheek. "They were committed, their marriage was spiritual as well as physical. They truly lived their marriage vows through good and bad times, health and sickness." Abbie took a deep breath. "Only death could have parted them and now it has." Her chin quivered. When Dane offered the comfort of his arms, she accepted, and he held her as she sobbed her grief.

He handed her a tissue and she repaired her face. "I'm sorry," she said, "but...but I...just can't help it. I feel so sorry for Eileen . . . and the children." She felt him lift her from the bed. "What are you doing?" she asked as she clutched the front of his shirt.

"I'm taking you where you belong," he murmured. "You can't stay here alone tonight." Dane carried her to a door in the room she had always assumed led to a closet. In the dim light from her lamp, she saw bathroom fixtures. He opened another door and they were in his room.

He laid her in his bed and pulled the covers up to her chin. "Sleep," he ordered, kissing her before leaving the room.

Abbie stared at the closed door, puzzled by his departure. After half an hour, she was still alone. Her thoughts returned to Eileen and the children. Eileen was strong. She would pick up the pieces of her life and carry on. With time to heal the sorrow, Eileen would manage. Money wouldn't be a problem. The potato farm was prosperous.

All Abbie could give her cousin would be emotional support in her time of mourning. Dane had told her nothing of the funeral arrangements, only that Duncan had died. Surely he would let her borrow one of the ranch vehicles and make a hurried trip to Idaho so she could be with Eileen. She could make up the time by extending the term of her internship.

She scanned the room, wondering if it had been used by Dane and his first wife. Had they made love in this bed? Fought here over his dedication to the family business?

The bedroom suite appeared to be antique. The dresser was massive, the chest on chest decorated with carved woodland scenes. She sat up and twisted around to see the headboard of the bed. Viking boats, rolling hills and valleys and pastoral scenes of farms with families and animals had been carved in minute detail across the wood. Considering how old she sensed it was, the headboard and bed were unusually large. She could imagine a mother making up stories about the figures, holding a child or two in her arms, with an attentive husband and father watching them benignly. Why, a whole family of tales could be created and passed from generation to generation.

Abbie wondered if she should return to her own room. She glanced toward the connecting bathroom and back to the headboard. She decided not to go. Dane had brought her to his room, and knowing that he wanted her with him, in his bed, was reason enough to stay.

She reached for the lamp on the other side of the bed and turned if off. Only a hint of light came from the bathroom between their rooms.

Suddenly the door to the hallway opened and Dane entered. She heard the sounds of the lock being set. His shadowy form moved to the bathroom and the door closed. When the door opened several minutes later, she listened to him approach and felt the bed sink under his weight. He slid beneath the sheets and turned to her.

"I'm glad you didn't leave," he said.

"I couldn't."

"I want to hold you."

"Yes."

"Comfort you . . ."

"Yes."

"And make love to you." His hand slid beneath the flannel gown she wore.

"Oh, yes," Abbie whispered as she pressed against him.

"This sexy gown must go," Dane said, gathering the material in his hand. There must be yards of fabric here," he hissed, frustrated at the challenge it presented.

"I made it and I know exactly how many yards are in it. Shall I tell you?"

"I'm not interested in a sewing lesson, Abbie love," he said, "just the woman who made this. Help me."

She knelt on the bed and he rose to his knees. As she held out her arms, he slowly lifted the gown up and over her head.

"You are unique . . . beautiful," he murmured as his hand reached out and touched her breast, tracing a pattern on her flesh but not touching the erect crest. He repeated the pattern on her other breast and her breathing became ragged.

Her hands touched the skin just below his armpits and slowly she caressed his ribs, feeling each one beneath the layers of muscle, until she met the hardness of his waist. His hips were lean and solid, his thighs conditioned and firm.

She read the passion in his eyes and the emotions churning within her overflowed. "I love you," she whispered.

His hands settled on her throat. Slowly he eased her face up to his, his mouth hovering above hers before he took her lips, easing them open, exploring the sweet crevice of her mouth. His tongue played with hers until, slowly, he pulled away. He nibbled at her lower lip. "And I love you," he whispered, as they both sank down on the bed.

Dane's mouth charted a trail of kisses down her body, leaving a path of moist skin to quiver with each new touch. He suckled at her breasts, tasted the taut skin of her abdomen, and buried his face against the auburn triangle. He exhaled a breath of hot air against her and sent such a powerful surge of passion through her body she feared she might climax before he was inside her.

When he parted her legs and kissed the satin smooth skin of her inner thigh, she bit her lip to keep from crying out. A lingering kiss at the bend of her knee was her undoing.

"Dane, please come here," she moaned.

He suspended himself above her and he began his entry, slow and sure, bringing her what she had longed for so desperately.

His thrusts were agonizingly slow but deep and steady, his rhythm confident as he met her needs, evoking an erotic nature she had denied since that first night.

When the moment of fulfillment came, they shared the blending of their souls as fate wove them into the weft of a special tapestry.

"ABBIE?" DANE'S VOICE CALLED as if from a distance.

"Please don't talk," Abbie said, burrowing into his shoulder. "If you're sorry you brought me here, if you regret saying you love me, tell me tomorrow."

He stroked her arm, sliding his hand down to hers and bringing her fingers to his mouth. "Abbie, love, I have no regrets. How could you think such a thing after what we've shared?"

"Are you sure?" she asked.

He nodded. "I love you. Period. I don't give a damn about our pasts or our futures. Right now, in this bed, I love you. I haven't said that to anyone for a long time. Maybe I've been saving my love for you."

She sighed and they lay quietly for several minutes. "I have a question," she said. "It may cause problems."

"What is it?"

"Was this room . . . this bed . . . ? When you were married, did you and . . . your wife sleep here?"

"No, love," he replied, kissing her lightly. "Until five years ago, this room belonged to my parents. Lil and I had a room upstairs. You're the only woman I've made love to in this bed. It's a beauty, isn't it? My grandfather had it sent from Denmark as a twenty-fifth anniversary gift to my parents. The irony is that I was conceived in this bed, by two passionate people still in love, in their middle years. So it has a reputation as well as a story to go with it.''

She toyed with a blond curl near his ear before nipping his earlobe. ''I'm glad. About so many things, but especially about this bed. I'm glad you carried me here and made love to me. I think about you so much. I try not to, but sometimes you take over my brain. You're with me when I'm busy doing my weaving, when I'm cleaning the jugs. I want to be free, but I want to be with you, too. Can I have it both ways?''

''I don't know,'' he replied. ''We'll work on it, think about it . . . but right now, we still need to discuss tomorrow.''

''What about . . . tomorrow?'' she asked.

''Abbie,'' he said, holding her chin and turning her face to his. ''The funeral. It's the day after tomorrow. I promised Jordan I would have you there tomorrow.''

She groaned. ''How could I have made love to you while my cousin lies alone and grieving over the loss of her beloved husband? I feel so ashamed.''

''Don't,'' he said, smoothing her hair from her forehead. ''They are two very different situations. Neither can be changed.''

''May I borrow a truck?'' she asked.

''No.''

She sprang from his arms. ''Why not?''

''I promised Jordan I would bring you,'' he said, smiling as her expression changed to one of disbelief.

''You're too busy. How can you possibly get away?'' she asked.

''Everyone needs a break now and then.''

''But in the middle of lambing? You're crazy.''

"We're between two lambing sessions...and you wouldn't want me to break my word to a young boy who is trying to be a man, would you?"

"Just let me borrow one of the trucks," she said. "I could take the motor home but that means I would have to disconnect..."

"There's also this rumor going around about me thinking I'm indispensable," he said. "Haven't you heard it?"

She blushed. "I didn't...mean anything..." she stammered. "I'm sorry. I was angry and...Moses has a very loose tongue."

"I agree, but I'll take you," he insisted, pulling her back into his arms. "I promised Jordan. I suspect Jordan is trying to protect his mother...and our being there will help him to succeed and still relieve some of the pressure."

"Thank you, Dane," she whispered. "Jordan is a very special child, almost too serious for one so young."

He chuckled. "I was accused of the same thing. Perhaps I could help him cope. I'm willing to try."

"That's very thoughtful, considering you've never met my family," she said.

"There's strength in your family. I can sense it. Maybe it's from your roots in the Kentucky soil, the pioneer heritage we read about. Your family fascinates me. I want to meet them. Besides, I've had some phone calls from my brothers and sisters and I need time away from this place to think about my own family. What's in the wind could have a major effect on the future of this ranch. So you see, my darling Abbie, you're stuck with me as your chauffeur for three days; one to go, the day of the funeral, and a day to come home."

She settled against him. "If you insist."

"I do." He pulled her into the spoon of his hips, cradling her head on his pillow. "Now sleep. You're still weak from the flu and we'll be leaving first thing in the morning." Folding his arms around her, he kissed the top of her head.

Within minutes she knew he was asleep. She wouldn't think of the future. She would live each day for what it held and not speculate about tomorrow.

CHAPTER FIFTEEN

WHEN MORNING CAME, Dane kissed her awake.

"I want to make love to you again, but there's no time," he said, touching her mouth with his. "A few more minutes and the house will be filled with people who will wonder why I haven't put in an appearance."

"The burden of being *the boss*?"

He smiled.

She traced the line of his collarbone. "We only make love when something tragic happens. First the poor lambs, now Duncan's death. Omens?"

"Of course not," Dane said, propping himself on one elbow and toying with an auburn curl near her temple, pulling it out and letting it spring back.

"Someday, will you make love to me just for the pleasure of it?" she asked, touching the tiny cleft in his chin.

"Making love to you is always pleasurable, but yes, someday," he promised.

His words stayed with her as he left the bed and headed for the shower. She made her way through the steamy bathroom and into her bedroom, closing the door carefully behind her. In minutes, she had dressed and was out in the motor home, packing a small suitcase and a garment bag. She carried them back to the kitchen and set them by the door.

"Going somewhere, Abbie?" Wilma asked. "Surely you're not leaving us."

Abbie explained the purpose of the trip to those already seated at the table. "Dane has offered to drive me," she added.

She caught the glances exchanged by Moses and Wilma, and wondered what secrets lay between them.

Moses patted her empty chair. "Sit down, Abbie. We've missed you, and we're glad you're feeling well enough to eat with us and travel, but we're sorry about the reason. We are a little surprised to hear about the boss. He don't usually leave the place in the spring. Our first Finn lambs were born yesterday. Healthy triplets," he boasted.

"I asked to borrow a vehicle but he refused," she said.

"For a man, loaning his vehicle is like loaning his woman or his gun," Moses replied, shaking his head confidently. "Most prefer not to do it."

"In that order?" Buck asked from across the table.

"You know better than that," Moses said as he glared at Buck. "A man who's true puts his woman first, then his gun, and his truck last. So if the boss don't loan his truck, you can draw your own conclusions about his gun and his woman."

"You make it sound as though he considers them all his possessions," Abbie said, pouring herself a cup of coffee. Without thinking, she filled Dane's cup.

Wilma came to Moses's chair and laid the damp dish towel against his neck. "Some modern women are more independent, old man, and you should accept it." She kissed his weathered cheek. "But a little sugar still goes a long way with women when they're trying to make up their minds."

The others at the table laughed while Moses sputtered at Wilma's display of affection.

"I understand, Moses," Abbie said, watching his face turn from tan to ruddy red and back again, "but a woman is always independent in her mind, in her emotions. She may be financially dependent on a man, but that doesn't mean she belongs to the man."

"That's right," Wilma chimed in, "and even an old dog like you can learn a new trick or two when it comes to romancing the opposite sex. Now can't he?"

Moses huffed. "Well, I'm glad you're taking the boss away for a while. He's been a bear these past several days. It will be right nice to have him gone for a spell. Take some of the cussedness out of him while you have him to yourself, okay? It don't matter how you do it."

Abbie smiled but didn't reply.

Dane entered the kitchen and the conversation stopped. The blue in his wool dress trousers was several shades darker than the pale blue of his oxford-cloth shirt. Tiny white buttons on the collar peeked over the crew neck of his navy pullover.

As he dropped into his chair at the end of the table, Moses looked his way. "You're late, boss, and from the looks of those duds you ain't going to the lambing shed. Abbie, here, beat you to the table, and don't she look purty this morning? Like her old self again. Ain't it great to have her back?"

Dane stared directly into her eyes, holding her gaze so long that she felt a wave of embarrassment sweep up her cheeks.

"Yes, she looks . . . beautiful this morning," he said, his words a caress as he spoke, "and yes, it's good to have her back."

He let the others carry the conversation when it resumed. Near the end of the meal, he gave instructions. "You're in charge, Moses, and if the rest of you want to keep your jobs through the summer, you abide by his orders. We'll be back the day after tomorrow. Surely, you can get through three days without a catastrophe, can't you? Abbie has written down the phone number where we'll be, but remember the purpose of this trip. Abbie isn't fully recovered and I don't want her having a relapse while she's on the interstate . . . in one of my borrowed vehicles.''

"Boss, you got big ears," Moses complained. "I was just explaining your philosophy about—"

"Too many of you have big ears and big curiosities and big mouths that don't know when to shut up," Wilma chimed in, stopping Moses before he could dig himself into deeper trouble.

After breakfast, Dane brought a garment bag and a suitcase from his room, and motioned for Abbie to follow.

She started to pick up her own luggage, but Moses took the two bags from her. "The boss is getting his car," Moses said.

"Car? What car?" Abbie asked. "I thought you only had trucks on the place."

Moses laughed. "Once in a while the boss gives in to a little bit of vanity. This is one of those once-in-a-whiles. He bought a car last fall after an extra good lamb crop was sold. He's only had it out a few times since." He scratched his thinning hair. "I wouldn't be surprised if the battery is dead."

They listened as a powerful engine roared to life.

Abbie smiled. "It's a good thing you didn't bet your paycheck on that dead battery. Thanks, but I can manage," she said, grabbing her luggage. "I'm one of those liberated women you were talking about." She ran down the steps, anxious to discover Dane Grasten's little bit of vanity.

Out of the garage rolled the rear end of a maroon and silver Eagle station wagon. As he put her luggage in the back and hung her garment bag next to his, she touched the shiny metal.

"Nice," she said, "but is it practical?"

"It has four-wheel drive," he replied as he opened her door and she slid inside. The pale gray leather upholstery was glove soft. The interior still had the smell of newness.

As they turned onto the dirt road she smiled. "This car is more out of character for you than your clothing. I have trouble getting used to you in anything but coveralls."

His stern features softened. "I've wanted a new car for years but couldn't justify it. Last fall, I was looking for a replacement tractor and stopped at a new car dealership in town just to browse." He smiled. "The salesman is a friend. He said this one had my name on it. Before I left town it was mine."

"And the tractor?"

He laughed. "I never found what I was looking for...and after paying cash for this, I wasn't sure I could afford the tractor."

"Well, I think it's very beautiful, luxurious but practical. How many miles have you put on it in...six months, is it?" She leaned toward him, trying to get a view of the odometer.

"One hundred eighty-six," he said, smiling as he shifted gears and roared down the dirt road toward the interstate highway.

"How many?" She leaned against his arm to see for herself. "You're right. Why so few?"

He shrugged. "Nowhere to go and no one to take with me."

Abbie settled into the bucket seat and closed her eyes. She wished the purpose of their trip wasn't such a sad one. What would it be like to lose a beloved husband? As she turned her head toward Dane, she fantasized about being his wife, sharing the work and trials of such a demanding life, enjoying the good times of going with him to the summer range and possibly living in a trailer or even a sheep wagon, the lovemaking that would surely become a significant part of their lives, the children that might come from that passion, children to bind them together forever, as a family.

But families were often destroyed by forces from within and without, unexpected forces that could come out of nowhere and...

She straightened in the seat and tore her eyes away from his profile. How quickly daydreams could evaporate.

"What were you thinking about?" he asked, as they turned onto the access road to the interstate.

"Families again. Eileen and Duncan...you and Lillian. You never did tell me what happened."

He glanced at her before concentrating on the highway. "I've never told anyone the full story, not even Moses or Wilma or my parents."

She glanced at his hands on the steering wheel, his knuckles white from the tight grip. "Perhaps it's time. I promise to listen and not to judge."

"We had a fight...words...cutting, insulting, damaging words. It was the evening she told me how she really felt about the child and how she hated being pregnant. I stormed out and went to the lambing shed, trying to calm down. It was dark when she came to see me at the shed. She said she was leaving . . . that she wouldn't be back. I assumed she would drive into Dillon and stay in a motel for a few days, cool off and return, and we'd work out our differences. It wasn't the first time she'd left. I was still too angry to try to stop her. My pride blinded me.

"About a half hour later I smelled smoke. At one end of the shed, she had poured gasoline all along the base of the building and splashed it up on the walls and set it afire. I had been in the other end and . . . God, I should have been aware of it sooner . . . but I wasn't.

"Wilma saw the flames from the house and called the rural fire department. Trucks from Ennis, Sheridan and Twin Bridges came and finally the firemen put it out. It could have been worse. We lost several ewes from smoke inhalation and quite a few lambs were trampled. Several weeks later she wrote from Texas. She had had an abortion. I've never heard from her since except for her response to the court when I filed for divorce. My only regret is the baby I'll never know." He turned to her. "So much for my family life experiences. Do you want to compare horror stories?"

"I've never married," she said.

"No children?"

Pursing her lips, she inhaled. "Sign of the times, isn't it, when marriage and children are separate facts of life?"

He shrugged. "One never knows. You're a beautiful woman. Surely you had a few close encounters."

"Just one but we had no plans to marry," she said. "I met him when I was a senior at the University of Utah. After graduation, I opened my own crafts shop and weavers gallery. He was a systems analyst at a high-tech manufacturing firm in Ogden. That's a fancy name for a high-level computer programmer. He wanted us to live together, to try the shoes on for size. Finally I agreed, and he moved into my apartment. The shoes fit reasonably well, but we decided there was no reason to complicate matters. I think we were just two lonely people who enjoyed each other's company for a while. I don't intend to ever get myself into that kind of situation again.''

''You don't sound like a heartbroken woman, only a little scorned.''

''Neither,'' she said. ''I found myself liberated and free to make my own choices. Frankly, I like it that way. When we parted company there were no assets to divide, no joint bank accounts, just his and mine, no ours, and thankfully no children.''

''You don't care for children?'' he asked.

''Oh, I love them, but the only ones I've been around are my cousins'. I just feel that if a woman has the babies, she should love the man enough to...to...keep her wedding vows through thick or thin.''

''Sometimes it doesn't work out that way,'' he warned.

''But surely if two people really want to make it work, shouldn't they be able to be successful? Maybe the answer is in compromising when they have disagreements. I don't know. I've never had to practice what I preach.'' She smiled. ''I sound like my conservative aunt and uncle, don't I, yet here I sit with you, a man I've made love with twice and neither of us has any plans to deepen the relationship.''

He drove in silence for several miles. ''Why did you and the programmer break up?'' he asked.

She frowned. ''As I became more successful with my tapestries, he began to make fun of me. He said it was child's play to weave strings together and find some sucker who is willing to pay an outrageous price for the results. He insisted on calling my tapestries rugs. I like to get up early, at the crack of dawn, and watch the first rays of a new morning break, but then when the sun goes down I'm bushed. He liked to go out to the singles' bars in the city but I'd yawn as the evening went on and he'd get angry.

"He never tried to understand what I went through when I was working on my designs. I do tend to get into moods when I work. When I'm sitting at my tapestry loom or the six-harness treadle loom, I can stay there for hours and hours. I lose track of the time. He resented that. Call it an obsession or whatever, but it's my chosen profession and no one is going to tell me I can't work at it!"

They were quiet for a while. "We'll eat in Idaho Falls," he said, then started to chuckle. "Let me rephrase that. Would you like to eat in Idaho Falls?"

She smiled. "It does make a difference in how it's phrased, doesn't it?"

He smiled, then signaled and took the first exit into the city. "You're six weeks into your internship," he said. "What do you plan to do after it ends?"

She caught the underlying message in his question. "I'll find a piece of land, build myself a studio and a home. I can live in the motor home until the studio is finished. It's the most important part of my plans. The house can be built later when I have more money."

He glanced her way. "Tell me about the studio."

She described her dream studio in minute detail, right down to the pit out in the yard for outdoor dyeing.

"I'm sure you'll have it all some day," he replied. "You have the determination to carry through on your plans."

"And you?" she asked. "What does your future hold? Do you foresee any changes?"

"That depends on several things. Some of my sisters and brothers want my folks to sell the place and divide the proceeds equally among them."

"Oh, Dane, that would be terrible," she exclaimed. "Could they force your parents to do that? That's not fair to you. You've stayed there, worked so hard and made it prosperous! How could they be so selfish?"

"It was a risk I took when I agreed to manage the operation. But I've held a few cards back, just in case I needed them. Now, why don't you choose a restaurant and we'll eat?"

During lunch they were somber, as each pondered the other's revelations.

"We'd better go," Abbie said. "It's only about fifteen more miles. Maybe we should have gone directly to Eileen's." She opened her purse and pulled out her wallet.

"This was better," Dane replied. "They would have invited us to eat and gone to extra trouble. Put your money away."

"But this trip is because of me," she said. "I'll pay for the meal and fill your gas tank and . . ."

"Please, Abbie, allow me the privilege of doing this because I want to," Dane said as he tucked the twenty-dollar bill back into her purse.

"I don't want you providing my meals or . . ."

"I've been providing your meals ever since I first laid eyes on you, Hardesty," he said. "Why change things now?" He reached for the check and dropped a tip on the table.

Outside, he unlocked and opened her door. She hesitated. "I won't know what to say to Eileen." She looked at him. "How do you console a woman who has lost everything?"

He put his hands on her shoulders. "She hasn't lost everything. She has the children. He will always be with her in them, and your being there will be consolation enough."

Sliding into the seat, she brushed the corners of her eyes and directed him out of town and south, to the small town of Shelley. "Turn here," she said. "It's about four miles. You can see it in the distance." She watched the white frame farmhouse grow larger in the distance. Suppressing the choking sensation that was building in her throat, she reached for his hand. "Thanks for coming with me," she murmured and he squeezed her hand reassuringly.

They were greeted at the door by the twins.

"Hi, Aunt Abbie, did you know our daddy got really bad sick...and now he's never coming back?" Jolene asked sadly.

"And Momma was crying but now she's stopped," Jodie said, "and Jordan is being bossy and..."

Abbie knelt on the top step of the porch and hugged them. "I know, darlings, I know, but soon you'll all feel much better. Your daddy would want you to be happy and keep loving each other. Be extra nice to your momma, you hear?"

They wiped their eyes and nodded their matching brown heads.

The girls spotted Dane standing near the unfamiliar automobile. "Who's that?" they said in unison, pointing at him.

"That is a friend of mine," Abbie said, rising and motioning Dane forward. "Girls, this is Dane Grasten. This is Jolene," she said, patting the girl on her right, "and this is Jodie. They're identical twins, just in case you hadn't noticed."

"I noticed," Dane replied, smiling and extending his hand to each girl.

They shook it, giggling as they raced into the house to announce the arrival of Abbie and Dane.

In seconds they were back at the front door. "Momma says to come into the kitchen," Jolene said. "She's making coffee. The neighbors have been bringing all kinds of food. It's everywhere!"

"Some of it is yucky," Jodie exclaimed.

Jolene elbowed her sister's ribs. "Momma said not to say that anymore, that we should be grateful. I like the peach pie Mrs. Miller brought."

In the kitchen, they found Eileen Mills. When she turned, Abbie was shocked at the weariness in her cousin's posture and features. Dark circles gave her hazel eyes a bewildered expression. Her brown hair had been pulled back in a single braid but wispy curls had escaped, making her appear much younger than her thirty-two years.

"Oh, Abbie," Eileen said, her voice breaking, "I'm so glad you came."

Abbie folded Eileen in her arms, holding her tightly as she sobbed against Abbie's shoulder. "It's all right, it's going to get better, I know it will. Cry, cry all you need to. That's why we're here." She patted Eileen's back, slowly rubbing it until some of the tension began to ease.

Finally Eileen withdrew and wiped her eyes. "I'm sorry," she murmured, turning away and blowing her nose. "Sit down, please. I'll get you some coffee."

"No, you sit down," Abbie insisted. "And I'll need another cup. I didn't come alone."

"The girls said you'd brought a friend." Eileen turned, spying Dane lingering in the doorway, watching the two women. "Oh," she gasped. "I didn't expect...oh, my!"

"Why don't you both sit down," Dane suggested, "and the girls and I will serve you two. Right, girls?"

"Yes," the twins cried.

He kept them occupied for several minutes as he lifted first one, then the other, while they surveyed the generous donations of food on the counter and side table. Finally the girls agreed on fudge brownie squares and celery sticks filled with cream cheese, and served them to Abbie and Eileen.

As Dane poured coffee, he caught the curious gaze of Eileen. "I'm Dane Grasten. I'm her boss," he said.

"Oh?" Eileen murmured.

Dane set the pot down and sat trying to fold his long legs beneath the table. "She's been sick," he said.

"It was just the flu," Abbie explained.

"No, it wasn't," he said. "Well, it was, but a very severe case of it, and I couldn't have her on the highway alone. She would have been a menace to herself and the other drivers. We would have worried about her."

"Oh, I see," said Eileen, studying Dane with new interest.

"She didn't have a car," he continued, "and I have this thing about loaning women, vehicles and guns. When my foreman explained that to her, she accepted my offer."

Abbie muffled a laugh with her hand.

"Oh." Eileen's eyes moved back and forth between Dane and Abbie. "I don't think either of you is quite telling the truth, but I'm glad you brought her." She extended her hand to Dane.

"Now tell us what we can do," Abbie said. "We didn't come to just visit, we came to help."

"Thanks," Eileen said. "There's visitation tonight, with services at the Baptist church in Shelley tomorrow at ten-thirty, followed by the usual graveside services in the Mills family plot." She stared wide-eyed at them and her eyes grew shimmery. "All those years when I was a child I hated funerals and my folks would make me go, 'so I'd know what to do,' they always said. And now... now I'm in the center of one... and I hate it just as much as I always did. Is that terrible?"

Abbie patted her hand. "No, Eileen, but you're a strong person. You'll make it through tomorrow and we'll be here."

"I've always believed in the hereafter but now I feel like my world ended yesterday," Eileen said sadly. "I miss him so much. Even while he was so sick, I still loved him very much. I don't know if I can keep going. I made all kinds of promises to Duncan, but that was when he was still alive. Now... I don't think I can fulfill any of them. I feel... so inadequate."

"It's normal to feel that way now," Abbie replied.

"Don't make any significant decisions for several months," Dane cautioned. "They can wait. I've seen too many widows regret decisions they were pressured into by well-meaning family members and friends."

"You're both wonderful," Eileen said, squeezing their hands.

"Where's your son?" Dane asked.

"He's out in one of the spud cellars," Eileen said. "He promised his father he would oversee the spring planting. If the weather holds up, we'll be planting in a few weeks. Jordan is so serious. He refuses to show any sign of weakness and he hasn't cried once. When I hug him, he's as stiff as a board. He has to break sometime."

"Point me in the right direction," Dane said. "I'll introduce myself. We talked on the phone and I'd like to meet him. Perhaps I can help."

Two hours later, as the others sat down to supper, Dane returned with Jordan. Jordan's eyes were red but dry, and he and Dane went to the sink and washed their hands.

After the meal, Jordan returned to the spud cellars, promising to return in an hour, and the girls went outside to play on the swing set in the backyard.

"I don't know what you did, but thank you," Eileen said. "Jordan is different, more relaxed."

"We just talked...sort of man to man," he said, looking solemnly at both women. "I haven't had a talk like that since I was a boy myself. Now, if we're finished here, tell me where we'll be staying and I'll bring in our luggage."

Eileen hesitated. "Do you...ah...what do you prefer?"

"Could I share Jordan's room?" he asked. "Jordan said he has twin beds."

"You're sure?" Eileen asked, glancing at Abbie.

"I'm sure," he replied.

After he left, Eileen said, "It would have been okay with me...if you had shared the same room. I'm no prude."

Abbie smiled. "This is fine."

Eileen frowned. "What's between you two? You both tiptoe around each other like you're afraid the other might figure out what you're really feeling. Is something wrong?"

Abbie shook her head from side to side.

"Then everything is just fine?"

Abbie shook her head again the same way.

Eileen studied Abbie more carefully. "So, you've only known each other a little while...and there's something developing . . . but neither of you is sure what to make of it?''

This time Abbie nodded.

"And it's too soon to tell what might happen?''

Abbie nodded again.

"Then good luck and may you both come out winners," Eileen said, her mouth softening into a smile.

Abbie turned to Eileen. "Who's coming from back home?''

"No one," Eileen replied grimly.

"But why not?''

"Daddy fell and broke his hip in a freak ice storm two weeks ago and Momma won't leave him. The others called and gave their regrets but they just can't afford the plane tickets with the economy so depressed back there. Dad says the tobacco crop doesn't look very promising. They've cut the quotas on Burley tobacco this year and they're predicting a dry summer. There's talk of a layoff at the Rainbow River Coal Mine Number Two any week. That would put most of the Hardesty men out of work. They've already closed Number Three for an indefinite period. You know how the area has always specialized in poverty? Well it hasn't changed. The unemployment rate in Muhlenberg County is well above the national average and the guys have to hang on as long as they can.''

"Sounds like farming and ranching," Dane observed.

"What about Callie?" Abbie asked. "Surely she'll be here.''

Eileen shook her head. "Callie is too broke even to buy a bus ticket to Central City. Momma is trying to get her to call me collect or call from Momma's house, but I don't expect her to do either. You know Callie—she's too proud to ask for help.''

"Callie," Abbie said derisively. "She never could hang onto her money. Is she still on . . . assistance?"

"She wouldn't take it if she didn't need it, Abbie," Eileen replied, coming to their cousin's defense. "And you shouldn't be so critical. Sometimes fate plays strange tricks on us."

"But she had it all," Abbie retorted. "The pampered baby in her family. She never had to work in the summers. She always started the school year with those pretty new dresses. Aunt Minnie made mine from her old dresses."

Eileen frowned. "You sound jealous."

"Of course not, but there's no excuse for her being on the dole. Surely her parents would help her," Abbie said.

"It's not her parents' problem, it's hers, and she'll work it out in time," Eileen said. "Aunt Ellen and Uncle Finis did their best but Callie was always so strong-willed. We all were. Have your forgotten?"

Abbie stiffened. "No, of course I haven't forgotten those years, but parents should...good grief, at least she *had* parents. If those of us who didn't have responsible parents can make it, why can't people like Callie?"

"You had a momma," Eileen reminded her, "and she stayed in touch. Doesn't she count?"

"If you mean those letters she wrote that no one could read, yes, she stayed in touch," Abbie said bitterly. "I still get one about Christmastime each year, but her return address is so scribbled, I've never been able to write back. She stopped in to visit Aunt Minnie once about four years ago and left before Aunt Min thought to get a better address. She's never been a dependable person or a good mother. When I have children, I'm going to be responsible for their care, no one else, and I'm going to give them all the love they need."

"What about the father?" Dane asked, leaning back in his chair and scrutinizing her. "Doesn't he have any say in the matter?"

"I...well, of course, but...I just meant..." Abbie stammered. "Never mind. How did we get on this subject anyway?"

"I've never heard you talk about having children," Eileen said. "Have you had a change of heart?" She glanced at Dane but he was staring at Abbie and didn't look her way.

"A person can always change his or her mind," Abbie said, feeling the heat of embarrassment on her cheeks. "It's all a part of maturing."

CHAPTER SIXTEEN

ABBIE, EILEEN AND DANE sat in the living room, and soon the conversation drifted to their childhoods. Dane told of being the sixth child in his family with everyone else at least twenty years older. Eileen and Abbie discussed their youthful years when they and Callie were the only girls in an extended family of three uncles and their wives, assorted in-laws and grandparents and lots of cousins.

The stories grew in outlandishness, and they all began to laugh. "Remember when..." each would begin, and one or the other would tell a new tale of summer fun or winter escapades, family gatherings on holidays, church potluck dinners on the grounds on Sunday afternoons, the religious revivals in the fall.

Eileen frowned. "The revivals always came after harvest, didn't they? Those preachers knew when they could get the men's attention. Crops first, spiritual matters second—that's the reality of it, isn't it?"

Abbie dropped her head against the high back of the sofa. She felt Dane's arm move out of her way. "Whatever happened?" she asked nostalgically. "We had so many dreams...and none of them have materialized. We all tried in our different ways. Eileen, you were going to run your own business, remember? You were always the organizer, the leader. Then you and Duncan met and you gave it all up for love, and babies and all this domesticity.''

Eileen smiled. "And you, Abbie, always wanted to be a weaver and make tapestries so big they would have to put up whole buildings just to house them."

"Yes," Abbie agreed, "and I didn't give a thought to money because I was used to getting my materials from our farms or the countryside or by raiding Aunt Minnie's sewing wall. Remember how she made it from vegetable crates and lined it with feed sacks?"

Eileen nodded. "And I remember the summer she showed us how to spin, to clean the fleeces and, best of all, to go to the hills and find the plants to use as dyes. Callie and I lost interest after a day or two but you were fascinated. You've certainly been successful."

Abbie shrugged. "I guess so, moderately."

"And poor little Callie," Eileen continued. "She always dreamed about being a singer or a musician and going to Nashville, and instead she married and had those babies and then that no-good Bobby Joe decided he had had enough and he skipped out, leaving Callie destitute, with all those medical bills. Men!"

"Now, ladies, don't be bitter or cynical about men," Dane warned. "They aren't the cause of your problems. Actually it sounds as if you all got what you dreamed about, but it's like answered prayers. You must be careful what you pray for because you might get it."

"Maybe you're right," Abbie said, "but Callie is the one I don't understand. She had everything and gave it all up when she got pregnant so young."

"I thought I had it all, too," Eileen said. "I thought Duncan and I would grow old together and instead, here I am, with my own business to run after all. What a cruel way to get what I asked for when I was so young and ignorant.''

Dane rose from the sofa. "I'm going to get some fresh air before going to bed. Want to come with me, either of you?''

Eileen declined. "You two go. You deserve some time alone. I'm very tired, and tomorrow will be...a difficult day. Thanks for reminiscing with me. It helps to forget. Good night," she called, and she left the room almost on a run.

Outside, Abbie drew her sweater closely around her and followed Dane down the steps and across the yard. He continued walking until he reached the first plowed potato field, running for acres across the farm.

He put his fists on his hips. "Sometimes I think farming and ranching are the two most miserable and least appreciated occupations a person could choose for making a living." He turned toward another plowed field. "Yet at other times I can't imagine doing anything else. There's something wholesome and basic about growing and raising what the rest of the country takes for granted. A man has to be a little crazy to care about such matters." He turned to her. "It's a very confusing world, isn't it, Abbie?''

"Yes," she replied, but as his arms went around her and he pulled her against him, she knew that together they could create order out of that chaos.

His mouth brushed her forehead. "I've never felt lonely until I met you, Abbie."

"I know," she whispered. "I've always enjoyed being alone, but now I think of you and wonder where you are and what you're doing...or thinking."

"I'm probably thinking of you," he confessed. "You've become a terrible distraction."

"What's ahead when we go back?" she asked.

"More lambing. The last week in May, the shearers come from Whitehall. It takes five of them to get it done. We inoculate for several maladies, dip or spray for sheep ticks, and if everything looks fine, we head for the high country in early June. We stay there until mid-September when we bring the sheep home and separate the lambs from the ewes and ship the lambs off to market. Then it starts all over again when we put the rams in with the ewes in October and November, depending on when we want lambing to occur."

"It never ends, does it?" Abbie asked.

"Not if you want to make a profit," Dane replied. "It's a business. I can't pay all the salaries, maintain the equipment, buy the vet supplies and the grain and feed we can't raise ourselves, set some aside for emergency hay purchases in case of a bad hay season and still have something left at the end of the year to divide among the family if I stop."

"What about you?" she asked, looking up at him. "Don't you get any extra above and beyond what the others get? After all, you're the one doing all the work!"

"I get a salary, plus a bonus, as well as my share." He touched her hair.

"Don't you ever get time off?" she asked. "You shouldn't be a slave to the place each and every day of the year."

"There are times when the work is slack. Winter if the weather is mild, or summer when I have enough sheep-herders to free me for some time off." His fingers slid through the curly strands of her hair. "It's grown since I first saw you. You have beautiful hair. I'll bet you were a holy terror when you were a kid, with a temper to match the hair. Did you freckle?"

"A little . . . and you?"

"I was a tow-headed Danish boy, stocky and stubborn."

"And cute as a button," she guessed, smiling.

He grew quiet. "Did you ever wonder what your own child might look like?"

"Not really," she admitted. "A blend of the husband and wife. Perhaps more of one than the other. Why do you ask?"

She waited for his reply, but instead of speaking, he pulled her close. "Enough of families and farming," he said and gently kissed her mouth, savoring the warm responsive feel of her lips beneath his. "You've a very special person, Abbie."

"So are you," she replied and her arms slid around his neck. "I wish . . . that we didn't have to go straight back to the ranch, that we could take an extra day or two and . . . just be together."

He shook his head. "We can't, not now when we're so busy. Perhaps when lambing and shearing are done."

"The next months will go by very fast," she murmured, resting her forehead against his shirt.

"Yes, and then you'll be on your way. Anxious to move on?"

In the darkness, she tried to think of an appropriate response but none came. His fingers touched the corners of her eyes and wiped the moisture away.

"We'll just have to enjoy this time we have, love, live each day to the fullest, as the philosophers would say." He kissed her once more before leading her back to the house.

THE FUNERAL WAS BRIEF, the church filled with friends and several Mills relatives. Eileen played the part of a gracious hostess when many came to her home after the internment.

Abbie assisted several women from the church in helping with the food, and insisted Eileen go outside for a few minutes. Later, when she looked out the window, she spotted Dane and Eileen, the three children and the reporter, Daniel Page, who had interviewed the Mills family a year earlier. They were strolling toward the plowed potato fields.

Good, Abbie thought as she turned her attention to the guests. Eileen needed the steady presence of her family today, and the two men with her would hopefully give her the emotional support she needed to sustain her loss. Dan Page had appeared at the cemetery, lingering after most of the mourners had left, then coming to visit privately with Eileen. He had the lean build of a runner and a quickness of eye typical of his profession. Eileen had invited him back to the house, where he had stayed in the background. Abbie sensed his protective manner with Eileen and the children, and wondered about it.

When Dan Page said his goodbyes in the yard, long after everyone else had left, he had eyes only for Eileen. "Here's my card. You call me if I can help in any way. If I'm out, leave a message and I'll get back to you." He turned to Abbie and Dane, his brown hair glistening in the sunshine, his green eyes serious. "Try to convince her to call me. There's no need to carry the burden alone. She has friends."

Dane nodded. "We're leaving tomorrow but we'll stay in touch. These Hardesty women can be overly proud. I've learned that the hard way. If you don't hear from her, take the initiative yourself. But you have to give them time and space. They're stubborn and quick to jump to wrong conclusions, but they smarten up sooner or later."

Before Abbie could react, he kissed her soundly in front of all the others. Amidst the laughter of the children, Dane, Abbie and Eileen waved goodbye to Daniel Page.

"I'm glad he came," Eileen said, watching the car disappear behind a cloud of dust. "He's the only other man other than Duncan I've felt I could talk to freely. I like him in a special way."

Dane and Abbie left shortly after noon the next day. The drive home was all too brief for Abbie, whose thoughts were divided among Eileen and the children, Daniel Page and his interest in Eileen, the sheep ranch and its people, her weaving career and her goals of having her own place, her own flock and studio, and Dane Grasten.

He had changed dramatically since that first meeting, yet his inconsistency made her hesitant to read more into his affection than was safe to allow. She wasn't sure what she actually wanted from him. She could think of nothing he could give up to be with her, and her future lay elsewhere.

They drove through Dillon and onto the Sweetwater Road, and Dane reached for her hand. "We'll be home in less than an hour."

"Yes. Thanks for the ride, boss," she replied, smiling at his rugged profile.

"You're welcome, Hardesty," he teased. "I can't think of any other employee I'd rather spend three days with than you." He braked and pulled off the gravel road. "Abbie," he said, taking her hands, "I don't know what lies ahead for us. I won't make promises because I don't know if I can keep them. The Finns and Lincolns are lambing. We'll be very busy. To make matters worse, all my sisters and brothers will be coming next week to discuss the future of the ranch. Maybe it has no future, I don't know. But I want you to know that although we'll have little or no time alone, it doesn't mean I don't want to be with you.''

He chuckled. ''Maybe I'll have to assign you to the feeding truck or the two of us to a night shift in the lambing shed in order to see you.'' He squeezed her hands. ''Do you understand?''

''I...think so,'' she replied. ''Just because we've been...close a few times, it doesn't mean we've put strings on each other.''

''We haven't just been 'close,' Abbie love,'' he assured her. ''We've made passionate and wonderful love together. Now we must consider the significance of that. We wouldn't want either of us to have regrets because we made the wrong choice, would we?'' His hands cupped her cheeks.

''No,'' she agreed, but the tremor in her voice belied her confident posture.

''Good,'' he said, drawing her face closer, brushing his lips against her eyes before claiming her mouth.

She rested her head against his shoulder. ''I can't believe I thought you were so terrible that first day,'' she said.

''And I can't believe I wanted to send you away.'' He traced the outline of her lips and she kissed his finger.

''We must thank Dr. Christensen for sending me to you,'' she said.

''And Moses for convincing me to let you stay,'' he replied.

Dane released her gently. ''Let's get out of here before I try to find out if we can make love right here in this brand-new station wagon. Damn it, I knew there was a reason for buying this car.'' He laughed as he turned the key in the ignition.

''You don't laugh very often,'' she remarked.

''I seldom have a reason.''

''Then I'm glad I've given you one,'' she replied.

When they drove under the towering log entrance and into the Sweetwater ranch yard, Abbie tensed. An unfamiliar automobile with Colorado license plates was parked beside another strange vehicle from Washington state.

''Who do they belong to?'' Abbie asked, turning to Dane.

''Ejner lives in Denver and Petra in Seattle,'' Dane replied. ''They're here early. Anna and Maren were flying into Great Falls and driving down with my oldest brother, Knud. It looks like the family confab is starting early. It won't be pleasant, but two of them are on my side.'' He turned to Abbie. ''How do you break a family deadlock over the future of thirty-six sections of land, several thousand sheep, a ranching business that's more than a century old and this lovely old house?''

''Very carefully,'' she said, ''and with a lot of tender loving care. The house and property and livestock should not be sacrificed for greed.''

He nodded, surprised at her depth of concern.

''What about your folks?'' she asked.

''That's what this is all about, Abbie,'' he said. ''My mother is eighty-three and my father is eighty-eight. They are both in incredibly good health. They would be crushed if they knew their children were having this meeting. You see, three of my own siblings want to divide their inheritance before Mom and Dad are dead. I suspect they're afraid their parents might outlive them. How's that for coldheartedness?''

He drove the car into the garage and turned off the ignition. Turning to her, he said, "Come inside with me and I'll introduce you."

"That won't be necessary," she replied. "They'll wonder why you're making a fuss about me. I'll go to the motor home and put my things away, then clear out the belongings I left in the house. You'll need that room for one of them, I'm sure."

"I'll help you."

"No, I can manage," she insisted, hefting the garment bag over her shoulder and marching toward the motor home.

Dane watched her go, realizing their time together was ending once again. Thoughts of Abbie weighed heavily on his mind as he entered the kitchen. All he wanted to do was make it to his bedroom before Petra and Ejner spotted him. He failed.

Moses and Wilma were seated near Petra and Ejner. Oscar was two chairs away. Trudy was busy refilling everyone's cup with fresh coffee.

He felt little affection for either of his relatives. Petra, smiling pretentiously, with her gray hair cut in the latest sophisticated city style, was the first to greet him.

"Hello, Dane," she said, rising from her chair and coming to him. She kissed him on each cheek and squeezed his shoulders. "It's so good to see you again. It's been such a long time." She took his arm and guided him to the others seated around the table. Her height was just under six feet, her figure still willowy. No one but a family member would guess her age to be fifty-eight.

"When did you get here?" Dane asked.

Ejner stood, extending his hand. At five-eight, he was considerably shorter than his sister. "Welcome home, Dane." His sixty years had been kind to him also.

"Wilma told us about the trip." He sat down again and took a long draw from his coffee mug.

"I didn't expect you until next week," Dane said, refusing a cup himself. "Why are you early?"

"Relax, little brother," Petra said. "Ejner and I felt we'd been away from home too long. We wanted to have a few days to relax, to enjoy the atmosphere. Living in a large city, we tend to forget what it's like here."

"The Finns are lambing," Moses piped up. "Did you bring your coveralls and overshoes? It can get messy, you know. Boss, yesterday we had five sets of triplets, a set of quaddies, several twins and not a single single!"

"That's good," Dane said, his gaze shifting from Petra to Ejner before turning his attention to Moses. "Are they doing okay?"

"Sure," Moses replied. "Wilma and me, we handled it all."

"From the looks of this kitchen, most of the crew is in, having a long coffee break. Who's minding the lambing shed?"

"It's covered, it's covered," Moses insisted. "Evie and a new man from the employment office in Sheridan are there. I hired the guy with the understanding you'd have to give your blessing. But he's a right sharp young feller. I think you'll like him. His father has sheep over near White Sulphur Springs, so he knows what it's all about."

"Good." Dane looked out at Abbie's motor home through the curtains but couldn't get a clear view. He returned his attention to his brother and sister. They continued to chat about their childhood on the ranch. Dane glanced toward the window once again.

Petra pursed her lips. "Are you listening to us, Dane? Who are you looking for?"

Wilma rose from the table and patted Dane's shoulder as she went past his chair. "I'll go welcome Abbie back and bring her in to meet everyone."

Several minutes later, Wilma returned with a reluctant Abbie in tow. She had changed into jeans topped with a loose knit shirt. Dane smiled. Across the front of the shirt was the cartoon character, Snoopy, wearing an oversized cowboy hat. Snoopy's rural mailbox read, "Joe Rancher." In spite of the informal clothing, Dane found Abbie beautiful.

Wilma pulled Abbie away from the door. "This is our intern from Utah. Abigail Hardesty, meet the boss's youngest sister, Petra, and his brother, Ejner. They gave up the country life for the big city years ago." As they shook hands, Wilma continued. "Abbie is from Kentucky. She's a farm girl and loves it here."

"Fits right in," Moses added. "Like she belongs here."

"Nice meeting you both," Abbie said politely. "Now, I'll get my things from the blue room and . . ."

"Oh, I cleared that stuff out hours ago," Petra said. "I prefer not to have to climb the stairs, and I've already moved my things in. I put your belonging on the porch, in a trash bag."

"What the hell did you do that for?" Dane exclaimed. "Abbie was staying in that room. You had no right."

"Calm down, Dane," Petra replied. "Trudy said your girlfriend here was due to go back to her motor home as soon as you two returned from your little trip anyway. I can imagine what kind of arrangement you had. All I found were nightgowns, no street clothes at all. Really, Dane."

"What she wore is no concern of yours," Dane said, his face flushed with anger. "You can just put them . . ."

Abbie laid her hand on his forearm. "It's fine, really," she insisted. "Trudy offered to do my laundry while we were gone. That's why there were no street clothes and I didn't need my work clothes. I stayed in that room only at Dane's insistence and only because I was ill."

"I'm sure," Petra murmured, the expression on her face skeptical.

Abbie pressed her fists against her thighs. "Dane is right. It's none of your business and I don't appreciate your treating my belongings in such a high-handed manner. I'd planned to move out and this proves I was right. I'm an outsider and I belong outside."

"You're not an outsider anymore," Dane said, putting his arm around her shoulders. "When we have our family meeting, I want you there."

"Why?" she asked.

"Yes, why?" Petra moved closer. "Our meeting is confidential."

A muscle in Dane's jaw twitched. "I want her there precisely because she is an outsider. I won't be part of this unless you all agree to someone recording the entire meeting. Abbie will change the cassette tapes and take notes and keep all our memories honest. Will you do that for me, Abbie?"

Before she could decline, Dane's brother sprang from his chair. "No," Ejner exclaimed. "She has no right to be there."

"No Abbie, no meeting," Dane said. "If we get out of hand, she'll bring us back to the subject. Will you do it, Abbie?"

She shook her head. "No, please don't ask me. I couldn't be impartial. I feel very strongly about this place."

He reached for her hand. "I need you."

She inhaled deeply, sensing she was making a mistake. "All right, Dane. If you insist."

CHAPTER SEVENTEEN

EARLY ON THE MORNING of the meeting, Abbie spent time in the den confirming she knew how to operate the cassette recorder. She stacked the blank tapes in two piles, made several marks on the legal pad to verify the pens would work, then sat down to await everyone's arrival. For the occasion, she wore a dress.

She glanced up as Dane and the others entered.

Dane decided he'd been right from the first time he'd seen her. Abbie sat perched on a high stool, a vision in black and gray. He couldn't get a full view of the dress she wore, but it appeared to be a soft woolen blend, its simple design accenting her slimness. His eyes traced a nylon-clad leg up to where it disappeared from sight at the end of a slit a few inches above her knee.

He smiled. His sister Petra would have a fit when she spotted the slit in Abbie's dress. Over the years, Petra had appointed herself the family arbiter.

Unable to resist, he strolled to Abbie's seat.

"You look lovely," he said softly. "I've always known you'd look great in black." He surprised them both by giving in to the urge to kiss her.

Abbie pulled away. "You mustn't. What will they think?" She peeked around his shoulder and caught Petra staring at them. "They're watching."

"Let them," Dane said, kissing her again lightly.

Abbie glanced at her watch. "Shouldn't we begin?"

"I suppose so."

Afraid he might kiss her a third time, she gathered her writing tablet. "Who's in charge?"

"Knud," Dane replied, stepping away a few inches. "He's the oldest and the most diplomatic." He touched her hand. "Abbie, you know how important this meeting is. If you think of anything we overlook feel free to speak up. I trust some of them more than others. And watch out for Ejner and Petra... and Maren."

She frowned. "Why are you so suspicious of your own family?"

His features softened. "It's in my genes, I think. The Danish people have spent too many generations being suspicious of the Swedes, the Norwegians and the Finns, and yet the rest of the world lump us all together. Ironic, isn't it?"

"You should all band together then, instead of letting your distrust undermine your strength," she scolded. "Families should do that, also. The Hardesty family learned that principle long, long ago."

"Tell that to my father and grandfather." He chuckled. "The Grasten family consists of generations of men who have operated with their backs against the wall in order to see who their enemies might be."

"But the enemies shouldn't be their own relatives." She peered around him. "They're getting restless. You'd better go protect your interests."

"You're right. Thanks for being here."

Knud, the oldest, took charge and laid out several legal options available to them. "Don't let your personal greed get the best of you. If you do, the Internal Revenue Service may come out the only winner."

"All we're asking for is our fair share," Ejner said, "and we'd like it before we're too old to enjoy it."

Petra took up the cause. "We've waited forty years and..."

"And for forty years you haven't lifted a finger to help with the work," Dane said, the color in his cheeks heightening. "You all left our parents with thousands of acres and no help...and now you want your share of the spoils like a bunch of scavengers."

Knud held up his hands. "Dane, that may be true but it won't help to start hurling insults."

"We should sell," Maren said and all heads turned to her. Her steel-gray hair was as harsh as her mouth. "I'm sixty-one years old and Max will be retiring next year. We want to go places, see things. At this rate I'll be dead before Mother and Father." She lifted her chin slightly. "I love our parents as much as the rest of you but, damn it, it's not fair to have all this land and just let it go to waste!"

"It's not going to waste," Dane challenged. "It's some of the best hay and grazing country in the area. How could we raise the sheep without the land? We have water rights that have been in the family since 1884 and have never been disputed. We've incorporated so you can all share in the profits without lifting a finger or risking your personal assets."

Maren sneered at Dane. "What good are the shares in the Grasten Sweetwater Livestock Company if I can't turn them into cash? I'm restricted from selling to an outsider. They're worthless this way!"

Anna, the oldest sister at sixty-four years, nodded to Knud and he gave the floor to the woman with the snow-white hair.

"We all have enough money to last us for the rest of our lives," she said. "Let's be generous and do what's right. Let's tell our parents to give it all to their youngest child.'' She turned and smiled at Dane. "He's the one who stayed here. He's devoted his entire life to this place, has kept it profitable and has seen to it that you each get a nice check every February. Be satisfied with—''

"No!'' Petra shouted. "He doesn't deserve it. If mother had been more careful, he wouldn't even be here. Why should they give all this wealth to an accidental...moment of passion in their old age? It's disgraceful for a woman to have a child when she's forty-five years old.''

"Shut up, Petra,'' Knud warned. "How can you call your own brother an accident?'' Again he led the discussion back to the subject by presenting their options, giving the tax advantages and the negative aspects of each plan. He looked at Dane, who had been sitting quietly, one hand covering the lower portion of his face. "Dane, you haven't said much. Give us some input.''

Dane straightened in his chair. "Whatever we do, I want the house.''

Petra laughed. "The house? Why would you want the house?''

"Because it's my home.''

Petra snorted. "Well, you can't have it because that's where the money will come from. The value of the place decreases greatly without a house.''

"You're wrong, Petra,'' Ejner said. "It's the land that's valuable. A new buyer would probably tear down the house.''

Abbie's gaze shifted to Dane as he stiffened in the chair.

"No one's laying a finger on my home. That's final,'' he said. "It has memories and I intend to keep it.''

"It's not your home until the deed says so,'' Maren said haughtily. "As far as I'm concerned, you're a tenant just like anyone we might have hired to run the place. You're the foreman and we're your bosses and you should remember that.''

''If I were only your foreman, I would have quit long ago because of the low wages,'' Dane retorted. ''I make a good salary because our parents understand the responsibilities, something the rest of you have long since forgotten.''

''Well, I think you're overpaid,'' Maren exclaimed. ''You make almost as much as Max does and he's much older and more experienced. You don't deserve it!''

''I have thirty-eight years in this damned sheep business,'' Dane replied, his voice rising in pitch as his face flushed. ''I've given my whole life to this ranch. If that isn't enough of a sacrifice, then what do you what? My blood? My life? I've already given up a family, freedom, time to call my own. And now you want to take the place away from me, too?''

Petra motioned toward Abbie. ''You've apparently found a way to compensate.''

''Leave her out of this,'' Dane said angrily. ''What I do here is none of your business. You get your profit share at year end. That's all that concerns you, so keep your dirty mind out of my affairs.''

''At least you've admitted it,'' Petra replied. ''Is she just one of many, or is there something special about her?''

Knud stood up. ''That's enough, Petra.''

''Our brother's relationship with Miss Hardesty is not the reason we've come together,'' Anna said. ''It's this family matter that needs to be settled once and for all.''

Abbie slid off the high stool. ''You should all be ashamed of yourselves.''

Dane rose from his seat. "Abbie, sit down. This is none of your affair."

"Then why is she here?" Petra asked. "Is she the reason you're determined to stay on here? An answer to your failure to keep your wife happy? What's really wrong with you, little brother?"

Dane glared at his sister.

"Shut up, all of you!" Abbie cried, throwing a handful of tapes at the six Grastens who were now all standing, staring at her. "You make me sick, every last one of you. You're a family, don't you know that? I never had real sisters or brothers and I always wanted them. My mother gave me away when I was only eight years old, after my father died in a coal mine cave-in."

Her vision clouded with tears. "Why don't you love each other and...and...count your blessings? Why don't you try to see what Dane goes through here? It's an endless job. There's always more work to be done than there are hours in the day. I don't think a single one of you would be strong enough or dedicated enough to do what Dane does while you're living in your fancy houses in the suburbs of some polluted crowded city. You're a bunch of fools! And Dane, so are you for putting up with them. After seeing you all together, I'm glad I never had any sisters or brothers. If they acted like you, they'd make me sick!"

As the tears began to flow, she ran from the room and out of the house.

IN THE MOTOR HOME, Abbie washed her face and applied a touch of red lipstick. She pushed the quarreling Grastens from her thoughts and changed into work clothes. She would walk to the lambing shed, where Wilma was working, and make up the time wasted in the family meeting. They were all acting like fools. Why should she care what they did with the sheep ranch?

She hurried down the dirt road, her fists jammed deep in her coverall pockets, wishing she had refused Dane's request. Now she knew more about the family business than she ever wanted to know, and the fighting and squabbling among the brothers and sisters had been emotionally draining.

Her adoptive brothers had squabbled and teased her, but still they had banded together whenever a problem had come up that affected them all. Recalling the black-haired, brown-eyed boys, her mouth softened.

A wave of homesickness swept over Abbie as the lambing shed came into view. She missed her family. She had never doubted Aunt Minnie's love. And Uncle Harry, with his less demonstrative manner, had taught her many practical approaches to solving life's problems that might come her way.

"Be honest," he had harped. "Look this old world straight in the eye each morning and meet it head-on," he had advised his sons and his redheaded adopted daughter. Now as she stepped into the lambing shed, she mouthed the words to herself. An independent woman about to have her thirtieth birthday shouldn't be suffering from homesickness, she thought, but she was. Perhaps she would give her aunt and uncle a call this evening.

And she would also give her cousin Callie a call, even if she had to ask one of her brothers to go find Callie and bring her to a phone. The rift between Callie and Abbie needed to be resolved. Best friends needed to swallow their pride and love each other. Wasn't that what Aunt Minnie had always said? Abbie thought of the lockets that had bound the three cousins together. Their pledge had been for a lifetime, not until they had a disagreement. If fate had handed Callie a burden heavier than she could carry alone, perhaps Abbie could convince her she sincerely wanted to help.

A few hours later, Abbie volunteered to stay with the lambs while Wilma and the others went to dinner. When the other workers returned for the afternoon shift, Dane was with them, but a string of problem deliveries prevented any normal conversations. He left in midafternoon and was missing at supper. The out-of-state automobiles were gone when Abbie returned from her shift.

For several days after that, Abbie didn't see much of Dane because Oscar Hansen had pulled a muscle in his shoulder and Dane filled in for him on the night shift.

Wilma and Moses took an afternoon off one day and went to Virginia City, the county seat. "To settle a legal problem," Wilma said, a grinning Moses in tow.

At supper that night, Moses rose from his chair and went to the head of the table, taking Dane's empty seat.

"Attention, folks," he said, his thin face beaming. Wilma joined him at the head of the table and he took her hand. "There's gonna be a wedding. Wilma and me, we've decided to stop fighting and do some loving. Come Sunday afternoon, Wilma and me are getting hitched in the living room right here. It's been our home for so long, but Wilma keeps leaving at the end of each summer, and . . . well, damn it, I miss her. So we talked it over and . . . she's promised to stop hitting me with that darn dish towel . . . if I marry her!"

He ducked as Wilma grabbed the towel. "We're not married yet, you old goat," she said, "so watch your mouth before you say something that might make me change my mind. It's about time this house got a woman

in it who could keep you two bachelors under control.''
She kissed him on his cheek and hurried back to her usual
seat at the end of the table.

"So everyone come to the wedding," Moses added.
"Two o'clock sharp. We've cornered the minister between preaching services. Then we'll throw a little
party...outside if the weather holds."

THE WEDDING TOOK PLACE on a sunny afternoon. The
evening before, Wilma had asked Abbie to stand with her
and she had accepted. She wasn't surprised that Moses
selected Dane as his best man. Dress was informal. Moses put on a new western shirt but wouldn't give up his
denim jeans. Wilma looked beautiful in an attractive
beige two-piece suit. The ruffles of a cream-colored silk
blouse gave her features a softer feminine appearance.

"You're lovely," Abbie said, handing Wilma a second brown pump. "I've never seen you so dressed up
before. You're really a very pretty woman."

"Oh, pooh on you," Wilma said, balancing on the
two-inch heels. "I can't remember the last time I got all
gussied up like this."

"Is this your second marriage?" Abbie asked.

"No, it isn't," Wilma retorted. "Imagine any woman
becoming a bride for the first time at my age. I never
would have thought it. Don't get me wrong, young lady,
I've had an opportunity or two to dillydally around and
it was right enjoyable, but Moses Parish is the first man
to make me a firm offer, and I'm glad 'cause I sure do
love that old man." She dabbed the corner of her eyes
with a blue tissue and turned away. "I'm turning into a
sentimental old woman."

Abbie gave her a hug. "Under the circumstances, I think it's just fine. Are you ready? Everyone is waiting."

Hoping she wasn't overdressed, Abbie followed Wilma down the stairs, the hem of her pale gray woolen skirt brushing against her calves. Her white-and-gray-striped jacket was worn over a cranberry chiffon blouse with a scoop neckline. Her only jewelry was the locket on a gold chain around her throat to match the gold loops in her ears. Gray pumps completed her outfit.

Wilma stopped on a landing halfway down the stairs. "You're a very pretty young woman yourself. You look like a junior executive in some high-rise corporation."

"Oh, this?" Abbie touched the edge of her jacket. "This is my Sunday morning best. I thought I might be attending church while I was here, but I've had to work every Sunday."

"Well lordy, tell the boss," Wilma scolded.

"No, I couldn't," Abbie said. "Work is work. I know it comes first with Dane."

"And how are you and the boss doing?" Wilma asked. "I thought that trip to your cousin's might help the two of you realize what was happening."

Abbie sobered. "It did, but his sisters and brothers put a damper on everything. I've tried to talk to him since, but he's always so busy. He's back to being the way he was when I first arrived—solemn, alone all the time, much too serious and determined to solve his problems by himself.

"Loners tend to be that way," Wilma said.

Abbie sighed. "I guess it's water under the bridge. He must have changed his mind about me and who knows what else. I don't even know what they decided in that terrible family conference."

"You never heard?"

"Is he going to have to sell?"

"Sort of."

"What do you mean, Wilma? Tell me." Abbie grabbed the older woman's arm.

"Easy, now," Wilma replied. "You really care, don't you? Well, if Moses has it right, the boss wants to buy the house and the land immediately around it including the lambing shed. They're going to get an appraisal on the rest of the property and all the equipment and improvements. He'll be swapping his ten sections for land up Springbrook Creek belonging to his dad and mom. Twenty-six minus ten and minus this one . . . that leaves fifteen sections. He can buy the fifteen sections, or they can go with the ten he's trading and all twenty-five will be sold together. Of course, the parents still have to agree to this."

"That's terrible," Abbie murmured. "He must be very disappointed to see the ranch broken up."

"The deal has its good points and bad points. He had first bids on the property, and if he buys it, the price is reduced by his share of the proceeds. Half of the money from the sale would go to his parents and the other half would be divided among the five of them. An attorney and tax man are looking into the inheritance and gift tax implications. There's a limit on how much each of them can receive each year tax free, so the transfer might be spread over a period of time. The funds would be in a separate trust account under the control of some outside trustee."

"Whatever happened to passing the family farm down to the children?" Abbie asked.

"That went out when the IRS got into the farming business." Wilma stared out the window. "The boss is pretty upset."

"I can understand why," Abbie said. "What's the bad part?"

"He would have to go into debt to buy the place that should have been his all along," Wilma replied. "The boss hates being in debt. I reckon he grew up hearing about the depression, bank failures, homesteaders not proving up. Cripes, for a young man, he's sure got his future dumped in the bankers' laps now. Of course, this is all on the condition that his folks agree to this scheme. He's promised to present the deal to them next month when they come for their visit. You'll like them, Abbie. They're both real sweet, and the boss looks just like his papa did years ago. The boss and his brother Knud are peas from their papa's pod, that's for sure."

Wilma took a few steps down. "Well, young woman, if we keep standing here much longer, I'll be late to my own wedding." They both descended the stairs.

Within the hour, the wedding was over, handshakes and kisses exchanged, and everyone began to work their way outside to the lawn. Trudy had outdone herself with the reception. As everyone gathered around the beaming bride and groom, Abbie excused herself and returned to the motor home where she changed into jeans.

She cut through the house on her way to the reception on the front lawn. In the shadowy living room, she caught sight of movement and turned. Dane was sitting in the corner, his legs stretched out in front of him. His head was resting against the back of the chair, his eyes closed. The fingers of one hand rapped a staccato beat on the arm of the chair, while his other hand clutched the silver dollar in his belt buckle.

"Dane?" Abbie said softly, "are you okay?"

He started, then relaxed. "Fine."

"I haven't seen much of you lately," she said.

"I've been busy."

"Is there something I can do for you?" she said. "Get you a drink or some of the wedding cake?"

"No."

She stepped away, reluctant to leave, yet sensing his wish to be alone.

"Abbie?"

She whirled around. "Yes?"

"Stay for a minute?"

"Sure." She pulled a hassock up to his chair and sat down. "What is it?"

"I...hell, I don't know." Leaning forward, he ran his fingers through his already tousled hair.

She took his hand. "Wilma told me about the outcome of the family meeting." She caressed the back of his hand. "Are you satisfied?"

"How could I be satisfied when the solution means the end of this business as we know it? I thought it would last all my lifetime and now...now they're getting their way. I feel so out of control. The feeling is new to me and I don't like it."

"Have you told your parents?" she asked.

He nodded. "I was going to wait until they arrived, but I called them a few days ago. They needed time to digest what their children want them to do. They're consulting our family lawyer again. At least no one is threatening to sue. The sale will give my folks enough funds to last them for the rest of their lives." His eyes sought hers and held them. "I know a family east of here where the daughter and son-in-law bought the place from her parents, and had to go into debt by borrowing to the limit. They had agreed to make her folks a monthly payment and a balloon payment each January.''

"Is it working out?"

"The daughter and son-in-law defaulted on their bank loans last year, and the place is up for sale. The old folks are out in the cold unless the sale brings in more than the amount due at the bank.''

"Why did they borrow so much money?'' she asked. "For improvement? Equipment? New breeding stock?''

He shook his head. "They bought two new cars, four-wheel all-terrain vehicles for each of their four children, took a two-week trip to Scotland and who knows what else. I promised my folks I'd never do that to them. At their age I didn't want them to worry...and now it doesn't matter.''

They sat quietly for several minutes. He turned to her. "But promises go both ways. I know another family where the father bypassed his son, who was managing the place, and willed everything to his grandchildren equally. The son had to buy out his own children and all his nieces and nephews. It was a mess. My folks have always said that would never happen here, but now it looks like it will, doesn't it?'' He paused. "Isn't that the outfit you were wearing when I first met you?'' he asked.

Abbie nodded.

"It was great for us while it lasted, wasn't it?'' he asked.

"Does it have to end for us, Dane?''

"I have nothing to offer you,'' Dane said, resting his head in his hand.

"I've never wanted your possessions,'' Abbie replied. "When I came here, I wanted to learn. Falling in love wasn't in my plans, but plans get changed. When I told you I loved you, I meant it. My feelings haven't changed.

If you have regrets, perhaps you should reexamine your own feelings. I've lived alone most of my life. I can do it again. But is it what we want?''

"You have your weaving career," Dane said. "I may have nothing if I can't arrange the financing I need. Damn it, how did I let it happen? I took my life for granted, and now the enemy has won the war because I let myself be caught off guard.''

"No family should destroy its own members," she said.

"Mine has.''

She reached for his other hand. "I'm sorry I walked out on the meeting. Whatever must they think of me, being such an outspoken outsider?''

To her surprise, he smiled. "They all accused you of being my lover.''

Her eyes widened. "Did you say anything in my defense?''

"I said they were right," he replied. "Petra was outraged. She said she couldn't stay in a bedroom where such immoral acts had taken place.''

"Oh, Dane, I'm so sorry.''

"Don't be," he said, sliding his hand up her arm. "I told her she needn't worry, that all our lovemaking had taken place in the master bedroom. She was more shocked than ever, accused me of running a brothel because I was paying you a salary. Knud and Anna wanted to go find you and bring you back...and congratulate us. Maren and Ejner were speechless, for once in their lives. They all left that same afternoon. Anna wanted me to promise to marry you and bring you to visit her in Colorado Springs. So you see, Abbie love, everyone knows about us now that it's over. But it was wonderful while it lasted.''

It still can be, she thought, torn between wanting to shake him and to run from the room.

"Do you have regrets about your internship?" he asked.

She shook her head. "I've learned more than I ever thought possible. I like it here. I've been here for two months and I know the next four will fly by." She glanced his way. "Do you have regrets about accepting me?"

Slowly, he pulled his hand free from hers. "I don't know," he said as he rose from the chair.

She stood up. "It doesn't have to end this way."

"I'm willing to void the rest of your contract if you want to leave," he said, the remoteness in his eyes frightening her.

Concerned about his mental state, she shook her head. "This is no time to make a decision. You're upset. You'll find a way out, but if you want to come to me . . . for anything, to talk, to make love, to accept my comfort, you know where to find me. I won't abandon you, Dane. I love you too much for that."

He turned toward the hallway.

"Dane?" she called.

He didn't answer. Several seconds later, she heard his bedroom door slam.

CHAPTER EIGHTEEN

THE SHEARING TEAM ARRIVED a week after Moses and Wilma's wedding. They set up their equipment outside near the old lambing tents, and the level of activity on the ranch escalated. While Dane and the other men brought the ewes and lambs from the far pastures and separated the lambs into a holding pen, Wilma and Abbie wrangled the ewes through the narrow wooden chutes to the stalls where the shearers were waiting. The shearers would push down the drop panel and roll out a sheep onto its rump, then begin removing the fleece with their electric shears. In less than two minutes, the animal was shorn and released, looking scrawny and bewildered by the experience.

The pace accelerated as the morning progressed. The shearers' wages were based on the number of fleeces removed, so they worked without talking, stopping only occasionally to replace the blades in their shears.

The sun beat down, dust mingled with the smell of sheep urine and flies and other insects came out. Abbie removed her cap and wiped her brow with her shirt sleeve. Compared with this, lambing had been a piece of cake, she concluded, recalling the tents and shed so nicely covered. Although the cold weather then was bone chilling, at least there had been no flies.

A sharp sting pricked her exposed neck. "Ouch!" she shrieked, slapping whatever had attacked her. The pain in her neck began to feel like a burning torch.

"What's the holdup?" Dane shouted.

Abbie glanced up and spotted the empty chute where several ewes had been just seconds before. Two of the shearers were standing idle. Her eyes traveled to the chute again. The sheep had moved backward, cramming into a solid mass of wool back at the entrance of the chute.

"Get them moving, Hardesty," Dane shouted.

His callous directive stung. She stood immobile, the pain in her neck numbing her legs as well as her mind.

"What the hell?" Dane charged past her, prodding the ewes with a sheep hook and moving them back through the chute. "Wilma, take over here. Andy, can you help?" When once again the chute was filled and the shearers bent over their sheep, Dane stomped to the edge of the work area. "Hardesty, over here, pronto!"

Anger at his insensitive treatment mixed with the searing pain in her neck. She blinked, trying to keep the tears from filling her eyes. She stopped a few feet away from where he stood. Dane's legs were spread apart, his hands in fists on his hips.

"Now, what the hell is the matter with you?" he asked.

"Something bit me," she mumbled.

"Where?"

"On my neck, but I can't . . . it must have been a bee."

"Let me see."

"No, I'll be all right," she insisted. A chill brought goose bumps to her skin as the burning escalated.

"Did you get the stinger out?" he asked, grabbing her arm.

She tried to pull free. "Take your hands off me, boss, or I'll accuse you of manhandling me."

"Shut up, Hardesty, and let me see." He spun her around, his hand brushing her auburn curls up and out of the way. With his other hand he pulled her collar down. Two red welts the size of chicken eggs distorted her slender neck. "The stingers are still in," he said, whipping his leather gloves off. "Hold these and lean against the fence."

She clutched the gloves and turned to grip the top rail. He laid one hand on her shoulder to steady her as he began to probe one of the stingers with his thumb and forefinger. Carefully he caught it and pulled it from her neck.

"Ouch!" she cried.

"Don't be a baby," he chided, "and don't move. There's another one." He propped his boot against a middle pole of the fence, his denim-covered thigh brushing against her hip. Her closeness started a stirring in his loins and he willed himself not to react. She was only a woman, one of many interns who would pass through the program. Or was it fate more than chance that had brought her into his life?

What did it matter now? Everything was changing, and much too fast to suit him. He concentrated on the remaining stinger. His fingers shook just enough to prevent him from capturing the evasive target.

"Hurry up," she pleaded.

He finally caught it and yanked it from her skin, immediately regretting his roughness when he felt her flinch. "Go to the house and get some ice on those stings," he said. "Take the rest of the morning off." He glanced at his watch. "We eat in a half hour. I'm sure you'll be ready to work again after dinner." He reached for the pair of gloves she was holding and slid them from her tight grip.

As he watched her walk stiffly away, his chest tightened. Did he love her enough to give her her freedom? he wondered.

Several days later, the shearing team packed their equipment and drove away. The work changed to irrigating the hay fields, and Abbie was assigned the dubious honor of moving irrigation pipe. Once again she discovered muscles she didn't know she had.

"YOU'VE GOT NO RIGHT!" Wilma said, as she sat in Dane Grasten's office. "She's a lady and you've got her moving irrigation pipe?"

Dane tipped his chair back on its spring. "She's an intern. I've always had the interns move pipe."

"This is different and you know it," Wilma replied. "Abbie has already taken more crap from you than she should have. If you keep on treating her like slave labor, you'll drive her away. Is that what you want?"

Dane frowned at the outspoken woman across the desk. "I offered to void the contract. She wanted to stay for the full six months. Then she can leave."

"Do you want her to leave?" Wilma asked.

"What I want or don't want is my private business," he replied, picking up a pencil and twirling it.

"You stubborn Danish . . ." Wilma sputtered. "Why, you're worse than your father used to be. The only reason I don't give up on you is that I saw your old man mellow and I know a Grasten can change. You've given Abbie every dirty job around this place but castrating the bull calves. I saw her running the scoop loader last week and helping Moses load the manure spreader. Shame on you for giving her jobs like that."

"She did a good job," Dane said, recalling the quickness with which Abbie had caught on to the operation of the controls. "She hasn't complained."

"I'm complaining for her," Wilma huffed. "Bring her into the kitchen where it's cool."

"I don't think she'd enjoy kitchen detail." Dane's thoughts went back to that early morning months ago when they had met before dawn in the kitchen. He smiled, remembering that they had never finished cooking their potatoes and onions.

"You like her, don't you?" Wilma asked.

He sobered. "That's my business."

"It's mine too," Wilma said. "Abbie is like a daughter to me. The two of you are meant for each other. Don't you see that? You act as if you hate her!"

He shook his head. "That's not the emotion she brings out in me." The instant he heard his own words, he regretted them.

Wilma leaned forward in her chair. "You love her, don't you?"

Dane remained silent. He had said he loved her that night when he'd carried her to his bed. Images of their passion filled his thoughts. He had almost allowed himself to think of the future, a future with Abbie at his side, a future with a wife and children. But that had all been washed away under the tidal wave of destruction left behind by his own family.

Now he spent all his free time preparing financial statements and filling out legal forms in an effort to arrange financing for the purchase of the property. He was choking on the bitter pill of going into debt so that his sisters and brothers could have money to squander. He was sure they would have it spent in a few years, while it would take him a decade or two to pay off the loans.

Where was the justice? Why hadn't he walked away years ago and taken up a different profession? But deep inside he knew that sheep raising was all he knew and all he wanted to do.

"I think you love Abbie and won't own up to it," Wilma murmured, bringing his thoughts back to their conversation.

He grew uncomfortable under her scrutiny. "Just because you and Moses have married, don't start playing matchmaker every time you find an available man and woman," he said.

She clapped her hand. "You love her! You might as well admit it."

His mouth clamped shut.

"I'm dealing with two fools here," Wilma said. "She's in love with you and you love her, and you're willing to let the months roll by and watch her drive that motor home away?"

"How do you know how she feels?" he asked, struggling to keep his expression blank.

"I can tell. She mopes around. I catch her staring off at the mountains, or watching you when you're around. Since you've been ignoring her, she's had a lot of time to watch you and I see the hurt in her eyes. Show her some love and she will return it tenfold."

"She's said she didn't want to get involved," he replied. "If she's allowed herself to fall in love, that's her problem. I can't control her thoughts or her emotions."

"No, I guess not," Wilma said pensively. "But the attraction between the two of you was instant, wasn't it?"

He frowned but remained silent.

"And by now that attraction has grown to love, hasn't it?" she said, pressing her point. "Dane, go to her and tell her how you feel. Give her some hope. Trust her, share your problems with her. That's what a wife is for."

"She's not my wife."

"She should be and she can be," Wilma retorted.

"She has plans," he replied. "I have none."

Wilma shot from her seat. "You damned fool. You're letting your silly male pride blind you."

He frowned. "She has her weaving career. She told me once that she would never give that up. If I lose this place, I have nothing to—"

"What is this? A corporate merger? A consolidation of assets? It's love we're talking about. What did Moses and I have to give each other? We both come with the clothes on our backs. I never gave it much thought until now, but maybe that's a blessing. We're husband and wife because we love each other. That's all."

He straightened, put down the pencil he had been twirling and folded his hands across his belt. "You make it sound so simple, Wilma. Where did you learn such wisdom?"

"Hard knocks," she said simply. "Abbie can't know you're still concerned about this financial matter if you don't tell her. You've cut her out, pushed her away. Can't you love her at the same time you're solving this? You're a man possessed by two different problems. With time, I know you'll arrange all this banking business, but the problem with Abbie can be resolved with just three little words."

Wilma's tone softened. "Don't be a fool, boss. Regrets can make for a mighty lonely life."

ABBIE ROLLED OVER, reluctant to leave the bed. Days off had been canceled during the shearing, but now on this first Friday in June, she had the whole day to herself. The weather was balmy with only a gentle breeze to move the grasses and the newly emerging leaves on the giant cottonwood trees surrounding the house.

She got up and perked a small pot of coffee. Today she would not join the others for breakfast. Why subject herself to another rebuff by Dane? Three times a day for almost three weeks was more punishment than any woman deserved. She was sure that by now everyone knew she and Dane had slept together. It had been shouted from the den during the family conference while the hands gathered in the kitchen for dinner.

The curious glances she had endured from her co-workers, mixed with Dane's continued rejection, was humiliating enough to toughen her skin.

She crawled back into bed, carefully balancing her cup and saucer. As she set it on a ledge near the novel she had been reading the night before, she peeked out the window. Early morning was her favorite time, and here in this mountain valley the mornings were more beautiful than in any place but Kentucky.

As she sipped her coffee, thoughts of Dane intruded. *Not today!* Abbie thought, rolling the window shades up and pushing the sliding windowpanes open. She savored the fresh air on her cheeks and relaxed again against the pillows.

Perhaps she could work on her tapestry. It now measured fifteen inches in length. Only the variegated blues of the sky remained to be woven. The tapestry had become a eulogy to their relationship, nipped in the bud by Dane's frosty manner. He still chose to keep to himself. Twice after the wedding, she tried to talk to him, but had been rebuffed. Now he would have to make the next gesture of reconciliation . . . if there was to be one.

Finishing her coffee, Abbie scampered out of bed and dressed in jeans and a red sweatshirt. The day was perfect for some outside dyeing, she decided. Weeks earlier, she had selected a spot to build her fire, far enough from the buildings not to endanger anyone. She had built a windbreak by piling rocks in a circle. The space was large enough in diameter and the windbreak was high enough for the iron grill she'd found in a junk shop. The grill would hold three large enameled kettles of water.

As she carried the grate outside and began to build her fire, Abbie glanced at the sky. Not a cloud in sight. A perfect day, indeed. She pulled a disposable lighter from her jeans pocket, touched it to the paper and kindling and laid it down nearby, in case she needed it again. When the fire was burning nicely, she returned to the motor home and brought out three lengths of garden hose. If she connected them to the spigot located beside the back porch of the house, she wouldn't have to transport the water for the kettles.

Two large cardboard boxes came next, one filled with her skeins of natural yarn, the other containing jars for dissolving the powdered chemical dyes, glass rods for stirring the hot wet yarn and another pot for wetting the yarn. As she brought the second box to the fire, she regretted the distance to be covered, but safety was paramount to her project. Although the grass was still green and moist, nearby sagebrush and wild vegetation was already showing signs of dryness.

The Australian shepherd puppies spotted her. Now almost three months old, they were playful and in constant motion. The three survivors from the poisoned litter came scampering toward her, followed closely by a year-old pup Dane had bought from a Ruby Valley rancher.

She dropped to her knees to pet and play with the animals for a few minutes before shooing them away. The puppies were soon curled in a pile asleep, while the year-old male named Duke continued to watch her every move, his handsome head turning and twisting, displaying the curiosity in his blue and brown eyes. After several minutes, he joined the younger puppies for a nap.

Abbie filled the kettles from the hose and set the heavy containers on the grate. It would be some time before the water was hot enough to use. She returned to the spigot, turned the water off and screwed on a nozzle to the end of the hose, then turned the water back on, checking the nozzle to see that it worked properly. Now she was ready.

Trudy waved to her from the kitchen window. The cook had agreed to stay on for another month. Occasionally, Abbie wondered if Trudy and Oscar might soon follow Wilma and Moses's example.

"Come taste my coffee cake," Trudy called. "It's fresh from the oven."

Abbie waved, her mouth watering at the thought of one of Trudy's delicious baked cakes. "I'll be right there," she called back.

Inside the kitchen, she was offered a generous slice of cake, filled with cinnamon and raisins and dripping with white frosting.

"There must be a thousand calories in this," Abbie exclaimed, "but I have no willpower."

Trudy laughed. "My own hips attest to the calories in my cooking, but you only live once."

"Where is everyone?" Abbie asked.

"Andy is moving pipe," Trudy said, laughing as Abbie made a face. "Wilma and Moses are checking out the sheep wagons for supplies. They're going to town tomorrow to buy the staples for the summer. Buck is repairing that used tractor the boss bought a couple of summers ago. Oscar is bringing in the horses from their winter range so they can gentle down before they're ridden again. Evelyn is checking the bands up Springbrook Creek way. Tomorrow is her last day. She's trying to convince the boss to keep her on.''

''And . . . Dane? Where is he?'' Abbie asked.

''In his office.''

''I'd better get back to my dyeing. I don't want to cross him today. He's been such a bear lately,'' Abbie said.

''You sit right there and eat. You're my guest and he has no right to interfere one way or another. Now eat and enjoy. Time off doesn't come along very often on this place.''

''That's for sure.'' Abbie took another bite of the moist cake, pressing the crumbs with her finger and eating them.

The women chatted over a second slice of cake and a coffee refill. Abbie glanced at the wall clock.

''Gracious, my water should be boiling by now.'' She rose from the table. ''Thanks, Trudy, it was great.'' She stepped outside.

In the distance, she spotted orange flames beneath billowing gray smoke. ''Oh, no,'' she cried, racing to her fire. The area behind her fire pit was ablaze. Through the flames she spotted Duke. He was dragging a three-foot piece of wood, one end in his mouth, the other end in smoldering flames trailing through the dirt. Tiny fingers of fire ignited the dry vegetation behind him as he trotted along.

''No, Duke,'' she screamed. ''Drop it!'' But Duke wagged his tail and trotted on. Panic turned her to stone for several seconds until she spotted the hose. She grabbed the end and turned the nozzle. The water spurted for an instant, then became a trickle and stopped, a few drops dripping onto the toe of her shoe. She followed the hose as it snaked back to the house. "Damn dog!" she cried, spotting the fragmented pieces of hose. "He chewed it up!"

She turned and screamed. "Trudy, ring the bell. I've started a fire!" As the dinner bell sounded the alarm, she ran back to the fire and began stomping it out, kicking dirt over the blaze where she could. Choking on the smoke, she covered her mouth and nose. The gentle breeze gusted and the fire shifted, creeping up the hill and out of sight on the other side.

DANE RETURNED THE TELEPHONE to its cradle, furious at the man on the other end of the line. The banker in Bozeman had turned down his request for a loan.

"We were unable to get a credit rating on you, Mr. Grasten," the banker had said.

"That's because I'm debt free," Dane had explained. "I pay cash. I write checks. Don't they count?"

"They don't prove you can pay on schedule," the banker had explained. "We've had too many farm loans go sour already. We just can't take a chance on a new-comer."

"My God," Dane shouted, "I've been a sheepman all my life and my father before me and his father. Doesn't that count for anything?"

"Your father's record is irrelevant in this matter, Mr. Grasten. I've seen too many young men who want to borrow their way into farming. It can't be done in this economy."

"But I'm already in the business," Dane had replied.

The banker had expressed his regrets and offered to send him an application for their newest credit card with its holographic design that prevented forgery. Dane had expressed his opinion by slamming down the phone.

He continued to stare at the phone, sure his head would explode if he didn't get himself under control. His world was caving in around him.

Through his muddled thoughts, he heard the dinner bell. He glanced at his watch, wondering why Trudy had moved the noon meal up to ten in the morning. As the ringing continued he realized that it meant fire. Fire, the most feared danger that could happen in their remote re-location. How did it start? Who had started it? he wondered.

He raced from his office and out the front door, but no one was in sight. Voices shouted from the backyard and he ran around the house. Moses was directing the other men as they dug a trench in a straight line parallel to the house through the burned area. He spotted three large pots on a fireplace made of stones arranged in a circle. What the hell was going on?

He kicked several pieces of hose aside and stared down at the water bubbling in the pots still on the fireplace, then spotted the box of natural yarn. Abbie? Had Abbie's carelessness started this fire? He spotted the cigarette lighter lying in the dust. Picking it up, he flicked it several times, watching the tiny flame come alive each time.

He searched the crew and found Abbie at the end of the line, digging alongside Oscar a quarter of a mile away. There was no time to investigate the cause of the fire now. The important thing was to put it out before it got out of control and took the house.

He grabbed a shovel and raced to the top of the hill. The fire had already burned several acres of sagebrush and weeds and was working its way north to Sweetwater

Creek and the road. The creek and the road would provide a natural firebreak unless the wind velocity increased. As he watched, the wind shifted again and the fire spread to fresh brush to the west. *My God,* he thought, *is the wind going in circles?*

He spotted Buck Jensen through the smoke. "Buck," he shouted, "get the backhoe and dig a trench on the other side of this ridge. He motioned the direction for Buck to take.

As he waited for the backhoe to work its way up the hill, he took the shovel and marked out a line for the ditch, which he hoped would deny the fire the fuel it needed, then he began to throw dirt on the nearest flames snaking their way to him. He felt the fruitlessness of his effort when the wind from his work fanned the fire. Still he persevered. The backhoe's engine mumbled behind him and he shouted instructions to Buck.

"The house," Dane shouted. "If the wind changes again..."

Buck waved to him. "They've dug a trench. Abbie's sure the house is safe now."

Abbie. As Dane worked on the section between the backhoe and the crew on the hillside, his thoughts focused on her act of carelessness.

Two hours later the last of the flames had been extinguished. Several acres of brush and sage had been blackened but no outbuildings were in the area. *It could have been much worse,* Dane thought, as he rejoined the others. He found Abbie standing near the pots cooling over the gray embers in the fire pit.

"Why did you do it?" he shouted. "Did you want to burn the whole damned house down?" Abbie's hair was singed, her face covered with soot, her sweatshirt turned brown with dust, smoke and sweat.

She whirled to face him, her posture stiff and unyielding. "I never...it was Duke. Oh, what does it matter? It's my fault."

The reality of how close he had come to losing everything that was important brought Dane's temper back to the boiling point. "You're a danger, Hardesty. You're a menace. Ever since you've been here things have gone wrong for me. You're a hex."

Abbie gasped. "You're crazy. Do you think I did this deliberately? How could you? I love this old house as much as you do. I love this place, every inch of it."

Rage distorted his flushed features. "Well, I want you off of it," he shouted. "I won't have you jeopardizing what little I have left. You're fired, now." He turned away in disgust.

She grabbed his shirt, but he pulled free. "I want you off the place in thirty minutes."

She studied the rigid set of his shoulders. "Dane, you can't mean it. You're upset...."

"You're damned right I'm upset. Just when I thought things couldn't get any worse, you almost burn me out. I should have sent you packing that first day. I regret every moment I've spent with you, Hardesty, every damned minute." He turned away, walking stiffly toward the house.

Anger surged through her. "Well, I do, too," she shouted. "I was a fool to believe your lies. I'll go," she promised, her head bobbing emphatically, "and it won't take me thirty minutes."

As Dane climbed the steps to the porch, he heard the squeal of tires and turned, just in time to see his own truck disappear behind a cloud of dust.

CHAPTER NINETEEN

"ARE YOU GOING TO REPORT the truck stolen?" Moses asked, as they gathered for the evening meal.

Dane stared at his untouched plate of food. He cut a piece of roast beef and took a bite, but as he tried to swallow the meat stuck in his throat. He left the table and didn't return.

After most of the workers had retired, Dane returned to the kitchen and found Wilma and Moses huddled over cups of coffee.

"Mind some company?" he asked.

"'Course not, boss," Moses replied. "It's your house."

"Yes, and for what? To live here alone again?" Dane grumbled.

"Coffee, boss?" Wilma asked, and without waiting for his reply went to the cupboard. When she returned, she set a steaming cup of coffee and a roast beef sandwich before him.

"Thanks," Dane said.

They sat quietly for several minutes while he ate part of the sandwich.

"Where do you think she is?" Moses asked, ignoring Wilma's tugging at his sleeve.

Dane shrugged. "Anywhere."

"Think she'll call?" Moses asked.

"If she does, are you going to ask her to come back?" Wilma asked.

Dane looked directly at the couple sitting across from him. "Why would she want to come back after the way I treated her?"

"Remember when she first got here?" Wilma said. "I warned you not to do anything to drive her away."

"And that's just what I've done," he admitted. He ate half the sandwich. "When she comes back, I'll apologize. She has to come back. Her motor home is here."

"It will take more than an apology to make her stay," Moses advised.

"You can't keep her as a permanent intern, that's for sure," Wilma said, laughing softly.

"Why don't you marry her, boss?" Moses asked with his usual straightforwardness.

"Ask her to marry me if she'll return my truck?" Dane asked, his mouth softening.

"Getting hitched takes a bit of compromising," Moses said. "Didn't Wilma promise to stop hitting me if I married her? And look how we've turned out. Still married and it's been almost a month, by golly." He kissed Wilma's cheek before she could get a word out.

"Trudy explained what happened with that darn pup eating the hose," Wilma said. "Abbie didn't mean you any harm. She loves you, boss, and you've been too hard on her, making her move pipe and clean manure piles and all those other jobs."

"Nothing that I haven't had to do myself," Dane argued. "She wanted to learn sheep raising and I've taught her."

"And she did everything," Moses said, "never complaining, at least to your face. She's one heck of a woman," he added, shaking his head.

"That she is," Dane agreed. "She was just stubborn enough to prove she could do it even when I expected her to fail. She could have refused."

"She's never failed you, boss," Wilma said, "but what about you? Have you failed her? Do you love her enough to admit it?"

Dane stared off out the window into the darkness. "Do you think she's sleeping in the truck somewhere? She shouldn't be alone. When she's upset she needs me." He rose from his chair. "If she calls, wake me."

The next two days passed in a blur for Dane. Unable to sleep at night, he took catnaps after dinner on the living room sofa. When the phone rang during his nap on the third day, he awoke instantly.

"It's for you," Trudy called from the kitchen.

Abbie. It must be Abbie, he thought. "I'll take it in the office."

He ignored the tremor in his hand as he reached for the phone. *The woman is making a wreck out of me.* He hadn't even returned the call from the Great Falls banker who had left a message the previous day. "Hello? Abbie, is that you?"

"This is Eileen Mills," the caller said. "I should have called yesterday but I couldn't. Abbie wants you to know your truck is here and—"

"Then I'm on my way," Dane exclaimed. "Keep her there!"

"But—"

He hung up the phone. It rang again as he left the house. "Take a message, Trudy. I'm going to find Moses. We're driving to Idaho this afternoon to get Abbie."

"But, boss—" Trudy called.

"No time," Dane replied, disappearing into the garage. As he backed the new station wagon out, Trudy came out onto the porch and waved frantically to him, but he ignored her.

Four hours later, he pulled into the yard of the potato farm near Shelley, Idaho. "Wait here," he said to Moses. "You can drive the truck back. Abbie will be more comfortable in the Eagle."

Parking near the front porch, he took the steps two at a time. Before he could knock, Eileen Mills opened the door.

"Where is she?" he asked. "Is she okay? I want to..."

"She's not here," Eileen said, holding the door wide. "Come in, Dane. I tried to explain, but you hung up too fast."

He stood rooted to the planks of the porch. "Not here?"

"No. Now please come in and let's talk." She took his hand, and as if he were a helpless child, she led him inside.

An hour later he came out again, his hat in his hand and his pale forehead furrowed. Without a word to Moses, who was still waiting in the Eagle, he strode to the blue pickup and climbed in. In minutes he was on the interstate headed north again, Moses and the Eagle in close pursuit.

WHEN THEY PULLED into the ranch yard, darkness had settled over the countryside, blanketing the mountains and valley as well as Dane's spirits. He looked around to confirm Abbie's motor home was still there.

Moses stormed into the kitchen on Dane's heels. "What the hell was that all about, boss? You could have told me what was going on! You leave a feller in the dark and he gets all kinds of horrible ideas. Now where is our Abbie?''

"I don't know," Dane replied. "I'm sorry. I was...too upset. When Eileen told me Abbie had left yesterday, I was afraid she might have come back here while we were gone. There was no time to explain. Sorry." He dropped into his chair. "Sit down and I'll tell you what happened."

Wilma and Moses sat silently while Dane brought them up to date. "She went to West Yellowstone. She had no cash because her purse with money and credit cards are here. She called Eileen collect and Eileen wired her some money. The gas tank was well below half full. It's a miracle she didn't get stranded somewhere."

He traced a coffee stain on the tablecloth with his index finger. "She went to Eileen's place near Shelley. Yesterday, she borrowed Eileen's car and left, making Eileen promise not to call me until this morning. Abbie told her she needed time to think. A problem in the fields prevented Eileen from phoning until this afternoon. She tried to warn me but I had hung up on her before she could explain that Abbie wasn't there." He turned to Moses. "Sorry, old friend, for leading you on such a wild-goose chase, but thanks for staying with me."

Wilma touched his hand. "What do we do now? We need to find her and convince her...make her understand...that you..." Her chin began to quiver and she burst into tears, burying her head against Moses's shoulder. Moses held her, helplessly patting her shoulder.

Watching the tough Wilma crying in her husband's arms was more than Dane could handle. "Don't cry, Wilma. Damn it, woman, if you keep that up we'll all be in tears."

She pulled free from Moses's arms and wiped her face. "I'm sorry for being a blubbering idiot, but she has to be found and brought home and home is right here." She stomped her foot.

"You're right," Dane said. "Eileen gave me the names of some of Abbie's weaving friends. Tomorrow I'll call them. Day after tomorrow I have to go to the Gilcrest place to look at some Romney sheep. Other than that I'll be here on the property somewhere. If Abbie returns, don't let her get away. Ring the bell and I'll come running. I love Abbie. I've got to make her believe that."

DANE PUSHED HIS CHAIR away from the breakfast table. "I'll be gone most of the morning," he said. "You know the number of the Gilcrest ranch. Call me if she comes back," he ordered Moses.

As Dane followed the dirt road along Little Willow Creek to the Gilcrest ranch, his thoughts were on Abbie. All of his calls to her friends had been futile. She was the reason he was going to the Gilcrest ranch. The owner had a small band of purebred Romney sheep for sale, sheep whose fleeces were prized by spinners and weavers, sheep who had been raised on grass pastures rather than open range.

Dane had planned to give fifty of them to Abbie along with fifty of the Lincolns to get her started in her own business, to give her the boost she would need.

He stared at the speedometer. *Damn it, I want to give them to her just because I love her.* No strings. He had even considered selling her a quarter section of his land, land near Springbrook Creek and the lambing shed so she could use his facilities until she could build her own. But now he knew he couldn't have her living a quarter mile away, alone at night, a constant distraction and worry.

He wanted her living in his house, in his bed so he could love her, share his joys and troubles, watch her work at the loom. He needed her as a sounding board when he told her of the other changes he was considering making. He didn't want her as a neighbor. He wanted her as his wife.

"SHE'S BACK!" WILMA WHISPERED, motioning to Moses as she peeked out the kitchen window. "Abbie's back."

Moses came to the window and looked over Wilma's shoulder. Abbie was climbing out of a small foreign automobile. Without a glance toward the house, she entered the motor home and closed the door behind her.

"Call the boss at the Gilcrest place," Moses said, waving his hand at his wife. "Tell him to hurry!" Glancing at the wall clock, he shook his head. "He probably ain't even got there yet. Damn! It'll take him almost an hour to get back. I'll go see her and find a way to keep her here until he gets back. We can't let her get away."

Moses knocked lightly on the motor home door a few minutes later. When he received no answer, he squinted at the door. "Come on in, Moses," he murmured to himself. "Why, thank you, ma'am, I believe I will," and with that he jerked the door open and went inside.

Abbie was in the rear, putting her belongings into the tall closets on either side of the vehicle. The upper half of her body was hidden behind the open doors.

"Hello, Abbie," he said.

She jerked away from the closet, her eyes wide with fright for an instant. When she saw him, she sighed, her hand pressed against her chest. "Moses, you frightened me."

"Are you leaving?" he asked.

"Of course," she replied. "I've been fired and ordered off the place. You heard him."

"Abbie, honey, he's sorry. He was really behind the eight ball that morning. The fire came at a bad time. He didn't really mean what he said."

She stiffened. "Then why did he say it? His meaning was quite clear to everyone. He said he regretted *everything* that's happened between us." She slammed the door shut and glared at him. "Do you know what that means, Moses? He made love to me. He told me he loved me! Those are his regrets. What kind of a fool do you take me for to stay here and work when he feels that way? I believed him!" Her eyes glistened and she turned away, busying herself behind the other closet door. "Now, if you don't mind, I have lots to do."

"He's been trying to find you," Moses said. "He's been looking everywhere. Why, I went with him all the way to Ide-ho to that cousin of yours . . . and . . . and he's been a-calling all of your friends and . . . and everything."

"Is he here?"

"No, ma'am."

"Good."

"Well," Moses said, scanning the interior of the motor home, "I reckon I'll be leaving. It's been nice working with you, Abbie. You're a natural with them ewes and lambs. Hope you find a place to your liking real soon." He got an idea when spotting her key ring hanging from the ignition.

"Goodbye, Moses," she called frostily from behind the door. "Tell Wilma goodbye for me, please. I really like you both. Maybe someday I'll write."

"Sure," he agreed, moving toward the front of the motor home. "Oh, Abbie?"

"Yes?"

"Your pots are still outside. I'd help you with them but I got to get back to work. We're stocking the sheep wagons. The boss's folks are coming next week, and Wilma is helping Trudy with the housecleaning. Two of the bands are moving to the summer pasture as soon as the wagons are ready. So you see, if Wilma and me weren't so busy, we'd sure help you pack up."

"That's okay," Abbie said, smiling. "I can do it by myself."

He trotted across the yard and back into the kitchen. "Did you get him?"

"Yes," Wilma replied, "but he won't make it back for another half hour. What if she's gone by then?"

"She's staying," he said confidently.

"How can you be so sure?"

He reached in his pocket and waved Abbie's key ring several times, then playfully tossed it to his wife. "Hide this somewhere. She ain't going no place, unless it's with the boss and on their honeymoon. She looks terrible, almost as bad as he does. Damn it, Wilma, this matchmaking is harder work than I ever figured."

ABBIE COMPLETED VARIOUS TASKS necessary to make the motor home ready for road travel, then went outside. She transported three kettles and the grill up the ladder and put them in the storage pods on the roof.

She locked the pods and rose from her kneeling position on the rooftop. She watched ewes and lambs in a distant pasture. Slowly she turned, gazing around the property, following the line of willows up the creek to where they disappeared into the next valley. Her gaze lingered on the lambing shed, which had been repaired, and she recalled the time Dane had come to the building after the snowstorm. He had found her, comforted her, given her the support she had needed, and later that evening he'd made love to her. A chill passed through her in spite of the warm June morning.

Her gaze caressed the land and buildings, as Abbie surrendered to the affection and memories they now held for her. When she turned to the west, the sight of the scorched hillside upset her. She hurried down the ladder, jumping the last several feet to the ground.

Lifting the door to the propane tanks, she turned off the gas, then unplugged the electrical cord. Only the boards Buck had used to balance the motor home remained to be put away.

She reentered the vehicle, anxious to get away. Someone might tell Dane she was here, and he was the last person in the world she wanted to see just now.

After crying her heart out at Eileen's kitchen table a few days earlier, she had borrowed her car and driven hundreds of miles, stopping at two hot springs for therapeutic swims, pulling into forest service campgrounds and staring into the trees, until finally the unfinished business at the ranch had become an obsession.

She had steeled herself to the possibility of seeing him. Each time her heart would flutter at the prospect, she would recall Dane's words, one word at a time, and repeat them aloud.

When she slid into the driver's seat and reached for the keys, her hand touched the empty ignition. Where were her keys? she wondered. Scrambling out of the seat, she dropped to her knees, searching the floor, running her hand beneath the seat, feeling around the gas and brake pedals, checking each and every crack of any size. She distinctly remembered taking the keys to the front of the vehicle.

Twenty minutes later, she dropped to the edge of the bed, unable to think clearly about where the keys might be. Her anger changed to a sense of entrapment and helplessness as she began to pace the aisle way. She stopped at the loom still on the table. Her eyes were drawn to the unfinished tapestry, its design tugging at her heart. She knew now the tapestry would never be finished. The tears she had been suppressing since her return began to spill down her cheeks as she touched the muted form of the man who represented Dane. She sobbed, covering her mouth with her other hand as her fingers lingered on the tapestry.

The door flew open and she whirled around. Dane Grasten entered. She heard the lock slip into place, trapping her inside with the very man she wanted to avoid.

"What do you want?" she asked, jerking her hand from the weaving and brushing the tears from her cheeks. "You're supposed to be gone," she said accusingly.

"I was at the Gilcrest place, looking at a small flock of Romneys," he said.

"Romneys?" she asked. "Their fleeces are fantastic for spinning."

"Yes, that's what I've heard," he replied.

She turned to him. "Why were you looking at Romney sheep?"

"I wanted to give them to someone special," he said. "A crazy redheaded weaving lady from Kentucky who had been making my life miserable ever since she came to my place looking for work."

She smiled through her tears. "Don't tease me, Dane. I can't take it anymore. It hurts. I don't want to ever hurt the way I did when you ordered me off the place. Why did you come back? I wouldn't be here now if I could find my keys."

He stepped closer. "Wilma called me and said I'd better get home quick."

Dane looked haggard but more open and vulnerable than she'd ever seen him.

"Moses said you had been looking for me," she said.

He nodded. "I came back, knowing you would have to return sooner or later. I had to be here to stop you, but you came back the one time I left." He reached out and touched her cheek. "That's not quite true. There was another time. When Eileen called, I drove to Shelley before she could tell me you weren't there." His finger touched the gold locket nesting against her throat. "Oh, Abbie, I said such terrible things to you. I was afraid you might send someone else to get the motor home. Why did you come back yourself?"

Thoughts of the future without him overwhelmed her. "I never wanted to leave," she said, her voice unsteady.

"Then stay." His hand caressed her quivering chin.

She shook her head. "I can't. The way everything has turned out, I couldn't stand it. My internship doesn't end until late September and...and I love you...but I'm not strong enough to work beside you, sit next to you at each meal knowing how you feel." She shook her head more emphatically and wiped her wet cheeks once more. "You've turned me into a crybaby, Dane, and I don't like it."

His hands settled on her shoulders. "Then stay a lifetime, with me, sweetheart," he said, enfolding her in his arms. "Marry me, become my wife. I love you, Abbie, so very much."

"Marry you?" The surprise in her eyes brought a smile to his. "Marry you after all I've done to you?"

"What you've done is love me, stand by me when we had the storm, make love with me and listen to me when

I had problems. I was at fault, Abbie, when I let the dispute with my family get to me so much that I took it out on you." His hands slid up to her cheeks. "Oh, Abbie, let me love you until our dying day. Have my children. Grow old with me."

She touched the pearl snaps on his shirt. "You have a mean streak, Dane, and you shut people out. I hate it. I won't stay if you expect me to tolerate such tactics. Verbal abuse is just as bad as any other kind of abuse. Maybe worse, because the scars form inside."

"I know that," he replied. "Wilma and Moses have been lecturing me each and every day about how to treat a wife." He touched her lips with his. "And I promise I'll never ask you to move irrigation pipe again."

Her hands slid up his chest to settle on his shoulders. "I hate moving pipe."

"I heard through the grapevine that you were complaining," he said. She had to take a step backward to keep her balance and she felt the edge of the bed against the back of her knees.

Passion ignited when Dane kissed her, nibbling at her cheek, her throat. He dropped to the bed, pulling her with him. She grabbed his face, holding it between her palms. "Kiss me, Dane, or I'll have to take the initiative and . . ." Before she could explain her threat, his mouth covered hers as he rolled her across the bed, tumbling against the pillows.

Relaxing in his arms, she studied his handsome face. "Do you really want to marry me?" she asked.

"More than anything else in the world."

"Enough to leave here and move to a city?" she asked.

"A city?" he said, as if she was asking him to move to another planet. "Why would you want to live in a city? Where would you keep your Romneys and your Lincolns? Where would the Finns do their lambing? And the Rambouillets and Targhees would make a city apartment awfully crowded. Don't your looms make it crowded enough already?" His features were somber but the twinkle in his blue eyes revealed his true feelings.

"So what shall we do?" she asked.

"Let's think about it later," he said, tracing her lower lip. "Right now I want to make love to you, just for the pure pleasure of it."

THEY LAY SATED in each other's arms. "We'll be making some changes around here," he said. "You should know."

"Because of your sisters and brothers?" she asked.

"Partly," he said. "I'm decreasing the number of bands to just two. I want more time with the Finns. I'll turn the Romneys and Lincolns over to you but I hope you'll accept my help with them."

"That's sweet of you, darling," she murmured, kissing his chin, and enjoying his laughter.

"I've always wanted to get into experimental breeding," he continued. "If I cut back on the commercial stock, I'll have time. And I want time with you, Abbie. I'm a workaholic but now I want to smell the flowers, with you by my side."

She nuzzled his neck, nipping the skin and enjoying his reaction. "Did you arrange all the financing you needed?"

"Partly."

She propped herself on an elbow. "Well, tell me. If I'm going to marry you, I need to know what I'm getting into."

He pulled her back into his arms. "My parents will be here next week. They had a few ideas of their own, contrary to what Ejner and the others expected. They want to give me the house and a section of the land. I offered to buy it, but they insist on it being payment for prior performance. The section of land includes the lambing shed. Dad had to remind Ejner, Petra and Maren that he could do whatever he chose with his assets. Knud told me Dad warned Petra he could cut any one of them out of his will completely if they get too pushy.''

"Does that mean you don't have to put the place up for sale?"

"Not really," he continued. "We'll still do the swap of my ten sections for ten of my folks' so as to put the house and lambing sheds and my ten sections together. The rest of the land will be put in a separate corporation and we'll borrow enough to buy out the three who want out.''

"Only three?"

"Yes," he said, rubbing his hand up and down her bare arm. "Knud and Anna never wanted to sell. They insist they don't need the money. Anna says her will leaves her shares to me and has for years. I never knew that."

"I liked her," Abbie said. "She and Knud are different from the others, more like you, my darling. Are they like your parents?"

He nodded. "Anna has been a high school counselor for years. Knud just retired from a commodity firm in Great Falls. He's introduced me to a Great Falls banker friend of his who has been looking for a grass-roots-level investment. He's agreed to loan us the amount we need to buy out the others, and his rate of interest is below that of the regional banks. He says he believes in keeping his money at home."

She smiled. "Then the ranch is still intact?"

He nodded. "Ready to operate for another century. Ejner, Maren and Petra have agreed to accept the proceeds of an early buy-out in the livestock company and not make claims against the estate at a later date. I'm sure Mom and Dad will leave them something but it won't be the property."

"That's wonderful," she said, stroking his bare shoulder. "What about me? I come with two large looms and all my weaving supplies. I won't give all that up."

"I'd never ask you to, love," he replied, as he kissed her forehead. "In my office is a sketch of a large room we can add to the main floor. It would have lots of windows so you can have good natural light...and so I can see you at the loom when I find an excuse to drive by."

"Oh, Dane, really? I could always work upstairs."

"No, you couldn't," he insisted. "When the babies are in the blue nursery, you'll want to be close by."

"Babies?" she asked, arching a brow.

"Yes, babies. Neither of us is getting any younger," he said, brushing her cheek with his hand. "We're not over the hill yet, but this house needs to be filled with children again. I hope you agree...maybe we can start trying this winter, when it's too cold to do anything else."

She nodded and he laughed again. "Good. You described your dream studio to me once. Now I want to give it to you. We're a long way from weaving shops, although I hear there is a terrific one in Missoula. You'll need a full range of materials. I don't want you having to run two hundred miles to town to buy a package of dye or a new book or..."

"You're very thoughtful," she said, kissing his chest. "I have some money. It's in a money market account in Salt Lake. Let me help pay for the studio." She told him the amount and he whistled softly.

"My future wife is a good financial manager," he said. "But no. The studio is my gift to you. If you want to buy shares in the operation, that would be fine. We can use the money to pay off some of the loan. I hate going into debt again. Ranching is hard enough without paying some banker your hard-earned money in interest. I'd rather the bank pay us on our investments."

They lay together quietly for several minutes.

"I'll have to notify Dr. Christensen about terminating my internship," she murmured.

He chuckled. "Emil called me a few weeks ago and asked me how you were working out. He confessed to setting us up...thought we deserved each other, thought I needed you to shake up my life. You certainly did that, my darling Abbie."

"Between Dr. Christensen and Wilma and Moses, we didn't have a chance, did we?" she asked.

"Smart people," he replied.

"Smarter than we are?" she asked.

"For a while, but not anymore, my love," he assured her. "We have the strength of our love and the wisdom of our mistakes to help us in the future. When shall we have the wedding and where?"

She considered his question. "The wedding should be at the church where your parents were married. I want it to be my only wedding so it must be special. I want Aunt Minnie and Uncle Harry to come, and my brothers, and Callie and Eileen and their families."

"Isn't Callie the cousin with financial problems?" he asked.

"Yes, but I'll buy the ticket and give it to her. We all made a pledge years ago to encourage one another to have dreams and to help one another to fulfill them. We also promised to ask for help if we needed it. That's the part of the pledge we've all fallen down on. Maybe if I help Callie now, she'll have her chance to find happiness and someday she can help me.''

"That sounds reasonable," he replied.

"But Uncle Harry can't leave the farm until after harvest time," Abbie said sadly.

"Then let's plan an October wedding," he suggested. "That's after the lambs go to market and everything slows down for a while. We'll be able to get away for a few weeks."

She gazed lovingly into his eyes. "What will we do until then?"

He kissed her tenderly. "We'll take one of the sheep wagons up to the mountains and I'll show you what summer herding is all about. And when we're not busy with the sheep, we'll make mad passionate love, just for the pure pleasure of it."

Abbie laid her head against his shoulder again. "That sounds wonderful, but what about the winters? What will we do then?"

"More of the same," Dane said, laughing as he pulled her close and sealed his promise with his lips.

FOLLOW THE RAINBOW...

Sally Garrett
RAINBOW HILLS SERIES

If you enjoyed *Weaver of Dreams*, Book One of
Sally Garrett's trilogy celebrating the inspiring
lives of three strong-willed American farm women,
you're sure to enjoy Book Two, *Visions*, even
more. Abbie's cousin, Eileen, discovers strength
and courage she didn't know she had when she
becomes a single parent struggling to save the
family farm. And in time she makes the greatest
discovery of all—broken hearts do mend when
healed by the transforming power of love!

Coming from Harlequin Superromance in
early summer, 1987, is *Visions*, Book Two of
Sally Garrett's Rainbow Hill Series.

Harlequin Superromance

COMING NEXT MONTH

#246 LOVE SONGS • Georgia Bockoven
Jo Williams's relationship with some of the senior
citizens who frequent her yogurt shop brings Brad Tyler
to her door one night, and once there, he never wants to
leave. But Jo soon realizes she'll have to help Brad over
the pain of a lost love for them to have their chance at
happiness. She'll have to risk losing him to gain his
heart forever.

#247 MASKS • Irma Walker
Despite appearances, Tracy Morrison is not a lonely
heiress. She's a reporter for the *Cincinnati Herald*,
working undercover to trap a couple of con artists—and
write the hottest story of the year. When Chris Collins
falls into her trap, she knows she's struck pay dirt. He is
manipulative, dangerous . . . and absolutely irresistible.
But, as Tracy will discover, he's not what he seems. . . .

#248 CHERISHED HARBOR • Kelly Walsh
U.S. Marshal Daniel Elliott and his latest assignment,
Marcy Keaton, are like night and day. Yet, as they fight
for their lives, they find themselves sharing passion-
filled nights and dreaming of a future they can't
possibly share. . . .

#249 BELONGING • Sandra James
Mayor Angie Hall believes the small city of Westridge
is hardly the place for a tough ex-cop from Chicago like
Matt Richardson. But her new chief of police proves
her wrong. He fits in perfectly . . . *too* perfectly for
Angie's liking.